Cheese

Deluxe

a Memoir

Greg Palmer

Foreword

Most of what follows is true. Almost all of the names have been changed, and some incidents and characters have been merged into new configurations, in part because the author didn't keep a journal of the Samoa years and certainly regrets it now because he has a lousy memory and frequently couldn't remember who actually did what, when, and with whom. And some of this is pure fiction, because things don't always work out the way they should.

If it were not for the encouragement and noble efforts of Maralyn Crosetto, and the technical support of Jack LeNoir of Day Moon Press, this book would still be a manuscript in an old cardboard box, so huge thanks to both of them. And thanks also to the people of the late Eastside Week, where seven early versions of these tales first appeared.

This is, of course, for Cathy.

And secondarily for all the real Samoans.

And in memory of Elliott, who was really my cat.

B&H Bennett &
Hastings Publishing

Specialties

No Substitutions, please

The Samoa

In March of 1965 Bud Hinkley was selected as the Rotary Club Boy of the Month. He was all set to go and had written a nice little speech for the Rotarian merchants about how as long as us youth have to follow our dreams, retail isn't a bad way to go. Bud would become an Arizona county commissioner 25 years later. He didn't give a rat's ass about retail, but even in high school his juices ran political. He would tell the Rotarians what they wanted to hear and knock 'em on their brown serge pants. Then a few days before the event Rotary President Stinky Lind heard that Bud was a big fairy.

Stinky was the town druggist, a college graduate who played around with narcotics all day so he thought of himself as a man of the world. But he was still shocked that such deviant aberrations as teen queens were present in our quiet Northwest suburb. He himself was as straight as the Kennedys, and to prove it he had been sexually harassing his only employee, Marge Collins, for 23 years. It gave Stinky and Marge something to do during slow afternoons around the Notions & Sundries. And as every local teen male knew, Stinky had a stack of ancient girlie magazines in his men's room at the back of the store. They weren't hard core stuff, more the Porn-Lite of the fifties, with big, grainy black&white ladies sitting at typewriters, doing laundry and tatting while wearing Sears underwear, with tinsel attached to pertinent points of interest. The magazines were for sale but nobody ever bought one. Counter Personnel Marge would have had the word out about such a purchase before the poor bastard got back to his car.

Not a lot of people have experienced a drugstore men's room. But from 1959 when Lind's Drugs opened, until

1978 when Stinky retired and turned the place over to his daughter Constance (who immediately dumpstered the men's room library, which had been an embarrassment to her since she was eight), a lot of Island guys did time in that biffy. Especially Stinky, who was chronically incontinent and so used that john ten times more than anybody else. He felt a little dirty whenever he visited the ladies, but at least his was good old-fashioned heterosexual degeneracy. This big fairy business was something much, much worse.

"We can't have that stuff in Rotary, Sweetcheeks," he told Marge. She was ordered to call Vice-Principal Murray at the high school and inform him that Bud Hinkley wouldn't do, Boy-of-the-Month-wise, for reasons she wasn't at liberty to discuss. Marge's husband was a lawyer, and she knew slander when she heard it. The Vice-Principal would have to select another outstanding local youth, and do it quickly.

"Impossible," Murray said.

"Not to have a Boy of the Month would imply that there aren't any senior boys worthy of the honor," Marge told him.

"There aren't," he answered. In his entire life Murray had never met anyone he considered an outstanding local youth. And by March he'd used up all the senior guys he thought were even close, which for him was exclusively the senior football players.

Marge Collins was not about to be pushed around by educational middle management, especially Murray. She knew he'd gotten some pretty odd prescriptions for ointments over the years. The man was a slave to chaffing.

"No worthwhile local Boy is not a message the Rotary Club wishes to send to the community," she told him tersely. "Find a replacement." Marge believed in honoring youth, but she also knew that Rotary had started its Boy of the Month program because the ritual provided twelve free speakers a year. If the assembled businessmen had to go through a meeting with nobody to listen to but themselves it could get ugly. They were tired of each other and had been for a long time. The only other speaker available was Pastor Olaffson, who had been bugging her to schedule his slide show presentation of "My Journey to the Holy Lands and Minneapolis." Marge knew that could get even uglier. She was not going to let the school off the hook for a presentable boy.

"I'll dig somebody up," Murray finally agreed, "but don't be surprised if he eats with his hands."

The guy he dug up was me, and it wasn't just because I knew my way around a place setting. Bud Hinkley had gotten the nod because he was playing one of the leads in *A Midsummer Night's Dream*, that year's all-school play. The Drama Club Promotion Committee believed that just by listening to a high school actor talk about the future lying ahead the Rotarians would develop an intense interest in Shakespeare and flock to the theater with their wives and children. (This turned out to be untrue.)

When Murray was presented with this doomed promotional plan he said, "What the hell, gimme a name." The first name that came up was Bud's.

It was ignorance of Shakespeare, not sexual orientation, that led to Bud's banishment by the Rotarians. In *Dream* he was playing Oberon, King of the Fairies. Stinky was unfamiliar with the Bard's early Comedies, even with a B.A. in Pharmacology from Montana State, so when he was told that the King of the Fairies was coming to mingle with his Rotarians he misunderstood. Thus I got tagged, because Dwelly Kelly and I were the only other senior boys in lead roles, and Dwelly had already been a Boy of the Month during football season. (In the fall he'd been a very small linebacker and now in the spring he was a very big Puck.)

"This is strictly to hype that theater crap, kid," Murray told me after I'd been summoned to his office. "Don't let it go to your head."

I went to the lunch, I ate the chicken, I read the speech Bud loaned me, and I didn't let it go to my head. Stinky and his fellow Rotarians seemed satisfied, although there was some concern that they had traded a King of the Fairies for a Bottom and what exactly was the connection there? (Apparently ignorance of the Bard's early Comedies was endemic among Rotarians.) During my speech I added a joke about Rotary scraping the "Bottom" of the barrel for their Boy of the Month, and instead of a laugh I got a lot of guys nodding their heads in agreement. Stinky misunderstood again and demanded that I put a quarter in the can for "sexual innuendo."

None of the day's events went to my head because my head was otherwise engaged. March of 1965 was a big month in my life. I was about to play my first lead on stage, wearing an ass's head composed of 85 pounds of lumpy brown papier-mâché globbed onto a chicken wire frame. The ass's head scenes in that production looked like Bottom had been transformed into a hunched and hobbling Quasimodo rather than a donkey; an interesting dramatic concept but not what the playwright had in mind. Academically high school had ceased to matter much because the University of Washington had just accepted me for next fall. And I was in love.

Cathy was the granddaughter of immigrant Italian coal miners—not fiery dark Southern Italians, but almost Germanic Northern Italians. Her people believed that if you worked hard at whatever you did you could do whatever it was. And she was the proof, very smart to begin with, and an extraordinary student because of the hours she put into it. We had been acquainted all of our lives, but nothing more than friends and classmates until we began sniffing around each other as sophomores. It still took me two more years of awkward maneuvers to ask her out on a date, after a *Midsummer Night's Dream* rehearsal when I was feeling particularly flush and self-confident, even if I could hardly move my neck thanks to the Head.

By chance we went to see the movie *Marriage Italian Style* on our first date, which romantically speaking was the smartest thing I ever did. The effect a roistering Marcello Mastroianni had on a young woman just beginning to get in touch with her Italian heritage was incalculable. Within a few days we were A Couple to everyone we knew and to ourselves—the first serious relationship for both of us. She had dated another guy earlier in high school, and to this day I can irritate her by casually mentioning how much he looked like a collie. I'd spent some time the previous summer with a girl who was five years older than I was, which made my parents very nervous and me a little astonished. But neither of us had played the game with much interest or intensity, and once we found each other we were both relieved not to have to play it at all. It freed up a lot of time, which was part of our initial attraction to each other, I think, a Courtship of Convenience that grew into something more.

She used her additional time (other than on me) to study, ski, and watch the NBA when the NBA on television was the Boston Celtics and whoever was playing the Celtics. I should have used the time to study, but other things seemed a lot more interesting—Cathy, the Drama Club, and especially my job. It was the first real job I ever had, and I was lucky to have it, because it gave me the opportunity to create masterpieces. You don't get many chances to do that in life. My œuvre wasn't art, however. It was eats. And the masterpiece was the Cheese Deluxe.

The Cheese Deluxe at the Samoa Drive–In on Mercer Island, Washington, was one of America's best burgers. Legendary burgers supposedly originated in eastern working class cities where two-fisted hard-hat guys spend their days carrying heavy objects from place to place. They want chow that reflects themselves—big, tough, sweaty burgers you have to bend over to eat. The Samoa Cheese Deluxe was close to that kind of burger, although it was rarely eaten by that kind of guy.

My being allowed to cook Deluxes was sheer dumb luck. In the summer before my senior year I started looking for a job. I needed the money to supplement a meager allowance. My parents were doing okay, but like everybody else's parents they grew up in the Depression. Through long experience and a lot of lamb patties and mac&cheese they had learned not to waste money no matter how much money they had. One of their definitions of wasting money was giving it to a kid who couldn't say exactly what he was going to spend it on, a kid who had not yet embraced the concept of investing.

I was drowning my employment sorrows in a Cheese Deluxe one afternoon at the Samoa when Josh came out from the back and joined me. He was a friend who had been the Samoa night and weekend cook for six months.

Josh was a solitary, outdoorsy type, the only guy I knew who drove a station wagon because he wanted to put large things in it, like canoes and backpacks, and not because it was his mother's car and he had no other options. The kitchen of the Samoa was about as outdoorsy as an ashtray, so Josh hated going to work, hated working, and hated leaving work because he knew he'd have to go back. He had taken the Samoa job to get money for his outdoor adventures, but the job consumed all of his energy and spare time so he never went anywhere. This nasty irony of life shouldn't hit you until you're at least 35, and Josh was only 17.

His salvation was a call from Recreational Equipment, Inc., the giant mail-order operation that supplies all those guys who want to climb things because they're there. They offered him an evening job doing repairs in the mountaineering department. We Samoans weren't quite sure what he was going to fix. We thought mountaineering repair was like parachute repair. If something you were using to climb to the top of a mountain broke, you weren't going to need it any more because you'd be dead at the bottom of the mountain. Apparently that wasn't the case with all the equipment. Clifford insisted Josh was going to be a crampon sharpener, but the rest of us didn't know what a crampon was except that it sounded like a feminine hygiene product, and we wanted nothing whatsoever to do with feminine hygiene products.

Josh was looking for somebody to take over his job at the Samoa. He knew that from a consumer standpoint I was intimately familiar with the operation, having put away quite a few Cheese Deluxes in the two years the place had been open. So he took me to see Betty.

Restaurants usually do not have Mission Statements. And if they do, the mission is: Sell Eats. But the Samoa actually existed for a reason other than comestible commerce. It looked, smelled and sounded just like any other hamburger joint, but a higher purpose was at work—Betty's purpose.

You could tell by looking at her that she wasn't your typical burger joint proprietor. Even on the days she cooked, she was always nicely dressed—no Spandex or lime-green double knits for our owner-operator. Betty knew her way around shops where the clothes are draped on pink padded hangers and they don't sell major appliances the next floor up. She was the kind of person who wouldn't have been caught dead in the Samoa if she didn't own it.

Betty's husband Chuck was Vice President of America's largest envelope maker. "There's a lot of money in envelopes," Chuck said truthfully but far too often, and as a result he and Betty were relatively loaded.

When their last child drove off to college, Betty waved goodbye at the curb and then went directly into her kitchen and started cooking. Chuck came home from the envelope marts that evening and found a six-course dinner waiting, and not a single dish included ground beef or Campbell's Cream of Mushroom soup. He was thrilled, and dove in with both hands. Chuck liked to eat as much as Betty liked to cook. Their Golden Years were going to work out just fine.

Three months later Chuck had gained 35 pounds and twice had to have all of his business suits let out. He started making up excuses to avoid coming home for dinner, doing all the ducking and dodging a guy with a mistress has to do without any of the benefits of a mistress. All he had was tight pants and a new chin tucked under the old one.

Finally, one hot night, Chuck pushed slowly back from a dinner table littered with the remains of stuffed mushroom cap canapés, asparagus spears au gratin, Lamb Shashlik, and thick wedges of seven-layer chocolate cake. He was feeling both light-headed and heavy-assed, and not sure he could stand up.

"Betty," Chuck moaned, "you're killing me. Do you know that?"

"It was the tier cake, wasn't it?" she answered. "I still can't figure out how to make it as light as it should be. I'll try again next week."

"No, God no!"

"Here," Betty said, smiling sweetly, "have a Bailey's Irish Cream. It'll settle your stomach." She aimed a lethal glass in his direction.

"For God's sake, no!" Chuck came as close as he ever would to knocking something from his wife's dainty hand. He told her that the big meals would have to stop or some day soon their kids would come over for a visit and find them both stone cold dead, face down in plates of Beef Bourguignon. She simply had to find something else to occupy her time.

"Isn't there anything you've always wanted to do, Sugar? Mah jongg? Club work? World travel? I don't care what it costs, as long as it keeps you busy and out of the kitchen."

Betty considered his offer for the week it took her to clean out all the leftovers and put them into Chuck. She remembered that when her kids were in high school they often had hung out at a place called The Burgerama. Once she even tried the place herself. As far as she could tell the Burgerama burger was made with beef patties that had been rejected by the military during the Korean Conflict—rejected by the Korean military. Some of her fries were still frozen. Her coffee was fresh that month. Her feet stuck to the floor.

"I know what I want to do," Betty said, visions of the Burgerama dancing in her head.

"Great!" Chuck was happy she'd found something. "What's it going to be?"

"I want to open a restaurant."

"A restaurant?" He couldn't believe it. "A restaurant? You don't want to get involved in the restaurant business, Sweetie. Restaurants are run by people with huge families they can exploit for cheap labor. The Chinese, the Mexicans, the Greeks. The Mafia. Those are restaurant people. All the family you've got left is me, and I'm too old to be a busboy. A restaurant! Christ Almighty!"

"A restaurant," Betty repeated calmly. She was going to wait him out.

Chuck tried reasoning with her. "It's one thing to make this gourmet stuff for me, but to make it for strangers is an entirely different..."

"I want to open a hamburger restaurant. Near a high school."

Now he was even more confused. "That's just...just nuts. The place will be full of kids. Teenagers. Baby, we've had kids. We've done teenagers."

"I want the kids. I want to make burgers for kids. Good burgers."

Betty's Folly was founded on an axiom that probably plagued the parents of ancient Egypt, and every civilization since: Kids Will Eat Crap. So she would open a restaurant for kids that had the food they wanted, but carefully prepared, using the best ingredients available, in surroundings where you weren't afraid to look too closely at the floor. It wouldn't be health food, but it wouldn't kill them either. It's what she could do to save a generation.

Chuck finally agreed, although he still thought that running a restaurant to help a lot of other people's kids was idiotic. He went out to find a location while Betty did research, visiting dozens of hamburger places all over the Northwest, testing the eats, investigating suppliers. During this period she ate 43 hamburgers and 26 orders of fish and chips. And people wondered why she brought a sack lunch to the Samoa.

When Chuck walked into his office and described what he wanted, a Mercer Island realtor saw his big chance to unload a difficult property.

"I have exactly the place you're looking for," said the realtor confidently, trying not to giggle. "Right here in this commercial zone, just down the hill from the high school. Easy access to the freeway, parking for ten cars, a lot of foot traffic nearby, and potential seating inside for twenty or so. But it won't last long."

They walked over to a small piece of land behind Arts Food Center at the eastern end of the Mercer Island Shopping Center. Chuck contemplated the only building on the property, a gas station that had been abandoned for years and looked like it. He started to laugh.

"When you said 'it won't last long,' I thought you meant somebody else was interested in buying it. Not that it won't last long."

"I agree it doesn't look like much now," the realtor replied, stepping between Chuck and the building, presenting his own plaid sports coat for view rather than the crumbling structure. "But with a little wood, a little paint, a lot of elbow grease and love, you could have yourself one going concern here, Buddy." And he was right.

Chuck and Betty decided to call her new enterprise The Samoa because of the island connection—Samoa and Mercer. And also because Chuck got a great deal on used Tiki Hut® Fire-Retardant Tropical Frond Wall Covering. So the place was going to look aloha-oi-ish no matter what they called it.

Chuck, Betty, and a handful of friends/suckers worked like dogs for two weeks to make The Samoa presentable. And when they were done it still looked just like an abandoned gas station—an abandoned gas station in Papeete maybe, but an abandoned gas station nonetheless. I could mop that floor a million times and nobody would mistake it for anything other than a stained, lopsided, concrete gas station floor. Health Department inspectors would get down on all fours to inspect that surface, only to discover that it was clean no matter how grotty it looked. Betty was very big on clean floors.

She made good on her vow to buy the best quality beef, cheese, buns and bacon she could find. The Samoa fish was fresh halibut, not last year's cod, the chips were spuds cut on the premises and bathed in fresh boiling fat, and the chicken hadn't been sitting frozen on a freight car siding in Arkansas for six months. The food Betty served was not only better for us, it tasted better too. Quality really does make a difference, something a lot of Samoa guys learned early thanks to Betty.

That day Josh brought me in as the possible new cook she and I met in the Samoa Employees' Lounge, which was a folding chair jammed in between the walk-in and the double sink. Betty recognized me as a regular customer but not somebody she'd ever thrown out of the place, so I was hired. Training took twenty minutes, and most of that time was spent on how to mop properly. I was a B+ senior in a good high school, so remembering to put the pickles, tomato and lettuce on the top bun and the mayonnaise and relish on the bottom wasn't much of a challenge. I never did get the Samoa Taco Excellante up to par. The shells kept cracking. Fortunately Betty didn't care all that much about tacos. They were a nostalgia item on the menu, as a kind of tribute to her life with Chuck. When they honey-mooned in Mexico in 1939 they were broke, and lived for two weeks on ten-centavo tacos, augmented towards the end by a lot of Kaopectate. The fact that her new cook lacked the patience and dexterity to squeeze open those crispy taco lips and insert the innards didn't bother her. "Work on it," was all she said.

That very first day, as soon as training was over, Betty handed me an apron, pointed at the grill, and she and Josh went out the back door together. They had a real lunch somewhere, with soup, salad and actual metal utensils. Back at the Samoa I didn't have the slightest idea what I was supposed to do next. Then Arlene the Counter Personnel stuck her head around the corner of the walk-in and said, "You've got six orders up: three Deluxe, one onion, one no pickle, fish two/double fries, chicken all white/slaw. Get your ass in gear."

For the next six months I slapped down patties, warmed fresh buns, dunked fine fish, watched and listened. On both sides of the counter we were all on the verge of adulthood in a quiet America that a few years later would blow up in our faces. We were strangers in a strange land, a land getting stranger all the time, who found comfort and some-times a lot more than comfort in each other. Clifford once said Will Rogers' claim that he never met a man he didn't like just proved that Will Rogers didn't get out much. After my time at the Samoa I was on Will Roger's side of the argument, but I could see Clifford's point too. I never could understand how Josh was able to walk away from an experience like that, from those people. But one of the things I learned at the Samoa is that we all hear different Sirens calling us to our fates. The trick is to find the Siren who's really calling to you, and not be afraid to follow her.

Just like Josh did. He's been at REI now for more than thirty years, nine station wagons, three great kids, and the summit of Annapurna.

Stackhouse

PARIS HAS THE EIFFEL TOWER. If the Eiffel Tower was moved to North Myrtle Beach, South Carolina (where they tried to buy it once) Paris would still be Paris, and North Myrtle Beach would still not be Paris. Interviewing the mayor of North Myrtle Beach in 1974, I asked him what you would be able to see from the top of the North Myrtle Beach Eiffel Tower. "23 golf courses," he said proudly. Not Paris.

The Cheese Deluxe was the Eiffel Tower for local teens, the big attraction that brought us in the door. And the Samoa Drive–In was our Paris, where we could sit with our friends and lovers at small tables by the side of the boulevard—Interstate 90—and watch life go by. The table, boulevard, friends and lovers were what made the experience ours, and the Cheese Deluxe was what made it special.

Children and parents were allowed to come in for eats and even linger a while. Denying the Cheese Deluxe to anybody who had the dollar would be like those creeps who buy great works of art and then stick them in their mansions, hidden from public view. That's a crime against culture, whether you're hoarding a Rembrandt or a truly outstanding burger. But those who came in for the burger alone could never be true Samoans. That distinction was reserved for us senior teens. After surviving eleven years of public education, this little hamburger joint was our final shelter from a world waiting patiently to chew us up. So we claimed the right of occupation for our year. Then we would disappear into the societal maelstrom and let the children have it.

The Samoa regulars were part of the teen social class usually identified as Underachievers. But what really distinguished them was that they didn't care if figures of authority thought they were Underachievers or not. 'Show me something worth achieving and I'll achieve it" could have been their motto. And when they eventually found that worthwhile goal they went for it, often with great success. But during high school they were still looking, and spent a lot of time looking over Samoa eats.

By the time I got to the Samoa as an employee the thrill of cooking was gone for Betty, so she wasn't around much anymore. The most regular Samoa female by then was Arlene, Counter Personnel Number One. She was attractive in her way and only a few years older than us. But her Untouchable status was obvious to even the most obtuse youth. Arlene was a single mother who had already seen enough horny guys to last her for eternity. She once told an inebriated All-Conference tackle three times her size that if he opened his big goddamned mouth one more time, "I'm going to box your ears." He didn't know what was involved in boxing his ears, though he guessed it had something to do with hitting him in the ears. That sounded unpleasant, and there was no question she was prepared to do it. So he stopped telling her what lovely eyes she had, took his burgers, and left. He was right, though. Arlene had lovely eyes.

Associate Counter Personnel Thelma would fill in at the Samoa whenever Arlene couldn't make it. Thelma was a short woman in her late fifties, with a tiny piece of brain lodged in her skull and an oddly shaped derriere. It was a classic rump, and not the kind a gentleman would give a lot of study. I wouldn't have known about its odd configuration except that it would get her into trouble. She'd disappear from the counter, and a few minutes later I'd hear her bawling for me from the bathroom out back. Her tush was so configured that it got stuck in the toilet seat. I'd have to get the broom and poke it through a crack in the bathroom door so she could grab the handle. I certainly wasn't going in there myself. She'd use the broom to pry herself free.

After this happened maybe fifty times she finally got smart and just took the broom with her every time nature called. After a few months I didn't hear that tush-freeing THWONGK any more so I thought she was probably sticking the handle in the bowl before she actually sat down, to prevent a seal forming. Which is why four dollars was my only out-of-pocket expense as a Samoa staff member. I bought my own broom, and kept it on a high shelf Thelma couldn't reach.

The other regular Samoa employee was DeeDee, a collegian who worked nights and weekends and hated every minute of it. Clifford insisted DeeDee was majoring in Penmanship in college, but he only did that to see if Wayne Whitley would buy it. I never knew what her real major was, but from her obsessions I assumed it had something to do with hygiene. DeeDee was always very clean, and cleanliness was the single thing she seemed to admire in others.

It would have been easy for us Samoa males to work up a sweat over the clean, attractive DeeDee. Some of my friends actually expressed envy at my continued association with her. Then they got a chance to see the whole picture, DeeDee-wise, and their envy turned to pity.

First there was her massive college boyfriend, Wolf. He was a rugby player, so he had that "invincibility" thing all rugby players try for, as well as an impressive array of scars. His forehead looked like a pink 3-by-5 card somebody had been doodling on with a red pen. It gave him an ominous, Frankensteinian look that went well with his name. Wolf could show up at the Samoa at any time, and did—an impressive argument for a cold shower if you were harboring unclean thoughts about DeeDee. Wolf assumed everyone was lusting after her, too. The first time we met he braced me up against the walk-in before I had a chance to introduce myself and told me he would break my legs if I even brushed up against her during the course of work. DeeDee thought he was cute, although their relationship had continual hygiene issues.

Even when Wolf wasn't around she had an extremely intractable personality where we youths were concerned. Or as Frank Forcade put it, "That's the coldest bitch I've ever met." The high school part of her life was over, but her tuition-paying father wouldn't give her an extra dime for any of life's essentials, like her own apartment or car. So she had to work, and being a person of somewhat limited skills outside the hygiene field, the Samoa was all she could get. She spent each shift terrified that a friend from the Graduate School of Penmanship would come in and see her peddling burgers, with children and to children. Twice when I was on duty DeeDee suddenly dropped to the floor behind the counter because a car-full of collegians had arrived. "You get this one," she snarled at me as she crawled out the back door. DeeDee was often *in* the Samoa, but she was never *of* the Samoa.

Geoff, who had decided to be a "sensualist" like Oscar Wilde when he grew up (well, not exactly like Oscar Wilde), once heard DeeDee mention that Wolf was off playing rugby in Idaho Falls. Her precise statement was, "Wolf is a man playing rugby in Idaho. You are boys eating hamburgers in a suburb." Geoff completely missed the spirit of her remarks. He asked DeeDee if she'd like to go to the drag races with him, as long as she was free. DeeDee just laughed at him. She laughed at Geoff every time she saw him for the next month. That was every day, because Geoff was the most regular of the Samoa regulars. No Cold Bitch Mocking Counter Personnel was going to keep him from his afternoon Cheese Deluxe, although for most of the winter of '64 he found reason to exit rapidly whenever Wolf came in.

For regulars like Geoff, when you didn't have anything to do you went to the Samoa. When you did have something to do you went to the Samoa before you did it and then again after you did it. This was especially true for boy/girl stuff. You didn't take a date to the Samoa, you took her somewhere else. Then you came back to the Samoa, sometimes with her and sometimes not depending on whether she wanted to be seen with you. Failure to file a report on the date within a day or two was considered extremely inconsiderate, especially by the many Samoa regulars who had never had a date in their lives.

Among the date-deprived was a guy named Stackhouse. He was unique among us because he alone declined to swear allegiance to the Cheese Deluxe as the World's Best Burger. At the Samoa he ate fish, but for burgers Stackhouse would drive ninety miles over Snoqualmie Pass to the Big Joy Drive In, in a little mining town called Cle Elum. He claimed the Big Joy Burger was better than the Cheese Deluxe.

It was a pathetic ruse. His real interest was getting girls to go over there with him, hoping his car would break down in the mountains so they'd have to huddle together for warmth. In the continual pursuit of the female that occupied so much of some guys' time, this was Stackhouse's only erotic fantasy. In the back booths of the Samoa he would describe the event as he imagined it, without any variation and damned little reality.

He was squat and complexion-challenged, with sandy hair combed straight back from his bumpy, pizza-esque forehead. He thought this wind-tunnel-hairstyle made him look older, but to the rest of us it made him look like a motel clerk in a place with hourly rates. And like many people who have a tendency to spit when they talk, he talked a lot, mostly about the mountain pass fantasy.

Two things made the fantasy unlikely. No girl would go with him, and for all his shortcomings he was an honorable guy, with a lot of integrity. That's why he hoped his car would break down in the mountains when a young lady was along but he wouldn't do anything to encourage it happening, like poking a hole in a water hose. "I don't have to go that far to get girls," he'd say indignantly, whenever somebody at the Samoa suggested that, yes indeed, he probably would have to go that far.

Given his nature and especially the spitting, mechanical breakdown was the only likely part of his dream date. That gaseous maroon Dodge wasn't going over too many mountain passes too many times. But the guys at the Samoa still felt any suggestion that the Big Joy was better than the Cheese Deluxe was treasonous. Our high school sports teams stank, no famous person ever came from Mercer Island, and we had the reputation of being rich jerks. We didn't even have a local movie theater, just a creepy bowling alley where the school bus drivers used to hang out. But by God the Cheese Deluxe was our burger and that meant a hell of a lot to us. So the crowd at the Samoa was quite pleased when Stackhouse's car finally did break down a few miles past the summit one June night and it still didn't get him laid.

It was the best chance he was ever going to have, and he knew it. The night was warm, the moon was full, and half a jar of Stridex Medicated Pads® had worked their odiferous magic on his major zits, even if his face had the raw look of human skin that's been buff sanded. He smelled like a big medicated pad with an overlay of Right Guard®, but that didn't matter because Janelle was along for the ride—Janelle, who certainly knew her way around a parked car on a dark road, Janelle, the gently-rounded star of many a guy's erotic fantasy. She went with him because it would piss Steve off, and in her turbulent relationship with Steve she thought he needed pissing off just then. A full moon, a dead Dodge, a bag full of burgers, and Janelle looking for ways to irritate Steve. We Samoans thought that if you couldn't get anywhere with a setup like that there was nothing left for you but the priesthood.

He and Janelle made it all the way to Cle Elum, bought the Big Joys, ate a pair, and then got another bag-full to bring back. Returning over the pass Stackhouse and the Dodge were overheating at about the same rate. The Dodge blew first, steam billowing out from under the hood. Trembling with anticipation, Stackhouse coasted over to the side of the road and shut her down. Then, with an expression on his face that would have frightened a career prostitute, he turned to Janelle sitting beside him.

Unfortunately for Stackhouse Janelle was not the cliché she appeared to be. Similar young ladies, in beach party movies and teen fiction of the period, went hormonal over good metal. A chopped-and-channeled cherry-red Chevy muscle car was supposed to turn an otherwise "good" girl into a moist, moaning animal. But Janelle thought General Motors shouldn't be involved in her romantic decisions.

Maybe it was because her father was the most successful Ford dealer in the area. Or maybe it was because she wasn't nearly as pliant as a lot of guys with Turtle Wax under their nails and horns on their heads wanted her to be. Whatever the reason, she didn't extend her considerable favors based solely on the splendor of a guy's wheels. She liked a good ride as well as the next youth, but there had to be something in the deal besides a groovy vehicle for Janelle. In Stackhouse she found nothing, and his vehicle was crap anyway. It was also dead by the side of the road—legitimately dead, which was a new experience for her—but dead nonetheless. So she regarded her leering companion for a moment in silence.

"It needs water," said Janelle at last, speaking with the authority that comes from being the only female graduate of Mercer Island High School Auto Shop. "You carry any water?"

Stackhouse hadn't been expecting a discussion of the Dodge's needs because he was concentrating so hard on his own. "Any what? Water?" he answered, as if he'd never heard of the substance before. "Water?"

"Yeah," said Janelle. "You gotta go get some water." And she kicked him out of the still steaming car with a peck on the cheek. She thought a quick kiss was the polite thing to do. He considered it foreplay. When she said, "I'll wait for you here," he misinterpreted her politeness for eagerness and came close to swooning. On the four-mile hike back to the deserted ski lodge at the summit he fantasized about every possible kind of sexual congress that might take place on his return. These fantasies were so vivid in his imagination that for long stretches of highway he had difficulty walking.

Janelle stayed in the car with her feet up on the dash and Stackhouse's letter-jacket (bowling) wrapped around her for additional warmth. For a while she watched the steam drift up from under the Dodge's hood, swirling through the trees into the soft glow of the full moon.

"It made the whole world shimmer," she told us later. "It was gorgeous, just like a picture on a calendar. Who knew?" She was not used to experiencing gorgeousness other than photographs of Paul McCartney and Richard Chamberlain in Teen Beat magazine. Janelle was a simple creature, with big appetites. That's why she ate all the spare burgers while she was waiting, plus an old Tootsie Roll she found in the glove compartment.

Janelle learned something that night. She learned that at the right time and the right place being alone in a parked car is just as enjoyable as being with someone. The youngest of four and popular in her way since the first grade, she had never really been alone before. Now she discovered that solitude has its attractions, as long as it isn't too cold, doesn't last too long, and there are eats. It made her want to get her own car and drive around in it all by herself. She was thinking maybe a Ford.

Stackhouse learned something that night too. He learned that the best laid plans of mice and men do indeed get screwed up, especially if you're a mouse. And that you don't always take the first ride that comes along.

With a borrowed jug full of water he was hiking back along the highway, oblivious to the moon, the forest, or anything else besides putting one foot in front of the other as quickly as possible. His imagination still teemed with images of the sweaty groping that was about to take place. Traffic was light, but not long after Stackhouse started back the growl of a semi came up behind him. The tense teen half-heartedly stuck out his thumb. Since the age of nine only four strangers had ever picked him up. Three of them were drunk, and the fourth was a guy who started driving with his knees so he could do things with his hands that forced Stackhouse to leap from the car and run like hell. So his expectations of getting a ride were low. But the big rig immediately pulled over and stopped.

The truck driver said his name was Low Ball, although the registration on the visor said his name was Montgomery Krasnowsky. He was hauling a load of sorghum from Great Falls, Montana to Elma, Washington, and was more than happy to give this teenager in trouble a ride down the mountain to his girl. "My God," Stackhouse said to himself as he climbed up into the cab, "my luck is finally changing." He leapt at the chance to get back to Janelle faster and fresher.

They hadn't gone two miles before Low Ball began telling Stackhouse about his trial separation from Louise-That-Bitch back in Helena. The more he talked the hotter and madder he got. By the time they reached Janelle Stackhouse was looking through the window of nineteen tons of sorghum going 108 miles an hour down a mountain pass under the control of a man who was frothing at the mouth.

In the months that followed, whenever Stackhouse told the Low Ball Story to a booth full of Samoans, this was always my favorite part. I could see his bumpy little nose pressed against the passenger side window, moving faster than he had ever traveled in his life. Yet that instant of confluence as he shot past his own car must have seemed like an eternity to him, an eternity in which he could see her in there, he must have seen her, pink tennis shoes up on the dash, legs apart, her skirt bunched up around her creamy white thighs. (Like I said, a lot of guys had fantasies about Janelle.) Maybe he saw a flash of lace; more likely he saw a flash of tinfoil, the half-wrapped Big Joy burger in her hand, Big Joy sauce running over her soft, downy forearm and dripping onto his Shucks Auto Supply seat covers. And the whole scene bathed in the glow of moonlight, filtered through a thick, ambrosial, evergreen forest.

And the sound! What did it sound like inside that cab? Surely a mélange of screaming, completely contrary to the visual beauty of the night and the moon and the forest green mountain pass. The big Kenworth's engine shrieking at the very edge of its capabilities. Over that mechanical howl, the angry, hurt voice of Low Ball and the desperate, adenoidal whine of Stackhouse:

"I tell ya, kid, women are no damn good...Stop here!... No damn good, ya give 'em everything they want...Please stop here please sir!....and they only want more and more and more...Oh God, no, pull over!...I love her, God I love her, but I just couldn't take it any more...Janelle!...Stay away from women, kid, you hear me?...Shit!...That's the word for it, I'll tell ya. Hey, ya want a cookie? I think you're sitting on some Fig Newtons." As Janelle disappeared into the night and the rear view mirror, gone from his life forever.

Stackhouse's Dream Date fantasy always ended with his return to the Samoa. For him it was to be a moment as good or better than the actual in-Dodge necking. He would stroll through the door. We would all look up from our petty concerns and meaningless conversations. We would know, just by the way he walked, that come among us was a laid man. We would be congratulatory. He would be humble. We would say, "Tell the story! Tell the story!" He would answer, "No big thing," and toss a bag of Big Joys on the table. "Now that's a burger," he would say triumphantly, sauntering back out into the night. We would chase after him begging for details, for the slightest crumb of information about his epic, erotic adventure. Then, over the next few months, he would tell the story to a constantly changing group of teen males who would never know the bliss he had found. It would be the most glorious time of his life, and it would never end. He even imagined gathering the grandchildren on his lap sometime in the next millennium and saying, "Lemme tell you young'uns about the night I nailed Janelle..."

So flying past her at 108 mph was tough, but fifty miles later, flying past the Samoa at a more sedate 75 was even tougher. All he saw in the glimpse he had was me, flicking off the readerboard sign ("Deluxe Burger and F ies, $1.50"), closing and locking the sliding glass front door for the night. Stackhouse was not a symbolism guy. In English class he never did get the "river" bit in *Huckleberry Finn* or the "highway" in *All The King's Men*. But that closing Samoa door meant something to him. He saw it as closing the door on his life as a child, like a symbolic Bar Mitzvah with F ies for Stackhouse. His juvenile fantasies would never again be able to overcome the adult realities that were beginning to plague him. He was screwed for life just like everybody else. And that night he knew it.

Low Ball finally came to a full stop at the Trucker's Rest in South Tacoma. He and Stackhouse ran into the restaurant men's room and pissed side by side for three minutes as their hideous lives flashed before them, Stackhouse lacking one Janelle to fulfill his dreams, Low Ball deficient by one Louise. Two men in love, two men alone.

"Hey, kid," the trucker said as they zipped up and came out together, "Whatdya say we go inside the joint here and I'll buy you a burger. The burgers are crap, but they're big."

"No," Stackhouse said sincerely, "I don't really like hamburgers much. I've got to get home. Thanks for the ride."

"No problem, kid," Low Ball answered, smacking Stackhouse on the back. "And you remember what I told you about women."

"I'll never forget it," Stackhouse answered honestly. He walked away toward Interstate 5 looking to hitch a ride back north. Home was only 50 miles away but it took him fourteen hours to get there. There was no hurry. He was in that frame of mind where you have so little to think about you have a lot to think about.

When he hadn't come back after a while and she was sated with the burgers and the gorgeousness of the mountains, Janelle fired up the cooled-down Dodge and drove home. She left his car at the Samoa, where Stackhouse tried to pick it up a few days later. Janelle had accidentally left the dome light on, so the battery was dead.

There was nobody around to give Stackhouse a jump-start when he arrived because it was four in the morning. It was four in the morning because he didn't dare show his face when the Samoa was occupied. He knew we were waiting for him, knew that Janelle had already been debriefed about the evening's events, knew that we knew he didn't get any. And that if he claimed he did we wouldn't believe him and Janelle would kick his ass for lying about it. Then Steve would really beat the crap out of him because he'd be the only guy who did believe it. Stackhouse was prepared to endure Steve's brutality for a night of passion with Janelle, but not for the night he'd actually had. When he finally did show his face it took us three weeks of relentless interrogation to hear about the truck, the sorghum, and what it's like in South Tacoma real early in the morning. Then he told it often. He cut all that about how good the Big Joy burger is. As far as I know he never went back for another.

The Golden Horseshoe

IN 1965 MERCER ISLAND Police Chief Gus Gilmore had a sheet of stained plywood nailed to the office wall behind his desk. Written across the top in large hand-painted letters was: "Dangerous Weapons Confiscated From Mercer Island Youth." The Chief was very proud of it. It showed that his officers could do something besides harass people who double parked in the shopping center or built their trash fires too high. They could stain big pieces of plywood, and were not afraid to confiscate dangerous weapons from us mad dog local youth.

The *Mercer Island Reporter* did a big feature on the Chief's homemade visual aid shortly after it went up. The Samoans were not impressed. Geoff eagerly showed everyone the front-page photograph of the Weapons Wall because what he called his "military assault slingshot" was prominently displayed. We found out later that the cops took it off him just as he was about to plink one of Mrs. McLaughlin's prize-winning Persian cats. At the time Geoff was six years old. So it took the authorities at least a decade to collect one plywood sheet full of Dangerous Weapons. No wonder they wanted hard evidence to prove they actually did something.

I saw the weapons in person just once, while visiting the Chief's office. It was during my four hours as the Designated Non-fairy Rotary Club Boy of the Month. Part of the honor, besides the Chicken Special in the back room of the Island Plaza Coffee Shop, was a ceremonial photograph published in the newspaper. This shot was always taken in Chief Gilmore's office on the way to the luncheon, I guess to demonstrate what arms-around-the-neck buddies we outstanding youth were with the cops. The guy from the *Reporter* who took the picture was in a hurry to get to an azalea show, which is why Friday morning's *Reporter* that week was of great amusement to the Samoans. The picture was hastily framed so it looked like my head was one of the Dangerous Weapons Confiscated from Mercer Island Youth.

Four years later I was back in the Chief's office, all growed up and doing some radio news work. Same chief, same government-issue furniture, same plywood Visual Aid on the wall. But the assault slingshots, peashooters, and the Swiss Army knife collected from Curtis' father were all gone. In their place were pill bottles and plastic bags, and a revised headline: "Dangerous Drugs Confiscated From Mercer Island Youth." The youth had been through a rough four years, and the bad times were far from over.

In 1965, though, if you tried to sell a local guy a "lid" he would have thought you were in the home canning supplies business or hocking your hat. Marijuana was what Russ Tamblyn kept in his hubcaps in *High School Confidential*. It was a movie prop, as relevant to our lives as Frankie Avalon's surfboard or *The Man From U.N.C.L.E.'s* primordial cell phone. Heroin was the stuff of jazz musicians and people lying on the street in downtown New York City. Cocaine didn't really exist outside of Sherlock Holmes stories and Fu Manchu novels. LSD had something to do with the Mormons. Crack was the result of bending over in loose pants.

Our sin of consumption was beer. A few guys actually liked the stuff. Others wanted to collect the labels from Ranier-brand beer bottles. The four dots on the back of some of the labels were a socio-sexual icon not worth explaining any more.

My particular group thought of beer as a kind of dorkiness inhibitor. We watched our parents drink it and even more exotic libations with their friends and become slightly less boring people than when they weren't drinking it. And we knew of places where our older brothers sat around, drank beer, and met big healthy girls whose inhibitions went out the window with the first sudsy sip—

Teen Heaven by any guy's definition. We yearned for that beer-induced camaraderie and those beer-infused women.

One evening a group of guys was in conference at the Samoa bemoaning the fact that there was no place a sixteen-year-old could go to have a couple of brewskis and be socially enchanting except the back seat of a dark car on a dead end road. We didn't want to get drunk. We just sought a convivial atmosphere conducive to light-hearted banter. The fact that we were in just such a place at the Samoa was lost on us. Somehow beer was the lubricant that made it all magical.

Geoff, the sensualist-in-training, was particularly vexed. "We're old enough to fight their wars but not old enough to drink their liquor!" he moaned rhetorically. He wasn't yet old enough to do either, and when he was old enough a few years later and there was a real war to go fight in he stumbled into the Selective Service Center for his physical wearing polio leg braces he got for fifteen bucks at the Salvation Army. (It didn't work. The braces were for a small child so it looked like Geoff's polio was restricted to his calves.)

The limited means by which we could attain our goal were pondered. Geoff introduced fake ID to the discussion, ironic because he had such a baby face he would be carded into his late 30s. He actually had some fake ID, identifying Geoff's alcoholic Mr. Hyde as Marine Corps Lieutenant Sylvan P. Peterson. The real Sylvan P. was a friend of Geoff's older brother who had carelessly left his wallet unattended one day while swimming.

We inspected the Marine Corps Identification Card carefully and in wonder, because Geoff looked about as much like the square-jawed, 28-year-old, six foot two Marine as a kitten looks like a Greyhound bus. "Has this ever worked, Sylvan?" Clifford finally asked. "Perhaps at a bar operated by the Lighthouse for the Blind?"

Geoff stared into his root beer float. "I don't know," he admitted, near tears. "I've never had the guts to try it."

One member of that night's discussion group hadn't said much, but then he rarely did. Roger was a shy guy from a shy family. I was his friend for a decade and I can't ever remember being in his home or meeting his parents. A year before he'd gotten a copy of *Catcher In The Rye* for Christmas from a liberal aunt, and the book had changed his life. He realized there was a world out there, and it was a lot more interesting than the world he was in. You had to know him pretty well to see the effect Holden Caulfield had on him, but it was profound. He went from being a guy most people assumed was dim to a guy who knew things—not just school things either, but small bits of information that moved life along, opened it up. If one of the categories in the school annual that year had been "The Guy Most Likely to Go to New York and Disappear Into Greenwich Village" Roger would have been the easy winner.

One of those things he knew about was just what we needed that night. Roger offered the information that there were taverns not far away where nobody would ask for ID. There wouldn't be any policemen around either.

"Where are these wonderful places?" Geoff inquired, amazed and intrigued. The only one Roger knew of for sure was called The Golden Horseshoe. It was located across the floating bridge in what was to become Seattle's tourist-ridden cutesy-pie Pioneer Square, but in the mid-1960's was a dump neighborhood full of broken down buildings and busted up men.

The Golden Horseshoe. I imagined a buffalo head above the bar and sawdust on the floor, an Old West sort of place with Buck Owens and Ernest Tubb on the juke. I pictured dusty cowboys with big hats and happy cowgirls with big butts encased in denim, laughing full loud laughs while they swilled Texas-brewed ale from frosty tankards.

A Field Trip to the Golden Horseshoe was immediately organized. Roger, Geoff, Clifford, Wayne Whitley and I would go directly to this Pilsner paradise and check it out, courageous scouts for what would surely become a mass migration of thirsty Island youth. Wayne was chosen as designated driver, mostly because Wayne was the only one who had a car.

Crossing the Mercer Island Floating Bridge twenty minutes later Clifford finally thought to ask Roger why this Golden Horseshoe was different from all the other beer joints that shunned our custom. Roger said that the reason underage people could get into the Golden Horseshoe was because it was a queer bar. By that he didn't mean odd, either, he meant a place for homosexuals. With homosexuality illegal, such places paid bribes to keep the police from harassing their clientele. Our patronage would just be a minor side benefit to the dearth of cops at the good old 'Shoe.

The first reaction to this news was silence. Then Wayne's brow descended a half inch, a sure sign that he was perplexed.

"Why are teenage homos allowed to drink beer," he asked, "when normal guys get thrown in jail for it? "

Clifford answered immediately. "It's because teenage homos have so little else." He could never resist an opportunity to slip a hook into Wayne's mouth and watch him dance on the water. "Washington and five other states let homos drink at fourteen. And drive too. To compensate for their lonely, degrading lives."

"Drive! They can drive at fourteen?" For Wayne this was a far greater outrage than juvenile drinking.

"Yes. In California it's age twelve, but then that's California for you. Chances are, if you see somebody very young driving, he's a homo. Or a homette, if he's a girl. "

"I'll be damned!"

"I thought girl homos were called something else," I offered from the back seat. I couldn't help myself. Feeding Clifford as he rearranged Wayne's world view was a favorite way for all of us to pass the time.

Clifford turned to look at me from the front seat, smiling his little smile, waiting for more. And I obliged. "I believe the proper term for the ladies you're talking about, Clifford, is 'Lesbians.'"

"That's correct, youngster," said Clifford, nodding in agreement. "But you have to understand that 'Lesbian' is a medical designation. It's like 'hemophiliac' for someone who bleeds a lot. 'Lesbian' is...it's medical, and mytho-logical as well. From the mystic Isle of Lesbos."

"The what? What island?" Wayne had bitten hard on the hook. It's only fair to say that he wouldn't have been nearly as gullible if he weren't also an inveterate seeker of knowledge. He wanted to know about everything, and all his life would assume that those around him knew more than he did. Usually this assumption was correct. In this case he thought there were only four islands of any impor-tance: Mercer, where he lived; Treasure, which he had once read about in a *Classic Stories* comic book; Iwo Jima, where his uncle had just missed being a world-famous hero because he was eating a sandwich and let some other guys put up the flag; and Thousand, where the salad dressing comes from.

Roger joined in. "Yes, Clifford," he asked, "Where is this fascinating island?" Clifford now turned his attention to the three of us in the back seat. All the troops were engaged except Geoff, who was lost in a beer reverie.

"The Isle of Lesbos is off the coast of...of California. Near Los Angeles." Clifford gave us his I-dare-you-to-laugh stare. "Twenty six miles." He turned to see Wayne's reaction. "Twenty six miles across the sea."

My turn. "But Clifford, isn't that where Santa Catalina is? Like the song? '26 miles across the sea, Santa Catalina come a'waitin' for me...'"

We all sang, even Geoff, "'Romance, romance, romance, romance...'"

Clifford: "There are actually three islands. It's a chain. No, it's an archipelago, like the Aleutians." His eyes gleamed in the dark. "There's Santa for homos, Catalina for cross-dressers, and Lesbos. For homettes." In the back seat we applauded. We couldn't help ourselves.

"Thank you very much," Clifford said politely.

"What's a cross-dresser?"

"Wayne, that's a person who prefers to wear the clothing of the opposite sex, whether they are a homo, a homette, or a person such as yourself." Clifford laid a friendly hand on Wayne's shoulder. "So that if you were to visit Catalina, the cross-dresser's island—and I think you'd have a lovely time there, I hear it can be quite charming—you would meet many attractive men and women. Only all the women would be men and all the men would be women. It would be an interesting time for you, I suspect. But confusing."

"Yeah, but I could tell them apart. No guy dressed as a girl could fool me. And the other way around."

"But if you visited you'd have to dress as a girl as well. That's the law on Catalina. And you could drink liquor freely. You'd want to drink, I suspect. A lot. You could put your huge, taffeta-wrapped butt on a stool right there at a real bar and order up cocktails with strange names. And all night long, girls—who would really be boys—would sit beside you and ask personal questions."

A more acute soul than Wayne Whitley would have smelled a rat some time earlier in this conversation. But blind faith and a short fuse were important aspects of his eternal quest for knowledge. He would always be a guy who believed that there was a place in the world called Santa that was 100% homosexual by government decree and that if he went there he'd be forced to be homosexual too. Wayne was a radio talk show listener just waiting for that time when radio talk shows would become offensively stupid. And like such listeners of the future his threshold for personal outrage was very low. He was outraged.

"Well I think it's a goddamned crime, these special privileges," he told us. "Nobody makes them be homos."

Clifford shook his head. "That's where you're wrong, my young friend. Many of them are the offspring of homosexual parents who are forced into the pervert life. America has millions of all-queer families."

Wayne thought this over. He did have his moments of clarity. "Wait a minute," he said finally. "If the parents are homos, where did the kids..."

"Imagine," Clifford interrupted, "how difficult it must be to tell your homette and homo mom and dad that, well, that you're a non-perv. That you don't want to vacation on Lesbos again, you want to go to Disneyland with the normal kids. Well, most guys would rather just pose as degenerates than break their parents' hearts like that. They become closet heterosexuals, and live sad, frustrating lives."

That's when the rest of us lost it, and Wayne got it. He was very gracious at these times. "Okay, I've been had," was all he ever said. We assumed that some day he'd get had once too often and beat the crap out of Clifford, but it never happened. The oddest thing about both of them was that they were best friends. You could argue that Wayne liked Clifford because he was the smartest guy he knew and he thought he could learn from him, and Clifford liked Wayne because his particular sense of humor required a stooge. But their relationship was far more than that. They were like Laurel and Hardy, who had their differences but were deeply fond of each other. Clifford and Wayne still are. Their houses are on the same street, they have nice wives and kids, and they regularly vacation together. One year they even went to Catalina. And Disneyland.

Roger was usually accurate about worldly things like cop-free homosexual bars, so we believed him. Still, some of us suspected that the moment we walked into the Golden Horseshoe we would be arrested. The *Seattle Times* would photograph us as we were led in handcuffs out the door to a paddy wagon, trying to hide our faces under our sweaters and letter jackets. The next day the front page of the *Times* would feature a shot of us drunken tots under the headline: "Mercer Island Teens/Too Much Money, Too Few Brains." (Subhead: "Also Fruits!") For the next forty years, every employer, landlord and potential girl friend would remember that picture when our names were mentioned. The fact that members of a sexual minority would witness our downfall seemed inconsequential.

It never occurred to us that as a result of our capture we might be identified as sexual minority members. We were so normal, so All-American, so butch, whereas we assumed all homos looked like Liberace, with makeup, jewelry, and flashy leather ensembles. Besides, Wayne and Roger were wearing their letter jackets. (Flashy leather ensembles, come to think of it.) Even though Roger's letter was in tennis, a potentially homo sport, Wayne was a football player, and surely no football player—at least no three-year Kingco League Honorable Mention offensive lineman—could be light in the cleats.

That's what we thought, but until that night none of us had experienced any contact with gay people, even though Wayne had heard some disturbing rumors about Bud Hinkley. The romantic interests of a very precise art teacher had been a lunchroom topic in the ninth grade, but Clifford said he was that way because he was Canadian. He was a nice guy too, so nobody cared much. Accusations of a particular homosexual practice were a standard part of most guys' insult repertoire, but that was just talk. For Mercer Island youth of the Sixties real live homosexuals were as scarce as Puerto Ricans, or so we believed at the time.

Now we weren't on the Island, however, we were driving around Pioneer Square looking for the Golden Horseshoe. And to the secret disappointment of some of us we found it, an average looking tavern with a small neon sign out front announcing Happy Hour details. It wasn't the "Teens Welcome" message we hoped to see, but we still felt committed. Wayne parked his Chevy facing out in case we had to Drink-n'-Dash, and together we approached the entrance, ready to run like cats at the slightest whiff of trouble.

Pushing through the barroom door I expected that moment in movie westerns when Alan Ladd walks into the saloon and everybody in the place goes quiet, and not just because he's four and a half feet tall. But it didn't happen at the Golden Horseshoe. We got looked at of course. It's only natural to glance over when a covey of quail come sliding into a room. But after an initial checkout it seemed like almost everybody in the place made a point of not looking at us. The bartender acted like we were regulars, directing us to the only table with room for five, watching over us pleasantly while we sat down. We all looked as sophisticated as possible when you're so frightened you're about to wet your pants.

"And what will you gentlemen have tonight?" the barman asked, with the half smile of someone enjoying a private joke.

Sylvan P. Peterson had been waiting for somebody to ask him this particular question since the sixth grade. "Do you have..." he asked, looking around casually, "do you have, uh, let's see...beer?"

"Yes we do," the bartender answered happily. "We have a great deal of it, as a matter of fact, in big shiny kegs. A pitcher, gentlemen?"

A pitcher! Genuine tavern talk! We were growing fond of this guy. He didn't look funny at all, but like your older brother, the Phi Delt. Maybe he wasn't one of "them." Just because he worked in such a place, it wasn't fair of us to assume he was a fairy. Probably he had a wife and kids at home and was just doing this in the evenings while he finished up his degree in dental college. His teeth looked like they had seen a lot of quality attention. And for the bartending job he was required to wear the magenta cashmere sweater and lime green Hush Puppies. They weren't a personal choice. It was kind of a queer bar uniform, like the red vests bartenders have to wear in non-queer bars.

With the beer ordered, the Rubicon crossed, we had a chance to look around. The Golden Horseshoe was more of a hallway than a room. The long wooden bar was up against one wall. Jammed against the opposite wall a few feet away were a dozen tiny tables, and there was a small dance floor in the back by the jukebox. The decoration looked like any other tavern's, with a few differences. Somebody had put full makeup and a golden Betty Grable wig on the promotional bust of the Rainier Beer Brewmaster. It made him look like Otto Preminger, if Otto Preminger was playing the title role in the Catalina production of *Mame*.

The clientele was what really set the Horseshoe apart. Except for a sleepy-looking woman perched on a barstool near our table, the place was full of nothing but men, all wearing gray suits. In the gloom they looked like very ordinary types, especially to guys like us, who were expecting an exultation of Liberaci.

More than anything else I remember how sad they all seemed. They were talking the way I assumed people did in taverns, but at the same time there was something furtive about everything they did. One eye always seemed to be on the door. They were just as afraid their parents would walk in as we were. No matter how the beer flowed there was none of the camaraderie or social ease we wanted so much for this place to have.

From the time we entered until the time we left the juke box played the same song over and over again: "Unchained Melody," the Righteous Brothers' swooping pop aria of loving, longing, and waiting: "Wait for me, wait for me, I'll be coming home, wait for meeeeee..." Couples danced, the blobs of gray suit shuffling slowly back and forth under Christmas tree lights that were stapled to the ceiling above the dance floor.

These were loving people, but obviously they had few opportunities to show it. They held onto each other as if every dance were the last dance, every moment another second closer to the time when they would have to walk off into the dark city, back to lives where nobody knew who they really were. The room was filled with passion, but no joy.

Just as our pitcher arrived the woman at the bar got up. She grabbed a chair and came over to our table. Of everybody in the place, she alone had been looking our way since we got there.

"Mind if I join you?" she asked pleasantly, sitting down before anybody could say anything. Not that anybody would have. I was trying to figure out what a woman was doing in such a place, assuming this was a real woman. She certainly looked like a real woman. She looked like... and then I glanced at Roger, who was staring at our new arrival with an expression that was partly fear but mostly fascination. I could see he was having a Holden Caulfield Moment, and I knew why.

Our guest was a prostitute. We were sitting with a woman of the evening. We Young Leaders of Tomorrow were three feet from the gateway to sin, disease, and community college. And this professional portal was interested in us because we were the only people in the place likely to be interested in her.

Her arrival had a strange effect on our little group. For the first time in our lives we were in the presence of a female who would sleep with us without question or complaint. She would let us touch her private parts and maybe she would touch ours and let us have our way with her, if we could figure out what our way was. The fact that money would have to change hands prior to the touching was inconsequential to her overwhelming aura of access. She was the only sure thing any of us had ever met. But far from being erotic or arousing, the accessibility of this person so close, so real, was frightening. She was scaring the hell out of us and knew it. It didn't seem to bother her much.

"I'm Rochelle," she said, pouring herself a beer from our pitcher. (Christ, I had a cousin named Rochelle!) "Where are you boys from? What's the big 'M.I.' for, Wayne?" It's hard to be that incognito when two of your party are wearing knit nametags and school logos.

"Michigan," Clifford answered quickly, before Wayne could give her our names, home addresses and phone numbers. "We are from Michigan. We are college people from Michigan."

"Uh huh," Rochelle said. "I thought maybe you were high school people from Mercer Island."

"That's an understandable mistake. But no."

The rest of us were perfectly willing to let Clifford carry our side of the conversation until we were 21. We mute goons stared at her and she smiled back. Rochelle reminded me of somebody. I did actually know another prostitute, but she was 101 and had been out of the business for 75 years. At last I got it. In the way she talked and dressed Rochelle was a lot like Shirley MacLaine. So either Shirley MacLaine was a very good actress in all those movies where she played hookers, or this hooker had seen the same movies and decided that's how prostitutes are supposed to act. Lust imitating art.

"Any of you Michigan college people looking for some real fun?" Rochelle purred. "Do you want to have a little private party?"

After a pause Clifford very politely said, "No, thank you," as if she'd just offered him half of her tuna sandwich.

"Maybe one of you others. Somebody who has some money. Anybody get their allowance today? We could go out to your car and I'd do things to you you've only imagined on the toilet in the middle of the night."

"Oh Jesus," Wayne Whitley said, lowering his head into our little bowl of beer nuts. Although I think Wayne was reacting to the possibility that these unnamed acts would take place on his upholstery, not the acts themselves. That's the way Wayne thought.

"I could take you all on at once if you really have some bread." I think she thought this would sweeten the deal for us but the effect was exactly the opposite. Rochelle wasn't as sensitive to her potential customers' desires as she thought she was.

I don't know why, but the rest of my colleagues were looking at me for our response to her enhanced offer. I sensed this as I stared intently at a spider on the ceiling above us. The spider was also looking at me expectantly. I had to say something. To just sit there would be rude, and our moms taught us never to be rude.

"While we appreciate your offer," I said as pleasantly as I could, "I think I speak for my friends when I say that, uh, that we're just here for refreshment this evening. Perhaps another time when, uh..." and I trailed off.

"You're really missing something." Rochelle was very matter-of-fact about it.

"I'm sure we are," said Roger, saving me and taking the conversational conch. Or I thought he was, but "I'm sure we are" was all he said. We sat quietly after that. Clifford told me later that he was trying to conjure up what he might be missing. The image of sharing the backseat of the Chevy with the four of us, plus a naked woman, was making him sick to his stomach. Roger was wondering what Holden would do in this situation. Geoff was horrified, but not by the fact that he'd just been propositioned. He was horrified to realize that he liked the taste of root beer a lot better than real beer. Wayne Whitley couldn't remember what he was thinking at the time, although he did like the beer nuts and wanted some more. And I was trying to come up with a way to tell Cathy that I'd spent the evening in a queer bar with a prostitute named Rochelle while she was home helping her mother paint their family room. ("Gee, I'd like to help you, honey, but I have to work.") I was contemplating a few weeks among the living dead.

As "Unchained Melody" ended for the eighth time and then immediately started up again, a soft-spoken, prosperous looking man in his fifties came out of the back and walked up to our table. "Good evening," he said politely. Then he asked Wayne Whitley if he was interested in dancing.

"What? What? Who?" Wayne could not believe that anybody in this place was speaking directly to him.

"A dance," the gentleman repeated. "Would you care to dance with me?"

"Go ahead, Wayne," Rochelle urged, "Give it a shot. Maybe this is what you're looking for." Even with such encouragement Wayne declined the gentleman's offer. He was quite gracious about it for someone who had never been asked to dance by anyone before, and certainly never by a guy wearing an ascot. It was quite a compliment actually, this man picking Wayne out of the crowd of us for a little genteel Righteous Brothers two-stepping.

Wayne didn't see it that way. As soon as the guy was out of earshot he said, "We're outta here right now." It was his car so he had the right to call the pass, but only Geoff objected. He had a bladder the size of a lima bean, and whispered to Wayne that he had to use the john first. I thought the whispering was kind of sweet. Geoff didn't want to say out loud that he needed to pee because he thought that might embarrass Rochelle. As if Geoff could say or do anything in this universe that would embarrass Rochelle.

"Hurry," said Wayne. Geoff jumped up and headed for the back of the Horseshoe.

"Where's he going?" Rochelle asked me. And when I told her Geoff was going to the can she shook her head and said, "That's not a real good idea, kids." We kids didn't know why, but none of us was going to rescue him from whatever horrible things were happening back there. We sat in silent expectation, watching the men's room door with interest.

Less than a minute later Geoff came shooting out of the john like he'd run into Godzilla in there taking a crap. He didn't stop walking real fast until he was out of the Golden Horseshoe, past the Chevy, and on the corner a block and half away. He still hasn't told any of us what he saw in the 'Shoe loo, and it's been more than forty years now.

As we were going out the door after him I glanced back at our table. Rochelle was laughing at something with the bartender and helping herself to the half pitcher of beer we left behind. Personally I'd had two small sips, and remaining on the table were three full glasses. There was one empty glass too. Sylvan P. Peterson was finally a man.

As far as I know, no other Island teen dropped by the Golden Horseshoe after that. Our report to the regulars back at the Samoa was shameful, variations of, "Yeah, there's no hassle, but it's a queer bar." That was all we needed to say. Once we had passed such a judgment no high school kid wanted a tavern brew badly enough to risk being associated with Them and then judged by Us.

After that we didn't talk about our adventure much. The Night of the Golden Horseshoe never became a big part of the Samoa oral history. I think my fellow adventurers felt as I did. We had landed on another planet. The natives weren't inhospitable, but they didn't need us or want us. They wanted to be left alone. Regardless of our benign intentions we were intruders who jeopardized whatever brief happiness they had been able to create for themselves.

I drove past the Golden Horseshoe a few times in the years that followed. Then one day it was gone. Now

I can't remember exactly where it was. The only immediate effect of our field trip was that Righteous Brothers
record sales to Island youth plummeted. To this day I can't
hear "Unchained Melody" without thinking about that
night and those men, wondering what happened to them,
wondering if they ever found the happiness we were all
looking for.

A decade later another gay bar opened in Pioneer
Square, but this one proudly identified itself as such on a
sign at the entrance: For The Gay Community and Their
Friends. It became the place to go for trendy Northwest
professionals regardless of their sexual preferences. The
night I stopped by it was a joyful gathering, gay indeed,
full of men and women who wanted to see and be seen.
A live band had replaced the jukebox, and there wasn't a
gray suit in the place.

"Time goes by so slowly, but time can do so much…"
Right you are, Righteous Brothers.

Don

THERE HAVE BEEN SOME legendary short order cooks in the history of West Coast beaneries. Marty Nylon at the Carnival Drive–In in Bellevue, Washington, was famous for saying things like, "As long as you've got hot water, you've got gravy." In Portland, Vince, an ancient black man, made sandwiches at a lunch counter without ever looking at his hands. He just knew where the fixings were, like Ray Charles just knew which piano keys played "Georgia On My Mind." At Juanita's Galley in Sausalito, the giant, woman-like Carmel-eata, whose bright blue hair matched her bright blue muumuu, made the best breakfast I ever had in a joint where no two pieces of furniture matched and you usually had to lift a cat off your chair before you could sit down. Perry, the Hash Browns Master at Seattle's Hasty Tasty, kept many UW students alive simply by putting a slice of American cheese on top of perfectly buttered and cooked spuds. And then there was Don, the Samoa Fish Man.

After a month I wasn't that bad as a short order man in Burgers. There were times at the Samoa when I was right spry in fact, never keeping anybody waiting for more than a few minutes, only screwing up one order in a hundred. Except on Friday nights, when I stank. Literally.

The Holy See was to blame. In the medieval mid-'60s, the Pontiff still insisted that his giant flock abstain from meat on Fridays. Unfortunately for me I worked in a place that turned out the best burger in the free world but also had an excellent, inexpensive fish & chips. So once a week it seemed like every Roman Catholic on our side of Minnesota dropped by the Samoa for a station wagon-full of halibut chunks. When I got home from work on Fridays my father would sniff the air and announce, "The fleet's in!"

The fish wasn't hard to prepare, just inconvenient in an otherwise burger-centric operation. I'd be in the middle of a brace of Cheese Deluxes and some couple would come in with their nine kids and order fish all around. I had to abandon the burgers, get the fish and its batter from the walk-in, and dunk the cold slimy flesh into the sticky yellow goo. Betty didn't allow us to pre-batter the fish because it would get soggy, God forbid anybody should have to eat soggy fish & chips the way they have in England for the last four centuries while they were also producing Bill Shakespeare, Chuck Dickens, Jane Austen and the Dave Clark Five.

Once battered, the messy little nuggets got dropped into the deep fat. I had to stand there watching so they emerged from that greasy little hot tub at the apex of crispy on the outside/tender on the inside. By then the burger meat would be inedible black crumbs. I'd been raised up Unitarianily to believe that everybody has a right to his or her own religious beliefs, but after just a few Fridays on the job I came to loathe Catholics and their doctrines, rituals, cars full of kids, and especially their food taboos. Samoa Friday nights had devolved into a pod of Irish and Italians of all sizes standing around the cramped area in front of the counter, waiting impatiently. I assume evil thoughts about me were turning up in a lot of the confessionals at St. Monica's. I didn't care.

Betty did care, so she found help. Don was a small, thin, intense man in his late 40s, whose dark jowls glistened with sweat after just a few minutes on the job. As Betty explained it, "On Friday nights, Don will come in and do fish, and you do everything else." That was dandy with me.

Conversationally great short order cooks are of two types. There are those who never shut up, even if they end up talking mostly to themselves. Carmel-eata would speak directly to each of the eggs cooking before her, informing them as to their final destiny in life; over easy, sunnyside, etc. The second type of short order person is the guy who can go for three eight-hour shifts in a row and never speak a word to anyone. Marty Nylon was like that. ("If I wanted to chat I'd be a bartender.") So was Don. He actually tried to carry on a conversation with a customer just once, the only time a famous person ever entered the Samoa.

Don and I were practicing Short Order Zen that night, staring silently at the deep fat and the grill, reciting our mantras to ourselves. I don't know what his mantra was, but mine was 'Let's have a fire so I can go home. Let's have a fire so I can go home.' It had a nice rhythm to it. 'Let's have a fire so I can go home.'

Counter Personnel Arlene interrupted our meditations. Nodding towards the front door, she whispered, "Am I crazy, or is that Roy Orbison?"

Arlene was not crazy, at least not about the guy in the doorway. The rock n' roll legend looked just like he did on *American Bandstand*. He was black and white and a little out of focus.

"What do you suppose he wants?" In the presence of this musical legend Arlene had forgotten where she was.

"Maybe he wants something to eat," I said. "Why don't you go recommend a good restaurant in the area."

"I'll handle this," Don said, untying his apron. It had never occurred to me that Don was a music lover, and if it had I would have thought he went more for Faron Young, Porter Wagoner—all those Grand Ole Opry types with the silhouettes of rhinestone farm animals sewed onto their clothing. Or given his religious beliefs, the Mighty Fortress that is George Beverly Shea. But clearly there were years of Roy Orbison appreciation in Don. What else would send a true cook to the counter, a place he had never been before even though it was only four feet as the fly flies from the deep fat?

While Arlene and I crouched behind the bun warmer and listened, Don slowly approached Roy and gave a little bow, like a schoolboy about to recite "The Boy Stood On the Burning Deck." "Good evening," he said. "Welcome to the Samoa. What can I get for you?" Don said it like anything was possible, from a full fish dinner to rotating Roy's tires.

Roy squinted up at the "Bill O' Fare" printed on the wall above the counter. It wasn't a complex menu, but it took him a while to make his choice, probably because the lighting in the Samoa wasn't meant for someone wearing dark glasses at 9:30 on a Friday night.

"Bucketa chicken, all dark," Roy finally mumbled, "n' a Doctor Pepper."

Don was disappointed. "And would you care for anything else, Mr. Orbison?" he asked. "Maybe some fish? It would be an honor to..."

"Yeah," Roy interrupted, peeking over his shades at Don. "Somethin' else. Where can I get a broad around here?"

The only noise in the next few seconds was Arlene and me trying to keep from laughing out loud. Don was a born-again Christian, not the kind who wears plaid suits and grins all the time, but a quiet one, who's found Jesus but doesn't feel any particular need to tell everybody else about his discovery. In his pre-Jesus days, when he'd still been born just the once, he may have had some experience finding broads for himself and others, but I doubt it. And those days were long gone. So when Roy made his inquiry Don just smiled a sweet, sad smile and backed away from the counter. Staring intently at the floor, Don kept retreating straight past the grill and out the back door of the Samoa. He got in his car and sat there for a while.

I cooked up a bucket of thighs and drumsticks while Arlene, though flattered, turned down Roy's invitations a few times. After the rock n' roll legend drove away we never mentioned Roy Orbison again around Don. And when somebody played "Pretty Woman" on the jukebox, he would stare into the fryer and suffer.

Don was a Master of the Deep Fat, and I was proud to work beside him. He never wasted a movement, directing all his time, energy and concentration towards those little bubbling brown bastards. He could even predict who was going to have fish, and how much, by the way they looked. So by the time all the Monihans reached the counter to order Don had the correct number of nuggets picked, dipped and cooking, just because Dad Monihan was driving a 1963 black Buick and Mrs. Monihan had something of the señorita about her. Don never explained how he knew, he just knew, the same way some mechanics know just by looking at your car that it's $846 from going anywhere. Don's prediction bit was just one of the skills he needed for the job.

He was something we suburban tots hadn't seen all that much of in action. He was a blue collar working man. Slowly, one sentence at a time, I heard his story—the one wife, four kids story. He'd learned to cook in the Merchant Marine. I suspect he'd been quite a rouser around the world until he finally came home, an alcoholic with a bad heart. He still had the bad heart, but now it was full of Jesus. That kept him going, as a junior high school janitor, a night watchman, and the Samoa Fish Man on Friday nights.

It seemed like a murderous life to me, a schedule no one should have to endure. But I don't think Don ever thought much about it. He did all the work because he could, because the work was available to him and you don't turn down work if your family is depending on you to bring home the halibut. And every Sunday, on his only day off, he did odd jobs around his church. He knew that his time, skills and devotion were worth far more than the cash he could afford to put in the plate. If you asked him why he was killing himself he'd say he had a wife and four kids. And though he wouldn't say it, he had dreams, too.

One Friday night between Catholics he turned to me and asked, "You goin' to college?" I was so startled I couldn't remember for a moment. He had never asked me a direct question before that wasn't specifically fish-related, and certainly had never shown the slightest interest in my life. When I answered yes he looked even more intense than he normally did and said, "I want my boys to go to college."

After another hour of fish, burgers and silence, he asked, "What's a good college to go to?" the way somebody else might ask what restaurant served the best lasagna. That was Don. He saw something that needed doing and he went over and did it, without any ritual. I really couldn't answer his question because I didn't know anything about his kids.

"Colleges are kind of like restaurants, they have different specialties. What are your sons interested in, what do they want to do with their lives?" I thought that might give me some idea.

Don looked at me for a long time and then said, "I don't know." He said it very quietly and went back to his fish. We never talked about colleges again. He was embarrassed, not by his dream, but by his fathering. He'd been working so hard for so long that he hadn't spent enough time with his family, and he knew it. I was sorry I asked and thought about apologizing. But it was too late for that.

He had the eerie calmness I've seen since in ex-cons, a snake-like placidity that doesn't quite hide the fire inside. I only saw Don's fire once, on a mad Friday evening when the fish were going into the deep fat in schools.

I was on my break, sitting in the Samoa lounge reading the specs on the AutoChlor dishwasher for the hundredth time. The Samoa didn't have an AutoChlor dishwasher because the Samoa didn't have any dishes. We just had the manual, and usually it was the only thing around to read. To this day I think I could field strip a 1963 AutoChlor Majestic 385 if I had to.

Out front, just on the other side of the wall, I heard a guy with little Indian Guides swirling around him order fifteen Smo burgers: "Three with mustard only, five with mustard and ketchup, six plain, no, make that five plain, one with mayo. Uh, how many is that now?" He was the kind of customer and it was the kind of order that drives cooks mad, especially for the Smo burger, a little nothing that was on the menu strictly for little kids and those people who think anything called Deluxe must weigh at least eight pounds.

I should have jumped up and helped Don, but a break is a break. I heard him slap the fifteen patties on the grill, and I went back to the energy-saving advantages of the Autochlor Majestic 385.

After a few minutes the first Smo flew past me, heading out the back door. Another one followed immediately, a little greasy flying saucer that smacked off the wall of the walk-in and then plopped to the concrete floor below. That wasn't the way we usually handed them out, so I peeked around the corner. Don was bouncing burgers sidearm off the walls, the ceiling, and then me.

I knew immediately what had happened because I'd done it myself more than once. He'd been concentrating on his fish and automatically dressed all the Smo buns standard—ketchup and mustard, one pickle slice on top. And when correcting that mistake made him lose an order of fish, he snapped. It was a very Don-like snap. From his expressionless face you would have thought the Burger Heave was a regular Samoa Friday night ritual, like changing the grease filters.

After all fifteen burgers had been launched into the atmosphere Don calmly got out fifteen more patties and flopped them down on the grill as if nothing had happened. Arlene and I scrambled around gathering the ex-food. It was understood that Don would never have anything to do with those particular Smos again. The black fish he set aside, and an hour later he ate it himself for dinner. It was a kind of self-imposed penance, I guess, a piscatorial hair shirt. And for the rest of the evening he didn't speak at all. Not a single word.

One Friday night I was off duty and hanging around the Samoa with the guys. We were discussing popular culture, which for us meant television. Wayne Whitley had been shocked earlier that day to learn that the laconic "Mingo" on the *Daniel Boone* television show wasn't a real Indian at all but a Las Vegas lounge singer named Ed who was wearing a wig. Wayne was a devoted reader of *TV Guide* and was constantly getting shocked by items in the "Inside Scoop" column. It was the only "news" he ever read.

"Mingo's a phony! I'm never going to watch *Daniel Boone* again!" Wayne Whitley said bitterly, his belief in television's honesty and integrity shaken forevermore. For much of his young life Wayne thought that *Gilligan's Island* was based on a real incident, that the ludicrous submarine in *Voyage to the Bottom of the Sea* really existed, and that there really was a Ponderosa covering three quarters of Nevada and operated entirely by four guys and a Chinese cook. Clifford was somewhat to blame for encouraging these beliefs. But now Doubt had settled in Wayne's heart, and it was sad to see.

Clifford tried to be soothing. "*TV Guide* is wrong, Wayne. I know for a fact that Ed Ames is a proud member of the Arapaho nation, a regular big-time brave. "

Geoff said that maybe they were both right, because his father told him Ed Ames was one of the Ames brothers. They were in show business so they had to be Jewish. His father said that the American Indians were the Lost Tribes of Israel. Israel is where all the Jewish people are; ergo, Ed Ames was an Indian, and a Las Vegas lounge singer, and a member of the Lost Tribes.

The arrival of the Lost Tribes into the conversation would have stopped a lot of people cold, but not us. We often heard about the Lost Tribes of Israel from Geoff, because his father thought that every group on earth he didn't understand was the Lost Tribes, including the Irish, the Basques, the Shriners, and the Southern Democrats. Geoff's father Hugh was a renowned crackpot. He was constantly writing Letters to an Editor somewhere about the issues of the day. A collection of these unpublished epistles would show that every issue on earth eventually had something to do with the danger of fluoridated water, the ubiquity of the Lost Tribes, or both. Fortunately Hugh was a benign crackpot. He didn't think there was anything wrong with the American Indians being the Lost Tribes, as long they didn't mess with the water. It was just a fact. And his one true believer was Geoff.

Clifford was having none of it and the Lost Tribes always gave Wayne Whitley a headache. "I can prove he's an Indian," Clifford insisted. "You remember the *Tonight Show* where Mingo was a guest, and he throws a tomahawk that hits the plywood human target right in the crotch?" (Of course we remembered. Who hasn't seen that? Johnny

Carson called it a 'frontier bris.') "Well, that's where his Indian name comes from. Ames. It's not spelled A-M-E-S. It's actually spelled A-I-M-S—short for AIMS LOW." Screaming and laughing at this stunning explanation rose up immediately in our booth and continued until Don came around the wall.

"If you boys can't behave you'll have to leave," he said quietly. His intense, forceful manner gave some of my colleagues the impression that he had a sharp knife hidden on his person and was prepared to use it on us. He glanced at me, very considerately passed on the "you should know better" stuff, and went back to his fish.

Geoff, who'd been in the Samoa every Friday night for two years, said, "Who the hell is that?"

"He's the Fish Man." I tried to explain. "That's Don. He cooks all the fish. You've seen him."

In fact they hadn't seen him, hadn't ever noticed the dark sweaty guy who peered out under the warming lights at them, guessing correctly that they weren't fish people. For months they had looked right through Don as if he didn't exist. And when I ran into some junior high kids I found out Don didn't exist for them either. He was just that guy, the one who wore the same gray Sears work clothes every day to school, the one who showed up with the mop and bucket whenever a kid threw up. For all I know the people at his church were just as unaware of the small, tired man who spent every Sunday painting and plumbing for the glory of his God.

Jim Wichterman was one of Mercer Island High's best teachers in the 1960s. He taught a lot of now very successful people how to think, not what to think. One day towards the end of the school year he told a roomful of smug, college-bound seniors that it would do us all a lot of good to work on a punch press in Detroit for a year before we inflicted ourselves on higher education. At the time, full of our own good fortune and bright prospects, we laughed him off. Working next to Don at the Samoa I began to get an inkling of what Wichterman was talking about. Knowing how to think, and knowing how to do a piece of work, are not the same thing. A guy needs both skills. And he usually needs the work skill first.

Don is dead now, the heart attack we all knew he would have one day. I never met his kids so I don't know if they went to college. In fact, I don't even know what Don's last name was. He was always just the Fish Man. One of the Greats.

Tucker

BY THE FALL OF '64 there were a handful of Latino families on the Island, one Native American family I knew about, Jill Lee's folks and a few other Asians. Everybody else seemed to be ex-European in some way. People thought you were real ethnic if you had the slightest accent—except Scandinavian—or your immediate ancestors came from farther east than Vienna. Jews less than two generations removed from Ellis Island were considered downright mysterious, although not always in a good way. At least that was Clifford's contention after someone accused him of being a member of the International Jewish Conspiracy.

"Damned right I am," Clifford responded. He bragged that the International Jewish Conspiracy had been awarded the 1958 Gold Prize in Krakow "for 'the best cuisine of any international conspiratorial organization.' We kicked the hell out of the Bildenbergers and the Illuminati. It was the latkes that put us over the top."

I suppose some people committed overt acts to turn Mercer Island into the golden ghetto it was, but mostly the Island was the way it was because that's just the way it worked out, given the cost of land and the folks who were around to buy it. Thirty years later the area would reflect the far greater ethnic diversity of the software/coffee/dot. com people, but in '64, at the Samoa, that hadn't happened yet. Microsoft wasn't selling for anything because little Billy Gates was wandering around Lakeside School in North Seattle carrying his *Lost In Space* lunchbox, with 25 cents milk money in his pocket. That's why I went through eleven years of public education and never sat in the same classroom with an African- American. Then came the twelfth year, and Tucker Reese.

My first day as a senior I was pretending to shoot the breeze along with twenty other guys in the high school's large entrance hall. It was before first period, and we were participating in a ritual being observed at that moment in every co-educational high school in the co-educational part of the Universe—checking out the new meat as it came in the door. Our primary interest was young ladies, but notice was also taken of new guys who were very tall (potential basketball players), very large (potential football players), or prematurely bald (potential beer buyers).

Tucker Reese showed up twenty minutes before the bell. He glanced back at the car that dropped him off, and then just came through the door like Archie Andrews. In the 1964 halls of Mercer Island High School he looked very alone, very nervous, and very black.

His arrival was not a surprise to some of us because of Neil Shulman. Neil and his sister Fawn were the most political people I knew, joining causes when they were still just mild concerns for most folks. As little kids they door-belled for John Kennedy with such ferocity they actually scared a lot of their neighbors. Fawn even made the AP wire in 1959 when she announced from the podium at some rally that Richard Nixon was "...evil incarnate, a blight on the nation!" Coming from a ten-year-old girl in a frilly white dress with a red-white-and-blue bow in her hair it made quite an impact. (She had a framed letter from the President-elect on her bedroom wall offering her a job as a speechwriter when she turned 21. It was still there, on a different wall in a different world, when she turned 35.)

Neil was the first person in our class who even knew there was a war going on in Vietnam. He was certainly one of the first kids in the country to propose at a student council meeting that the Associated Students of Mercer Island High School officially take a stand opposing American involvement in Southeast Asia. Advisor Vice–Principal Murray just laughed.

"Your anti-American crap will never fly as long as there's breath in my body," Murray barked at Neil. Later that day Murray called the local FBI office and told them that, "because I'm a patriotic American," they ought to look into the loyalties of the Shulmans.

"Oh, we already know all about them," said the FBI.

"I'm not the least surprised," Murray said gleefully.

"Thank you for your call," the FBI said politely.

The FBI was actually telling the truth (imagine!) when they admitted they knew the Shulmans. Neil's father Herb worked for the government. Clifford claimed he was a CIA operative, but that was principally for Wayne Whitley's benefit. And Wayne believed it, even though spies were supposed to look like James Bond back then and Neil's father looked more like James Thurber.

Herb Shulman, I was to learn, was one of the top legal commandos in the Justice Department, a civil rights expert who was so good at his job he was allowed to live where he chose to live. He wanted good public schools and a decent environment for his wife and kids because he'd seen so many bad public schools and awful environments in his work. But that meant he was on the road a lot, around the South in the '50s and '60s, around the North in the '70s and '80s. Neil and Fawn worshipped him, even as they fought off the unsettling suspicion that their father cared more about injustices to strangers than he cared about his own family. It wasn't true, but it looked that way a lot of the time.

I used to wonder why Neil hung around the Samoa as much as he did. He was a vegetarian—the Lone Vegetarian in the Mercer Island student body, as far as I knew—in a place where the very air we breathed had a lot of vaporized animal flesh in it. His regular Samoa order was renowned: "Cheese Deluxe, extra onions, extra lettuce and tomato, extra cheese, five pickle slices, hold the meat." I had one with him once out of curiosity. It wasn't bad, but it needed something. Meat, I thought. Bean curd, Neil thought.

I think Neil liked us but I also think he saw us as The Masses and he thought he should be One with the Masses. The closest he ever really got, at least at the Samoa, was a Friday fish night when he spotted Don hiding behind the Deep Fat.

"Who's that?" Neil asked me. I told him what I could about Don, how much I admired his ability to do what he always called 'a piece of work,' no matter how dull, difficult or dirty it was. Neil began to swoon. Before I could stop him he rushed back behind the counter, grabbed Don's hand and started pumping it, calling Don 'brother worker.' This made Don extremely nervous. Friday nights after that he'd duck out the back door whenever Neil showed up to talk about The People's Struggle.

We masses once rose up at Neil's request. The previous spring Murray announced that students would no longer be allowed to wear shorts to school on hot spring days, not even the knee-length surfer's baggies some guys had been wearing for years. Neil never wore anything but full-length corduroy pants with cuffs; still, he was the first guy to protest this arbitrary ruling. The next day he wore borrowed knee-length shorts to school, and at his urging so did Phil, Dennis, Curtis, Geoff and Jesse. They were all suspended, "until you can return to school properly attired," was how the pink slips read.

What returned to school the next morning, however, were four lawyer-dads, led by The Fuehrer and Herb Shulman. They suggested to Vice–Principal Murray that if all the school administration had to worry about was the erotic effect Curtis' and Neil's scarred and knobby knees might have on teenage girls then the school system was wasting its money on a Vice–Principal for Student Affairs. The students weren't having any affairs, and that salary might better be spent on books and lab equipment. They concluded by saying that they were ready and able to discuss a reallocation of administrative compensation at the next school board meeting.

Faced with the Four Lawyers of his personal Apocalypse Murray immediately caved. The proletariat, backed up by good lawyering, had won the day. It was a particularly useful lesson for all of us who would become more intense masses in the turbulent times later that decade.

Sunday night before the start of our senior year a group of guys gathered at the Samoa to hoist one last Cheese

Deluxe to the lazy crazy hazy days of summer. It was the occasion of another of our undeclared tribal rituals—The Late-Summer Night's Dreams, a round table discussion when we lied to each other about our activities of the three months past. Generally the conversation ran to stories of steamy romantic conquests that couldn't be verified because they always took place somewhere else.

When Neil showed up for this ritual I was surprised. Affairs of the heart and other organs never seemed to interest him much. But there he was, clutching his meat-less, vegetable-laden Cheese Deluxe. He arrived just as Geoff was giving us intimate details of Naomi, a 28-year-old waitress at the Dew Drop Inn on Lake Chelan, where Geoff's family had a summer place.

Neil waited about a minute and then jumped in. He said he had something important we needed to hear. Nothing important anybody needed to hear had ever been said before in the Samoa, so we passed him the conch.

"Have any of you been paying attention to what's going on in the South?" This was Neil, so I knew we weren't about to hear about the sexual conquest of some hot-blooded Alabama Mama. Because Neil was interested in the civil rights movement, I guessed that he wanted to tell us something about that. Freedom Summer had just ended with three murders. But that happened thousands of miles from us. We didn't know any black people. As far as that goes we didn't know any redneck peckerhead racists either.

"You can't think that way," Neil said. "It's our country, and if, if people are being killed for what they are, for what they believe in, no matter where that happens it's our business."

"My dad says it's not as bad as it looks," Wayne Whitley put in. "He says the newspapers and TV are blowing it out of proportion."

"Your dad doesn't know his ass from his elbow," Neil said matter-of-factly. Had it been any other person this statement would have led directly to Wayne grabbing the speaker by the neck and hitting him in the beezer. But Wayne just said, "Okay, yeah, maybe." We cut Neil a lot of slack.

"So what can we do about it?" Phil asked. He cared, but he was also looking for something to do.

"Nothing while we're here. Next summer, after we've graduated, that's when we can go down south and help with voter registration and stuff like that. Maybe we'll get beaten up, but we'll do whatever we can for our Negro brothers and sisters."

I looked at my friends around the table. For this crowd Neil wasn't going to have to save too many places in his Volkswagen bus for that trip southward. We were mostly the offspring of good Northern liberals, but that sounded like a long drive to a hot place that was either deadly or just deadly dull.

Neil wasn't finished. "There's something we can do here, now, tomorrow. The government has this program in the South. Any family that's had a problem because they're Negro, anybody who's been a victim of race hatred, they get the people out of there. They relocate the family if the family wants. They just pick them up and put them down somewhere else. My father is involved in it."

"What's this have to do with the CIA?" Wayne asked.

Neil ignored him. "So there's these people. Named Reese. The father led a march, or a sit-in, something, whatever the reason, he got identified. Two weeks ago in some small Alabama farming town, the Ku Klux Klan burned down his house."

"My God!" Geoff said. "Were they killed, was the family killed?"

"No, they got out, but only with what they could carry. They lost everything else."

"Didn't they have any insurance?" It was Tess, who had just arrived.

Neil looked at her for a moment to see if she was kidding. But Tess was serious. After her father got out of football with most of his brains he went into the insurance selling game and made a bundle. Tess had been told from infancy that if you just have enough insurance you really won't have any serious problems for your entire life. She believed it.

"Tess," Neil explained, in a tone you might use to tell a three-year-old about the importance of washing her hands, "this is a very small town they come from, a farming town. These people don't have indoor plumbing, or, or anything. And the whole system down there has been screwed up. The white power structure has spent a hundred years screwing up the system so black people never will have anything. They'll never have a chance.

"So anyway, this family, the Reeses, the Justice Department is moving them. They're coming here. Actually they're already here. They got the father a job with the city as a policeman."

"Oh, that explains it," Frank Forcade mumbled to himself. Frank's knowledge of the personnel of the Mercer Island Police Department was involuntary, but comprehensive.

"They have a daughter who's like 14 and a son who's 16. His name is Tucker. He'll be at school tomorrow. My dad wanted me to ask you to, to accept him, to be nice to him, help him get adjusted. Not give him any trouble. Can you do that?"

He looked anxiously in all of our faces. I could tell this Tucker guy and his family were very important to Neil, maybe the most important thing that was going to happen in his whole time in high school. But he was still pissing me off.

"Neil, do you really think any of us would give this guy heat?"

"Well, no, but, you never can tell what people are going to do..."

"Neil, you should know us better than that."

Neil looked at me, and for the first time since he came in the door he stopped talking like we were slightly dim strangers.

"You're right. I'm sorry. It's just..."

"And Neil?" Clifford interrupted, before Neil could go into the whole pitch again. "The next time you want to have an intimate little chat like this, don't get the onions on the burger." We returned to the thrilling saga of Naomi and Lake Chelan.

Given his story it wasn't surprising that Tucker Reese looked a little tense the next morning. In his entire life he had never been in a school building where everybody else wasn't black. Now his was the only black face out of more than a thousand other faces, most of them in that hallway trying not to stare at him. I'm sure a lot of adults worked hard to convince Tucker that Mercer Island was an entirely different world from the one his family had just escaped, but it still took guts to walk through that door. And he did it alone, which had to be his choice. Out in the car that dropped him off were parents who were even more anxious than he was. They knew what could happen, but he was just beginning to learn. That's where they stayed, though, out in the car. So let it be remembered: On September 5, 1964, Tucker Reese integrated Mercer Island High School all by himself, without any help from lawyers, cops, Federal Marshals, the National Guard, or Nicholas Katzenbach.

From across the room we saw Neil run in from the parking lot where he'd been lurking behind a tree and grab Tucker before he'd gotten ten feet into the building. Neil had his hand out and a smile on his face like he was Chief Mouseketeer Jimmy Dodd and Tucker was Annette. His quarry jumped back a little at this apparition. Tucker had surely considered the possibility that no matter what he'd been told these strange white boys were going to beat him senseless and hang him from a majestic evergreen the moment he set foot in the school. It just hadn't occurred to him that the attack would be lead by a smiling guy in baggy corduroy pants and an MIT sweatshirt.

Neil went for the Stanley-and-Livingstone opening. "You must be Tucker!" he boomed, grabbing Tucker's hand and pumping it. "I'm Neil Shulman. Welcome to Mercer Island High!"

"Hi. Yeah," Tucker seemed to be saying, although his voice was so soft we really didn't hear much from forty feet away. But we could certainly hear Neil. You would have thought Tucker was Helen Keller, not just a slightly confused, nervous, sixteen-year-old kid.

"We've got a few minutes before first class," Neil bellowed, pointing at that new and marvelous invention, his wristwatch. "Are you supposed to check in at the office?"

"Yeah. Think so."

"Well, let me show you where that is." Neil took Tucker by the upper arm, like he was making an arrest, and wheeled his captive in the direction of the office. Then he stopped, wheeled him back around, and pointed at us.

"But I'm sure you'd like to meet some of the guys first!"

Neil was clearly wrong about that. Tucker Reese looked like he wanted to meet some of the guys never. But Neil had pictured exactly how this morning was going to go and he wasn't about to be thwarted, just because Tucker had an entirely different picture in mind, one that involved not talking to anybody about anything, but sliding in quiet.

"Fellows," Neil said grandly, pulling Tucker in our direction, "I'd like you all to meet Tucker Reese. He's new to the school. A junior. He hails from down south." From what Neil said and the way he said it, I got two messages. First, that he planned to play this like a chapter from a Hardy Boys novel—all this 'fellows' and 'hails from' stuff. And second, that we were supposed to dummy up about what we already knew of Tucker and his family—the Klan, the fire and the big trip north.

Neil went around the group with individual introductions, adding positive personal notes. Clifford was a star of the debate team. I was in the school plays and was actually in a few honors classes. (Thanks a lot, Neil.) Wayne Whitley played football. Frank Forcade was an automotive genius "who has apparently met your father." Curtis... Curtis...Neil struggled a little with Curtis, and finally came up with "Curtis' family hails from Switzerland, and he drives a...a car."

We mumbled our hellos and shook Tucker's hand as our turn came. It was a big hand, warm and wet, at the end of a long arm that hung from a tall, thin body. In the 1960s, even with Wilt Chamberlain and Bill Russell dominating the game, it wasn't yet a stereotype to think that every tall black male must be a great basketball player. But Tucker looked like a great basketball player. He had never played on a basketball team in his life, and never would. His interests lay elsewhere.

After the introductions we just stood there. I didn't see that there was much we could talk about right then, but I had underestimated Wayne Whitley.

"So Tucker," Wayne said, "I hear you been through some shit."

Neil gave a slight whinny. Tucker first looked surprised, and then shot Wayne a quick, shy smile.

"Yeah," he said, "I've been through some of that."

Wayne had some follow-up questions but Neil was too fast for him. He had Tucker down the hall and into the school office before another word was spoken.

For the rest of that week Neil never seemed to let Tucker out of his sight. He even got permission to go to Tucker's classes. Before and after each class the introductions continued, and like ours they were all very positive. If they'd run into an ax murderer Neil would have described him as "handy with tools." At lunch they went from table to table, Neil pulling Tucker by the arm, grinning and introducing, while Tucker spoke only when he had to and only as much as he had to. Clifford said they looked like a road show production of *The Defiant Ones*.

The first Friday night of the school year was always bursting with teen activities. The Evolving Episcopal Youth were holding a get-acquainted dance, the bowling alley had two-for-one student night, and up at the high school the football team was playing the opening game of the season against the powerhouse Lake Washington High Kangaroos. Football players, including Highly Offensive Guard Wayne Whitley, had been practicing for weeks, as if it would help. According to Coach Gruner, it was a "building year" for the Islanders, which meant the team was probably as bad or worse than it had been the year before (2-11). Still, hope springs eternal in the high school heart, so the stands were full. A lot of those people wouldn't bother to see another game all season, so there was a festive once-in-a-lifetime spirit in the crowd, aided considerably by the musical accompaniment. Even though Music Director Jack Hibbard refused to have anything to do with the pep band, it was quite good. And this year they had a new attraction—saxophone player Tucker Reese.

There was also romance in the air, which is another reason the stands were full. The first game of the football season was also the first social event of the school year, a time to see what couples were still together after the summer, who was newly available, who was still single. If you were going to have a meaningful relationship for the new year the game was your first chance to find someone with whom to get meaningful and begin the meaningful process. There were many unattached young men and women who didn't see a single scrimmage that night, but for two hours stood down front with their backs to the field, scanning the stands.

I didn't go that far, but it is also true that I had grown tired of advising other people about their romantic pursuits and wanted some of my own. And because I wasn't particularly looking for an evolving Episcopalian or a two-for-one bowler, I prowled the game. Not for long, because I spotted Cathy sitting alone up behind the band after only a few minutes. Her escort for some of the previous year, the collie, was nowhere in sight, so I hoped that he had become an ex-escort. I went for her like a well-thrown pass, and then did the whole pathetically nonchalant "Oh, is this seat taken?" bit. I'd need three more months of these "accidental" social meetings before I actually had the nerve to ask her out on a date, but that game was where it started. And at least we were relatively alone up in the stands.

Alone lasted for almost two minutes before Curtis joined us. He was in exile. The cheerleaders had told him that he was not to sit in the front row of the bleachers as he had all the previous year. His unwavering stare made them extremely nervous, especially during high kicks and cartwheels. Curtis protested that he was simply a big fan of the cheerleading arts and there was nothing else worth watching on the field. They responded that if he sat in the front row again this year they would tell their football player boyfriends, who were fully prepared to beat Curtis up for ogling.

So he joined us in the back, but he came prepared. Around his neck were binoculars that General Patton would have been proud to own. He had borrowed them from his father, although his father was unaware of it.

Using the glasses, Curtis' concentration on the sideline pep activity was so unwavering that Cathy and I were still alone more or less. Then Clifford came up and sat down on the other side. He was in anguish because the Islanders were doing so poorly. Clifford was devoted to his local teams, but each week his willpower was put to the test. He wanted to stand up and cheer the few good plays, boo the officials, and scream death threats at Coach Gruner. But he had devoted his life to avoiding Outward Displays of Emotion. So he just sat and suffered, making sure everyone around him suffered as well.

Midway through the second quarter (Kangs 22, Islanders 3) Neil appeared from nowhere and flopped down beside Clifford. It was the first time all week I'd seen him without Tucker attached. Apparently it had been a long week for Neil, because he looked like a deflated balloon. He sighed a very long sigh.

Curtis didn't even notice Neil was there. He had cheerleader Missy Sagerson in his sights and was watching her every move with almost clinical interest. That vague feeling you get when you think someone's watching you? Missy had that feeling down to her heels, and she knew who was causing it. She kept jerking her head around, thinking she would catch him somewhere down front leering at her. She could feel Curtis' eyes on her important body parts, but she couldn't spot him. The more she tried the more Curtis chuckled to himself, until Cathy told him to knock it off. Cathy didn't much care for Missy Sagerson—nobody did, really—but just like guys, girls have to stick together about some things no matter how much they dislike each other. Stalking is one of those things.

Curtis had his Missy to watch, but for the rest of us the football field was devoid of anything even remotely interesting. So along with Neil we stared down at the top of Tucker's head. When a time-out was called the pep band immediately stood up and played "The Theme From Peter Gunn" for the sixth time. Far below us, cheer-persons bumped and ground, except for Missy, who had stopped cheering entirely and was standing stock still on the edge of the field, inspecting every single person in the stands one face at a time.

"She's looking for you, Curtis," Cathy said.

"She started in the front row," Curtis answered, still staring through his binoculars. "I figure with the big crowd here tonight I've got three minutes before I have to go hide behind the refreshment stand."

Neil sighed another long sigh, but none of us responded so he finally had to speak.

"It's not going well," he said as if we'd asked.

"When has it ever gone well for this team?" Clifford was testy. "We are an embarrassment to the school, the league, and the sport. And I'll tell you why. Our tradition here is an owner tradition, not a player tradition. The boys down there subconsciously resent the fact that they have to play at all. They were born to be supervisors, not workers. So they think poorer guys should be playing for them while they reap the rewards. And that's why we stink."

"I'm not talking about the team," said Neil, who had never talked about the team. "I'm talking about Tucker."

"You mean people have been giving him trouble?" I asked. "I can't believe..."

"Nobody's given him any trouble. Nobody's given him anything. I figured if he could just get to know people and they got to know him he'd feel at home, he could...I don't know, become part of everything. Be one of us."

Neil stared at his shoes, the band finished, the game started again.

"They say he's a good sax player," Clifford offered as consolation. "My people tell me he's a real asset in the pep band."

Wait a minute. "Clifford," I asked, "do you really have 'people' in the pep band?"

"That's the great thing about pep bands," Clifford continued, ignoring the question. "It's going to take Tucker months to learn the orchestra repertoire, but after only a week at school he's got all the pep band stuff down pat. Because every pep band in America plays the same six numbers. All those pep bands, every Friday night, playing 'Peter Gunn.' 'On Wisconsin.' Whatever that thing is about the Irish."

"'The Notre Dame Fight Song.'" Cathy said. "Unless you're confusing that with 'Stars and Stripes.' Or 'Buckle Down, Wynsocki.'" She'd been a pep band clarinetist but had given it up the previous winter when a large basketball player chasing a loose ball came flying into the stands where the band was set up. He took out all the clarinets, the flute, two snare drummers and Student Conductor Big Ed Fenster. Cathy didn't mind getting pasted by this giant. It was part of being in the pep band. But he was covered with sweat, most of which clung to the musicians. They mopped up the playing floor with towels but the band was left to drip dry. For the next three days, no matter how many times she showered, washed her hair and changed her clothes, Cathy still smelled like Sonny Liston's sweat suit after a long day in training camp. Or at least she thought she did. That was more of a sacrifice than she cared to make in the name of pep.

"Surely 'Louie Louie' is regional," I argued with Clifford. "The Kingsmen—local boys and all that."

"No, it's all over the country. For three reasons. It's easy to play, it's dirty, and even the clumsiest cheerleader can find the beat and dance to it. I bet every high school pep band in America that's allowed to play it plays it. And they'll still be playing it fifty years from now." (Indeed.)

"How is it dirty?" Curtis was still concentrating on Missy and her cheerleading colleagues but he was trying to follow the conversation too.

"Are you guys listening to me!?" Neil was hot. "Can we possibly discuss the pep band repertoire some other time?"

There was something quite endearing about Neil Shulman. His social skills were nonexistent, especially for a bright, well-brought-up guy. He had no sense of humor to speak of. He wore what seemed to be the same pair of pants every day of his life, plus one of his limitless collection of college sweatshirts. He was sensitive to peoples but could be brutally oblivious to individuals. And he couldn't tell a Pontiac Grand Am from a Model A Ford. Yet you would have been hard pressed to find anybody outside the four members of the Islander Young Republican Club who actively disliked him. Neil was that rarity among us, a kid with genuine passion. And there was something attractive about that.

"So what's the problem with Tucker?" I asked.

"You want to know the problem? I'll tell you the problem! He calls me 'Sir.'"

Sir. It hung in the air in front of us like a little dark cloud.

"And you'd prefer 'Neil.'"

"I'd prefer anything to 'Sir.' I'd prefer 'whitey' or 'peckerhead' to 'Sir.'"

"Could he possibly be making fun of you?" Clifford was trying to be conciliatory. "If he was making fun of you that would be a good sign. It would show he wasn't afraid of you."

"How could anyone make fun of me?" The idea never occurred to Neil that he could be a source of amusement. He was so serious, and what he said was so important, and the times were so bad.

"Lighten up, Neil," I said. But he was obviously prepared to be offended by the very idea of Neil-inspired amusement.

"I just mean that joking with you, with anybody, would show that he was beginning to...to be comfortable around us. Is he funny?" Clifford asked.

Neil shook his head. "How should I know? He hardly ever talks, and never starts the conversation. And...and well, when he does talk I have a hell of a time understanding him. It's that accent. It's from another world."

"Why don't you try leaving him alone?" I jumped a little hearing Curtis' voice. I had forgotten he was there. And that was his point.

"Leave the guy alone, that's what he wants. Ignore him, like you ignore me. Who needs another dad?"

"I'm not trying to be his dad."

Curtis finally put his glasses down to look at Neil. "What are you trying to be?"

"I'm trying to be his friend. I thought that was obvious."

"Bull," Curtis said, getting up. "He doesn't want you to be his friend. That's what's obvious. And if he wasn't a Negro you wouldn't pay the slightest attention to him. He's a junior, for Christ's sake. Who needs 'em?"

"This is a different..."

"Bull again. Ignore him, Neil. There's a lot to be said for being ignored. Take it from me." Curtis strolled casually away towards the refreshment stand just as Missy Sagerson started working her way across the top row of the stands.

"He's right, Neil," Clifford said. "Isn't it time you treated this guy like, like he was just another guy and not some class project?"

"Maybe." Self-doubt was a new experience for Neil. He wasn't sure he liked it.

Clifford suddenly laughed. "You know who had it right, from the beginning? Wayne."

"Whitley?"

"That first day, Wayne was the only one of us who talked to Tucker like he was just another guy. 'I hear you been through some shit,' isn't that what he said? That's what anybody would have said to a guy whose house had been burned down by creeps."

Neil got a very strange look on his face. "Whitley is the only guy he asked me about all week long. Wayne Whitley. Jesus. I'm taking advice from Curtis and Wayne Whitley. What is going on?"

Clifford laughed. "They're the masses, Neil, the proletariat. You're supposed to listen to them sometimes. How else can you tell them what they want to hear?"

A few minutes later the whistle blew for halftime (Kangs 33, Islanders 6) and people came trudging past us up the grandstand aisle. The pep band finished their final first half number ("Louie Louie") and came up last. Tucker was walking with Big Ed Fenster and Chuck Deeter, talking pep band talk. He spotted Neil on the top row next to the aisle and fear came into his eyes. But Neil just said "Hey," and turned back to his conversation with Cathy about their World History class. It was a small but important moment for both guys. It was the moment Neil let Tucker go off to be Tucker, whoever that might turn out to be.

Tucker found his own friends, and it didn't take very long. The first one was Big Ed. Using some sheet music mailed out from Tucker's old school they transformed the Pep Band into one of the funkiest high school sports music ensembles north of L.A. As word spread, even Jack Hibbard came to the games to hear them, especially the Deeter/Reese duets. At first Missy Sagerson and her cheerleading colleagues had trouble with the new material. It's not that easy to do splits, cartwheels and pyramids to a medley that begins with a cornet solo of "At the Jazz Band Ball" and four minutes later has evolved into jazz riffs by two guys who worship Miles Davis and Charlie Parker. The cheer squad eventually adjusted after they got help from Tucker's sister Artis, who knew some steps, who had some moves. Artis would become a cheerleader herself two years later. To this day remnants of the Fenster-Reese Repertoire can be heard in Northwest pep bands. They still do "Louie Louie," but usually only once a night, as a kind of sop to us old timers who show up for the games.

Tucker, Artis and their folks came into the Samoa occasionally, one of the only families that always came in together. They'd been through some trouble and it made them a much closer group than your average Mom, Dad and two kids. Although you wouldn't have known it by their eats. They boxed the menu; Tucker had a Cheese Deluxe, Artis had a Taco Excellante, Mrs. Reese had fish, and Officer Reese had chicken. And all of it to go, which is why I never really got to know them. I don't think they felt comfortable taking a table at the Samoa. Old habits, I guess, old fears. Even though standing out in the crowd was no longer dangerous for the Reeses, they still stood out, and that made them uneasy.

Ten years later I had a business lunch at a fancy steakhouse in the big city. The maitre d' was a handsome black man who saw me come in the door, stuck out his hand and grabbed mine. I wouldn't have recognized him. He'd put on forty pounds, and all of it style. He was quintessentially urban, and only if you knew the way he used to talk would you have noticed the trace of Alabama in his accent. In his suede jacket and moderate Afro he was as Inside as you could get in 1974.

By then Neil Shulman had been hiding in Canada for five years. He finally came home with the amnesty President Carter declared, but he came home to Boston and stayed there. I've never seen him again, except occasionally on the news, so I don't know if he's aware of the successful Urbanization of Tucker or how he might feel about it. I know I feel like we lost something, like somewhere out there is a sweet, shy farm boy from another world who deserved to survive. Tucker would certainly tell me I'm full of it.

At the prom that spring of 1965 Tucker escorted Miss Fawn Shulman. This was no friendship date; some real feelings were there on both sides. That night they were cuter together than a box full of kittens. They won the evening's election for 'King and Queen of the Dance' by a landslide. But when the award was announced and the crowning took place, the winners were Missy Sagerson and her quarterback beau, who both loved the attention.

Because Cathy and I were the Awards Committee and counted the votes, that's why.

The Fight

A FEW WEEKS AFTER I started cooking at the Samoa I was at a church social. It wasn't on the Island, and it wasn't all that social, but it was something to do. Like a lot of guys I went to church youth group meetings as an excuse to get out of the house during the week. For a while a bunch of us were Evolving Episcopal Youth every Tuesday night, Little Lutherans every Wednesday, and Liberal Religious Unitarian Youth every Thursday. We avoided the Catholics and the Jews because we heard that they required their youth groups to do a lot of memorization, and who needs that? And nobody went back to Young Life after the first meeting, when we were asked to take Jesus Christ as our personal savior.

"What do you mean, 'take'?" Clifford inquired of YL Youth Leader Dewey Monson, a very large collegian with a beatific smirk. "'Take' as in how?"

Dewey turned the smirk up a notch. "Take as in 'take Jesus into your heart and live forever with him,' Cliff."

"I see. And it's Clifford. But doesn't the Bible say that Jesus is already in my heart? That Jesus is in fact in all things, which would include my heart? And that chair? And these delicious snickerdoodles?"

"Well, yes, but..."

"And so how can I take something into my heart that's already there?"

"It's an expression. It's faith. It's..."

"Don't you really mean I should acknowledge and embrace Jesus' already existing presence in my heart?"

Dewey looked relieved. He thought Clifford was leading him out of the wilderness. Those of us who knew Clifford knew that the wilderness still loomed and Dewey was in trouble.

"Yes, that's exactly what I mean, Clifford, and very well said. Listen everybody. You should acknowledge and embrace the presence of Jesus in your heart. That's a wonderful way to..."

"Anybody else in there?" Clifford had that smile again.

"I'm sorry?"

"Is Jesus the only religious figure who's in my heart?"

"Hahaha!" Dewey laughed robustly. "You're taking this much too literally, Clifford. Jesus is..."

"Moses. If Jesus is in my heart, where's Moses? Besides the bulrushes."

"Moses is not God so of course he's not..."

"Yahweh then. And Shiva. Ta'aroa, the Rainbow Serpent of the Bungalung people of Australia. Zeus. Allah. Are they in my heart too?"

Clifford surprised me. While the rest of us had been dozing he must have been paying attention at all these religious youth group meetings we attended.

"They are not in your heart!" Dewey's smirk had faded. "Only Jesus is in your heart!"

"But isn't Young Life non-denominational? You said a few minutes ago that we are all welcome under the tent of God's love. You seem to be guarding the tent, so I thought..."

It was Dewey's turn to interrupt. "Yes, we are non-denominational, all are welcome, but we are non-denominational entirely for Jesus and none of those other people!"

"Ah, I see. There is no Jesus but Jesus, and Dewey is his prophet."

"Listen, kid..."

"Well," Clifford said, calmly and succinctly, "that's just the shits."

Dewey turned bright red and leapt from his seat like non-denominational demons were after him. Clifford quickly tried to look as if he were having a Moment of Bliss, along with his fourth snickerdoodle. But Bliss didn't save him. Dewey picked up Clifford's chair with Clifford still in it and threw blasphemer and chair out into the hall. The chair was eventually allowed to return.

We came and went at some of the other denominations, too. When the Lutherans changed their meeting night to Friday their youth group shrank from 25 Little Lutes to one Ardith Stixrud in the space of one week. But before we abandoned Lute-land Pastor Olaffson said something that was to be repeated many times at the Samoa.

We were planning a Youth Group dance, and Geoff had just suggested actual live music because his older sister was dating the drummer of Sin! and she could get them to play for practically nothing. Pastor Olaffson, having already given us his inspirational message, was dozing in the corner. He roused briefly and found himself in the middle of an enthusiastic discussion of sin, how it was cheap, drew a big crowd, and could spark up any gathering. The Pastor was shocked. We tried to explain, it's just the name of a rock and roll band, kind of a joke name, really wonderful young persons. Pastor Olaffson eventually said "I see," but he didn't.

"A dance," he said. "Yes, a dance. What exactly is the Christian purpose of that?" For a room full of teens, contemplating an evening of inappropriate touching in a church basement, the question was unanswerable. And unforgettable.

The religious social I went to right after starting at the Samoa was most likely Unitarian, because it was in a home, not the church basement, and the parents stood around in the kitchen drinking wine and pretending they weren't eavesdropping, which is a very Unitarian thing to do. A guy there I didn't know was talking about the high schools in the area. He was saying Mercer Island was okay but there was one place where somebody from somewhere else could get into trouble on the Island, "could get the stuffings knocked out of him" was how he put it because the parents were listening. And that was the Samoa. He'd never been there himself but he'd heard it from a lot of people: Stay away from the Samoa if you like your teeth. I should have put him right but I kept quiet. Why argue with a guy who thinks about places in terms of how dangerous they might be?

So listen up now, buster. There were a lot of Island types who hung around the Samoa, and they could be tough if they had to be. Some of them looked tough all the time, but with a few exceptions that was more of a fashion statement than anything else. The way a stranger could get roughed up at the Samoa was almost always verbal. We were wise asses, not hard asses.

Like one night a guy pulls up in a black Buick Starfire with a white racing stripe. It looks like Hot Rod Magazine's Car of the Year, and somebody's worked very hard to achieve that. There's enough wax on the hood to make candles for the entire Archdiocese. He's with a girl who's practically sitting in his lap. She's a Dorothy Provine type, with teased blond hair, big makeup, and that continual look of somebody who's just been goosed. There's room for a month's groceries on the seat beside her, only this is a guy who has never allowed a brown paper bag full of produce to touch his tuck-and-roll upholstery.

She stays in the car doing mirror makeup while the guy saunters through the Samoa door and up to the counter, wearing a letter jacket from a school we don't recognize. If you know your way around a jacket though, you know this is a four-letter man in football and wrestling from Unknown High. He looks like a wrestler too, big but solid, with one large muscle going from the top of his head straight down his back until it splits into his butt cheeks. The guy ripples all over, even in the jacket.

The letter he's won is a blue and orange M that takes up most of his upper left quadrant. It's a huge M, probably the biggest M you can order from the Athletic Supply Company catalogue. And you can tell by the way this guy moves that having a big M to flash around means a hell of a lot where he comes from.

Big M gives the assembled Samoans his "don't mess with me" look. It's a reflex action with him. He probably does it when he struts into his Lutheran Youth Group.

The Samoa goes very quiet. He assumes the crowd is awed by the very magnificence of him, his car, his girl, his M. We listen silently as he pops for a Cheese Deluxe, single fish, fries, chocolate shake and a Coke for the little lady. Soundless minutes pass as I cook his eats and that big M shines in all of our faces. Just about the time I hand the paper bags off to Arlene, a pleasant, conversational voice rises out of a Samoa back booth.

"Maybe it stands for 'Mother'," says the voice. The Samoa instantly goes up for grabs. Big M, who's had no experience with people laughing at his M (at least not to his face) has another reflex action. He swells up like he's going to pound everybody in the joint. Which just makes everybody laugh even more, because he may be a big tough wrestler from M High but there are ten of us, and it's our venue. The action he's considering will last no more than a few seconds and is a guaranteed loss for him. He's been around enough to realize that. So he throws a five down on the counter, grabs his food from Arlene—who's biting her lip hard, with tears and a little mascara rolling down her cheeks—and marches back to the Starfire. It's a real long walk for him by now, what with the laughing going on. As he gets to the car the girl grabs the bags like nothing's happened and starts rummaging through them. Her voice cuts through the night like bad brakes.

"Didja get any tar tar?" she says. "Richie, didja forget the tar tar again? What's the matter with you?"

"Shut up," Richie explains. And the Samoa goes up for grabs a second time. Richie throws a lot of gravel around getting out of the parking lot.

One real fight, that's all I ever saw at the Samoa. And that was no gangland dispute between strangers. The combatants had spent their lives together. They'd slept in each other's homes dozens of times, and from the age of three had always attended each other's birthday parties. But that's the way it is sometimes. Some little thing happens and you want to beat your best friend's brains out.

The little thing that came between Dennis and Phil was a chair; or more accurately a particular place on a high school cafeteria bench. It would probably be a lot more romantic to say they fought over a girl, but the fact is teenagers don't fight over girls—at least they didn't where I came from. Girls were too damned ephemeral to fight about. A guy wants to fight about real stuff he can understand; a scratch in the paint, a cheap hit on the field, a seat on a bench.

That particular Friday lunch period Dennis was in Phil's spot, a spot Phil had scent-marked when school started in September. It was 'Where Phil Sat' and everybody knew it. Certainly Dennis knew it, because 'Where Dennis Sat' was on the bench right across the table. But for reasons we will never know Dennis decided to mess with the Order of the Universe. He got there first, he sat in Phil's place, and he liked it.

Phil arrived a few minutes later, assessed the situation, and thought it was some kind of joke. "Get your butt outta my seat," he said pleasantly. Dennis didn't even turn to look at him. So Phil said exactly the same thing two more times, each time a little louder, a little angrier. His mounting agitation was due to Dennis' responses, which were: A. silence; B. "Who are you, the principal?"; and C. "Screw you."

That's when Phil grabbed Dennis by the neck, pulled him straight back from the table like pulling a dipstick out of a crankcase, and threw him in a southerly direction. Dennis landed flat out on a table full of trays and fish sticks. He didn't appreciate this trip at all and quickly returned to Phil's location. But before an escalation of hostilities could take place some kid near the door yelled "Teacher!" Instantly Dennis and Phil were sitting side by side, munching other people's fish sticks and discussing the nuances of spot welding. The teacher, James Dimwiddie, arrived on a run, charging dramatically into a roomful of teens trying hard to look like the Mormon Tabernacle Choir on a five-minute break.

"All right, what's going on?" Dimwit demanded of the room. It was his week to maintain cafeteria order but as usual he'd been out behind the incinerator sucking on a Lucky.

Everyone in the place assumed his question was rhetorical, because not even Ardith Stixrud answered. So Dimwit stood there for a moment looking around ferociously. Then he went into The Walk, slowly stalking up and down between the tables, glaring at all the angelic fish stick eaters around him. He acted as if the Black Hand of Guilt was somehow going to appear magically over the evildoers' heads if he just waited long enough and walked slowly enough.

There were still a lot of greasy fish sticks on the floor because of Dennis' landing. Dimwit finally stepped on one, which shot out from under his shoe like it was still a living fish. Down he went, his head disappearing from sight between the tables. The laughter lasted as long as it took that head to reappear. Then the laughter started again when we saw that there were two more fish sticks stuck, like organic Velcro, to the back of his sports jacket. Dimwit was furious. He looked at the guy nearest him.

"I saw that, Forcade!" Dimwit shouted.

"What?" Frank answered. "What are you talking about?"

Too late. Dimwit grabbed Frank and marched him out of the room, snarling the usual threats while Frank made the usual protestations of innocence. Murray gave him three days of after-school detention. He spent the time in the auto shop installing a Continental Kit on his aunt's Pontiac.

The moment the doors closed and we were teacher-free again every kid in the building turned to look at Dennis and Phil. They glared at each other for a long, cold moment. Then each man rose and marched out a different exit. There would be no more lunchroom entertainment.

We knew the dispute wouldn't end there. Dennis and Phil hung out with the same people, and those were the people who hung out at the Samoa. For those two guys not to make a Saturday night appearance at the little Tiki Hut® shack by the freeway was as unlikely as the Beatles® splitting up.

The next night the sky was clear, the stars were many, the air was crisp and invigorating. It was a beautiful Saturday evening in a great Northwest winter. The Samoa glowed like an oasis, calling out to weary travelers everywhere. Betty had even put up a new message on the readerboard out front: TIM TO EAT! DELU E BURGER & F IES $1.50. (I got very tired of telling smartasses who Tim was. Then the T fell off so the sign made at least a little sense. IM TO EAT!, and so are you!) But that night the place was not full of weary travelers with tim to eat, it was full of people who wanted to see Dennis and Phil resolve their differences in an uncivilized manner.

I was working the grill and working hard. With the fight crowd on hand business was very good, to the surprise of Counter Personnel Thelma. Being an old woman from off the Island she was ignorant of the situation. When I wised her up she wanted to know what I was going to do about it.

"It's the duty of the cook, not the Counter Personnel, to maintain order," she told me like she was reading from some ancient manual of the Short Order Arts. "If you get into trouble I'll call the cops." Thelma could be a real pain in the ass.

When Phil showed up with his people a few minutes later I had two choices. I could hit him with the Samoa Crowd Controller or take him aside for sage counsel. I chose the counsel because I didn't want to have to eat my Louisville Slugger on a future occasion when he had recovered and returned.

Phil and I were more than strangers but less than friends. We'd had a few classes together over the years, and I knew his secret. His secret was that he was very smart and a voracious reader, especially of histories and biographies. He could have done extremely well in school. But as Phil and his parents had been told repeatedly since he was six, "Phil isn't applying himself," which is what they said when they thought you were dumb but suspected you might not be as dumb as they thought. Phil had a disadvantage with teachers, too. His eyelids drooped so he always looked half-asleep even though he wasn't. They kept putting him in dumber and dumber classes where he didn't apply himself even more because he was so bored. That was his problem, but nobody in any school ever figured it out or had the consideration to ask him what his problem was. Instead they told him what it was. They were wrong.

When Phil hit junior high he chose to join those guys whose under-achievement wasn't intentional like his. Phil found that they weren't nearly as boring as the not-quite-smart/not-quite-stupid with whom he had been grouped until then. When your life is driven by boredom-avoidance as Phil's was you go to almost any lengths for interesting possibilities, even intellectual slumming.

Phil was an okay guy but I could guess how receptive he'd be to getting advice from me, fight night or any other time. So talking him out of What He Came To Do was not going to happen. But I wasn't a lawyer's kid for nothing. I negotiated a deal.

"Phil, here's the situation," I said. "If this fight happens inside the Samoa I'll get blamed, I'll lose my job, Thelma's gonna call the cops and you'll go to jail. But if this fight happens twenty feet that way, off the property, it won't be my fault and I can keep Thelma from hitting the button. What do you say?"

Even with testosterone squirting out of his ears Phil was sensible. "No sweat," he said.

It wasn't long before Dennis arrived with his people. They could just as easily have been Phil's people, and Phil's could have been Dennis', but during the previous 24 hours their mutual acquaintances had been forced to choose sides. This allocation of allies could have been traumatic for a lot of guys, but most of them were surprised at how simple it was. Finding something to dislike about someone else, even someone who has been a friend, was far too easy. But not universally so. Wayne Whitley had been a good pal of both Dennis and Phil since they were all in eighth grade detention together. I had been wondering which guy would arrive with Wayne in his corner. But I underestimated Wayne. That was the first time in eighteen months that he didn't show up for Saturday Night at the Samoa. I asked Clifford where he was.

"Washing his hair," Clifford said smiling. Good old Wayne.

With Dennis and Company at last on the grounds both groups went through the traditional pre-fight ritual. Phil and his guys got there first so they stayed inside the Samoa, while Dennis and his guys stood around in the parking lot rearranging little piles of gravel with the toes of their shoes and trying to look nonchalant. This phase of the proceedings was highlighted by sporadic group laughter and surreptitious glances from combatant to combatant. Otherwise they tried to look like they were ignoring each other. Then Dennis announced as how a Cheese Deluxe might just hit the spot. He entered the building, breaking the proximity barrier. Soon a few uncomplimentary remarks were spoken a bit too loudly. Toe-to-toe verbal confrontation followed.

The original subject of their dispute, Dennis' usurpation of Phil's lunch spot, was not mentioned in this discussion. Instead the parley touched on themes familiar to us all—the nature of each party's mother and what the respective party did to her, the sphincter, and human waste masquerading as brain tissue. But because these two knew each other so well there was also a special, intimate quality to their face-off, with references to past incidents and imagined slights that only they understood.

Later that night in the post-fight discussion many Samoa observers found Phil's body language during this period of the ritual contrary to the bravado of his remarks. He seemed to be continually backing away, out the Samoa's sliding glass door and into the parking lot, as Dennis advanced menacingly. Some felt this indicated reluctance on Phil's part to fight. Anybody could understand Phil's apparent hesitation. Dennis had been in Golden Gloves for a while. Although short he was the last person you'd have chosen to belt it out with. Phil probably felt that way too, and to the Samoans his movements seemed to prove it. But I knew what he was doing. He was leading Dennis across the twenty-foot line into the supermarket parking lot next door. It may not have made sense to the regulars, but I appreciated the consideration.

Guys will chew on each other for hours before they actually fight and then they won't fight at all but just stalk away, accusing each other of no guts. We'd seen it happen a dozen times at the Samoa, in the school hallways, in an assortment of parking lots. So I suspect Dennis thought there would be a lot more verbal activity before any real action began. In that he was mistaken, and the consequences of his miscalculation were electrifying. As soon as they both reached Art's property Phil hit Dennis as hard as he could right on the button.

I can still see that punch, still feel it somewhere inside me, still hear the Samoa regulars gasp as Dennis fell to the blacktop, blood spurting from what was left of his nose. It was a profoundly effective punch. My father once told me that if I was ever in a fight I wanted to end quickly I should hit the other guy in the nose as hard as I could. Fortunately I've never had to test his advice. But thanks to Phil I know Dad's strategy is right on the money.

In this case it was more than a fight-winning punch. Even best friends drift apart sometimes. They develop different interests, they want to go in different directions. But the process is usually a slow one. One day you realize you haven't talked to your old pal for a long time. And there's always the possibility that you'll get back together.

Not Phil and Dennis, though. That punch was the precise instant a lifelong friendship ended forever. If each man had walked away that night, or even if they just rolled around in the gravel for a while and then stopped, they could have reconciled eventually. Friendship was the most important thing in both their lives. But the punch, the unexpected viciousness of it, was terminal. And they realized it. As Dennis went down and Phil watched him fall the look on both their faces wasn't anger. It was surprise. Their worlds would never be the same, and the suddenness of the change scared them. It scared all of us. If a guy you've known and trusted all your life can do that to you, can you ever really know and trust anyone?

Dennis got up, of course. Although different types physically they were evenly matched. Phil was tall, lean and graceful. He was a natural athlete, like Muhammad Ali, and obviously those guys can make formidable fighters. Dennis was more experienced, well muscled, and fearless—like a pit bull. In a long fight he probably could have taken Phil, and Phil probably knew it. But not after that punch. Dennis was hurt. Short of killing Phil he had already lost. But there are standards to maintain, and giving up without using everything he had left was inconceivable to Dennis. Blinded by his blood and his rage he charged forward and knocked Phil back into the supermarket garbage cans. They rolled off onto the ground, Phil on top, Dennis hitting him in the ribs as hard as he could. Phil was able to pin one flailing arm, and then another, and then it was over. For just a moment he looked down at the mutilated face of this friend he had known since they were toddlers. Nothing was said. Phil got up and walked away and Dennis did not follow. They left in different directions, clutching their bloody, ripped shirts and their own friends around them.

Afterwards the crowd decided to call it a draw, not out of respect for Dennis' feelings but because we wanted it to be a draw. We wanted it not to have happened. This was no clean bloodless series of haymakers in a John Wayne western. This was short, brutal and sickening, physically and emotionally. It was something horrible happening to people we knew, people we liked. For the regulars, to see it for real was to want no part of it. After that you couldn't have gotten beat up at the Samoa if you tried. Humiliated yes, but not hit.

We teens lived a sheltered existence in the mid-1960s. That entire year I saw only one guy who said he'd been smoking marijuana, and nobody believed him. Beer was the controlled substance of choice, but only consumed seriously by a relative few. And there was very little violence by or to kids. It was the kind of place where one of the "gangs" in high school was made up of Drama Club members.

Not long afterwards some of us had to grow up fast. The class of 1965 really did have Dimwit's Black Hand hanging over it, but it wasn't the Hand of Guilt. It was the Hand of Doom, especially for those guys who spent their days in remedial English and their nights at the Samoa. During the next five years, without the shelter of college, a lot of them enlisted or got drafted into the service, and many ended up in Vietnam.

Dennis and Phil actually wanted to go. It was still early enough in the war that enthusiasm for the fighting wasn't limited to old men hiding behind flags and lecterns. Dennis was a natural warrior so it made sense for him. Phil thought it sounded anything but boring. After two desultory years in community college he went down and enlisted in the Marines.

When Dennis tried to do the same thing in the spring of 1967 he was informed he had a medical problem. Apparently he'd broken his nose badly, and as a result his breathing was affected. Dennis argued with the recruiter that he could still fight. That's probably true, he was told, but the Marines have standards to maintain.

"We can't take the chance that your abilities will be impaired at the exact moment your brother Marines are depending on you for their lives," the recruiter told him, like he was reading it off a wall. Dennis went home and cried for the first time since he was four years old. In the next few weeks every other branch of the service rejected him, the Army three times in recruiting offices in Portland, San Francisco and Reno. Dennis was ashamed, and went to work for the railroad out of Spokane.

The last time I saw him was that long afternoon in 1970 when we buried Phil.

Happy Motoring

THERE IS A CONNECTION between coordination and intelligence that's far too common to be coincidental. Although there are many exceptions, a lot of dumb guys throw like Peyton Manning and a lot of smart guys throw like a girl. The lucky ones have adjusted to this biological justice. You couldn't get Noël Coward's goat because he was a sucker for a fastball on the inside corner any more than Johnny Bench was embarrassed because he couldn't whistle the score of *Cosí fan tutte*.

Clifford was no exception to the all brains/no brawn phenomenon. He was the second smartest person I've ever known and also the most uncoordinated. Whenever he attempted anything physical, Clifford looked beset by bees. He didn't help himself through years of P.E. classes by wearing gym shorts from the Diamond Jim Brady Collection; huge white trunks that seemed even bigger and whiter than they really were because his P.E. tee shirt was two sizes too small and slightly pink from a washing mishap. Clifford's legs sticking down out of those shorts looked like pretzel sticks protruding from a sea of billowing white foam. I was in gym class with him for six years and in that time he never hit a pitched ball, never caught anything thrown at him, never made a flying object go into anything else, whether a hoop, a net, or somebody else's hands. Even outside gym class furniture would scuttle into his path to smash him in the ankles whenever he walked by.

He never said much about it, but I know his lack of coordination infuriated him. For an intellectual person Clifford had a secret passion; sports of all kinds. He was like those guys you meet who are obviously intelligent, sophisticated types, and yet they've been keeping score on Pittsburgh Pirates baseball games since they were nine. And they have all the paperwork to prove it. The inability to make his body do what he knew other bodies could do was what led Clifford to first question God's existence, when he was about four. Eventually he decided that there is a God but He's a nasty, vindictive Son of a Bitch. It's not surprising Clifford felt that way. The Big Coach had blessed him with an abundance of mental facility but cursed him with no physical dexterity at all.

Both traits affected his life in many ways. Late in our junior year when we were discussing the universities we might like to attend, Clifford's initial choices—obscure Midwest religious institutions, California surfer colleges—seemed odd given his intellect and interests. He finally admitted that his first criterion for selecting a college wasn't its academic standing, prestige, location or cost, but whether physical education was a mandatory requirement. If it was required, it was off Clifford's list, and that excluded a lot of places where he might have been very successful. I think his happiest moment in high school was the last day of the last gym class he would ever have to take.

His coordination deficit started very early. Clifford's parents were pleased when their weird little baby was talking in complete sentences by his first birthday, months before Dr. Spock said he would. They were concerned that he wasn't walking months after Dr. Spock said he would. When neighborhood mothers gathered with their offspring Clifford's mom propped him up in a corner, where he sat and commented on the other toddlers moving around the room. She hoped no one would notice he wasn't toddling himself, because they'd be so impressed with how verbal he was. Eventually she had to stop attending such gatherings, after little Clifford remarked one afternoon that Joey DeFalco's mom looked like "a great big sack of potatoes." It was a precisely accurate description, but Mrs. DeFalco was not amused. Clifford's mother really didn't mind having to stay away after that. She didn't like being around babies. Babies made her nervous, especially her own.

That was the beginning of Clifford's dominant conversational characteristic. He developed verbal defenses that were sometimes breathtaking in their viciousness. Instinctively he saw where you were the weakest, and that's where he'd hit you the hardest. (Mrs. DeFalco had been on a diet for 28 years and had lost a total of nine pounds.)

As he got older you'd think Clifford's prime targets would be the athletes he envied. But he had too much respect for the physically superior. I think that's one of the reasons why he befriended Wayne Whitley. Wayne was a natural athlete, especially in those sports where Extra Large is an advantage, and Clifford recognized that when they were both still Extra Small. The victims of his cruelest comments were always shlubs who were almost as awkward as he was, or people who tried to be athletic and didn't have it. "Try, try again" was not a doctrine Clifford admired. "Quit trying and make way for people who know what they're doing" was more his credo. Part of his contempt for the athletically inept was self-loathing, but he didn't worry about that. "I loathe so many people for so many things it would be hypocritical not to include myself," he would say. "And I loathe hypocrites."

Once we went to the last Seattle Sonics home game of the year, against the hated L.A. Lakers. One Laker, a highly touted rookie, had been a major disappointment all season. If he got in the game at all it was usually in the last five minutes when the outcome was already decided. So it was that final night of the season for both teams. With 28 seconds to go and the Lakers up by 14, he got fouled in the act of missing and went to the line for two. In that brief moment of silence right before he took his first shot Clifford snarled loud enough for the entire arena to hear, "So, Laker boy, are you enjoying your last 28 seconds in the NBA?" The kid missed both shots—the first one went over the backboard. He played pro ball for two more years, in the Australian League.

Our school system tried very hard to turn out well-rounded young ladies and gentlemen. The Samoa regulars thought this objective was a waste of effort. We believed that there were areas of knowledge and skill that would never be of use in the real world, and mostly we were right. Spanish, Geometry, Botany—we haven't needed any of these things we endured in high school, since high school.

Clifford, however, was not as lucky as the rest of us. No matter how careful you are, life does require some personal coordination. And the first big test comes in the mid-teens.

He skipped a grade early in elementary school so he was younger than the rest of us. It didn't make any difference to him or anybody else, until all his friends turned sixteen months before he did. For a teen male the sixteenth birthday means just one thing: you can drive, but only after you pass the state test. Clifford sat at the Samoa and watched as we regulars went off to the city, one by one, and passed the test on the second or third try. We got our licenses, and felt like real grownup human beings. Clifford alone was left license-free and dependent on us to haul him around. He insisted that he enjoyed exploiting us like that. It was one of only two times in my life when I felt truly sorry for him.

In the spring of 1965, the day he turned 15½, Clifford took the written test and got his Learner's Permit, as the law allowed. It meant that he could take the wheel as long as an adult was in the car teaching him what to do. This was before Driver's Education was a mandatory class in high school, so we drive-ready youngsters were expected to get educated any way we could. For most of us the in-car instructional adult was one of our parents. But not for Clifford.

None of us really understood his relationship with his folks. For them, Clifford was more than an acquaintance but less than a friend. One night at the Samoa, when Jesse's problems trying to shake his father were under discussion, Clifford mentioned that he couldn't remember ever hugging his father, or the last time he was kissed by his mother. We were shocked, but he said it proudly, as if that's the way it should be and any other kind of relationship with your parents is excessive. All we could figure was that early in their lives together Clifford's family decided to share a last name, a house, occasional meals, two cats and a few ancestors. Other than that they would go their own ways, with their own interests, being supportive only if asked.

His mom was a medical librarian at the University and his father had an office in their basement where he wrote technical articles for various publications. I tried to read one of his pieces once and got lost in the title. His mom and dad were very quiet, very bright people, who treated each other as acquaintances too, so much so that you wondered why—and how—they ever had children together. Clifford used to say he owed his existence to an error in timing and an impertinent Bordeaux.

While they showed mild interest in their children's activities, neither Dad nor Mom ever left the house to attend anything the kids did. In his senior year Clifford won a huge trophy in the Impromptu Speaking competition at the State Debate Championships. On five minutes' notice he delivered a reasoned yet passionate defense of capital punishment that had half the audience eager to string up the first shoplifter they found. That night his parents had a rare evening out. They went to a performance of *Aida*.

Given their relationship Clifford was as likely to ask his father to teach him to drive as ask Vice–Principal Murray. That was probably just as well, because Clifford's father was a famously bad driver. He had a Saab, avocado green and avocado shaped, the first Saab on the island. Just the sight of it on the road up ahead was enough to convince people taking their mothers to the hospital to wait a few hours until the roads were clear.

It wasn't that he was reckless. He was exactly the opposite. Clifford's dad never drove more than 25 miles an hour, and usually a lot less, regardless of the road or the speed limit. He was the kind of driver who has never had an accident himself but caused dozens of them, as other frustrated motorists tried to get around him. Most of Clifford's extensive knowledge of profanity came from things he heard strangers yell at his father on those rare occasions when they went somewhere together. No wonder he had strong feelings about making way for people who know what they're doing.

Clifford turned naturally to his friend Wayne Whitley to teach him how to drive. It was a measure of Wayne's loyalty that he agreed to do it and even agreed to use the Chevy for the purpose. Wayne as Drivers Ed teacher wasn't strictly legal—the learner's permit was valid only if the other person in the car was at least 21. But given the players and the training vehicle, that was a minor problem. Wayne was so protective of that car he was even difficult about people who just wanted to ride in it. You had to check your back pockets for sharp objects and your shoes for dog crap before he'd let you get in. Then when you rode along with him, half the time he was watching his passengers rather than the road, sneaking glances if you were riding shotgun, adjusting his mirrors so he could constantly check anyone in the back seat. I don't know what he was watching for. The Samoa regulars had a lot of problems but incontinence wasn't one of them. That such a person was going to let somebody else drive his prized possession, some-body who had never driven before, somebody who was Clifford, was almost incomprehensible to the Samoa regulars.

The day after Clifford got his permit, he and Wayne were to meet at the Samoa for Lesson Number One. For different reasons both guys tried to keep this rendezvous quiet. Nevertheless, a large crowd was on hand for what promised to be a great show. A few people had cameras to record the event.

When Wayne pulled up in front of the Samoa a laugh arose and cameras flashed. He had tied two-by-fours to the front and rear bumpers of the Chevy. In each of the back side windows was a large, hand-lettered sign that read: BEWARE! BEGINING DRIVER! PLEASE STAY BACK!

Wayne climbed out, looking like a guy who's been called to identify his dad at the city morgue. Clifford arrived on foot a few minutes later, saw the Chevy and its additions, and sighed a very long sigh. He walked around to the driver's side door like he was going to get in, but Wayne stopped him. He checked Clifford's back pockets and shoes and then pointed to the passenger seat. Wayne assumed his regular place behind the wheel, and Clifford his regular place up front right. There they sat.

The windows were up and Wayne had already told the rest of us to stay clear of the vehicle, so we couldn't hear what was happening. But we could see that for the first time in their lives, Wayne was doing all the talking and Clifford was doing all the listening. 23 minutes passed without incident, as a dozen faces watched and waited for some kind of explosion. Just as boredom was setting in the Chevy's wiper blades swished across, just once, with that rough squeak of blades on dry glass. A few minutes later the headlights came on, then the brights, then the lights went off. Then parking lights, on and off. Shortly after that the horn honked briefly. Turn signals came next—left, right, then nothing. By this time the Samoans were making bets on what would follow. Janelle picked up half a buck for sun visors down and up, and nobody got wind wings opened and closed. There was a period of inactivity after that and then the entire sequence was repeated. And repeated again. The Chevy still hadn't moved an inch, and Wayne was still in the driver's seat.

Clifford told me later that Wayne began their session by outlining the entire instruction period, from first entrance to solo driving. "He had a check list. With

146 numbered items. A check list." From the check-list and what Wayne said it sounded to Clifford like he would be ready to take the state driver's test sometime in 1988.

From inside the Samoa we had observed #1 on Wayne's list: Vehicle Orientation. Speaking very slowly and care-fully, as one might to a two-year-old in the early stages of potty training, Wayne demonstrated every single demon-strable item inside the car three times. During this period he did not allow Clifford to touch any of these items himself, only watch. Trying desperately to control his annoyance, Clifford finally asked when he might actually be allowed to operate anything personally.

"That'll be in Lesson Three," Wayne answered. "Now let's go over that cigarette lighter once again..."

"And when, just out of curiosity, do you expect we'll get to the more important items, like turning on the goddamned motor?"

"It's an engine, not a motor."

"Actually, you idiot," Clifford snapped, "it's both. Although 'engine' implies liquid fuel and 'motor' implies some other form of energy like electricity, the words are interchangeable as far as designating machines that convert energy into mechanical force or motion. So when are we going to turn on the goddamned motor, and get into mechanical force or motion?"

Wayne looked at his friend calmly, although Clifford later insisted there was the hint of a smirk on his large face. "And how," Wayne asked, "do you expect to learn anything if you're not going to pay attention?" It was a question Wayne himself had been asked a thousand times by teachers and Clifford had never been asked before. They contemplated each other in silence. Then Clifford took a dive.

"I'm sorry," he said, with all the sincerity he could muster. "Please go on."

"All right then," Wayne answered. He was tempted to say, "Don't let it happen again," but thought better of it. Instead he returned to the cigarette lighter, the glove compartment, the heater and radio—items we couldn't see from inside the Samoa.

After one hour and 26 minutes of Vehicle Orientation, Wayne smiled broadly at Clifford and said, "I think that's enough for one day. I wouldn't want to overload you." He took out his list and grandly checked off #1, leaving 145 items to go. "We've done so well," he told Clifford magnanimously, "that we may just jump the schedule and actually fire her up the next time. Can I give you a ride home?"

Clifford declined the ride and came inside the Samoa instead. He told me that if he had to spend another second sitting in that car watching Wayne operate switches and levers he would die. Wayne drove home alone, grinning all the way. He and the Chevy had survived Lesson Number One without bruise or blemish.

The next afternoon the crowd at the Samoa was smaller but just as ready for a memorable moment. And they got it, when Wayne finally started the engine after showing Clifford what a "key" is and how it has to be inserted into a special place in the steering column for the car to start. "Not just any key, either," Wayne cautioned. "Each car has its own special key."

"Really!"

"Absolutely. You twist the key one-quarter turn until the engine starts. Then you immediately stop twisting. You never twist the key when the engine is already running because it makes a horrible grating noise and it must be bad for the car. Because it's such a horrible noise, see. If it weren't bad for the car I don't think it would make that..."

"I think I have the concept," Clifford interrupted, as he wrote down 'Don't twist when running/horrible noise/ God help me!' in the spiral notebook Wayne had thought-fully provided. He looked up at his instructor, encouraged at last by the throaty growl of the Chevy engine. "So now that it's running,' Clifford asked hopefully, "are we going to..." That's when Wayne shut the engine off, and the throaty growl went away.

Wayne put the keys in his pocket and turned to Clifford beside him. "I'd show you again how to start the engine but that might drain the battery, and that's one thing you never want to do. Even though a car runs on gasoline, it has to have a battery as well, which is electricity." Wayne paused to give Clifford time to write down this scientific insight but Clifford just stared back at him.

"Is there a problem?" Wayne asked. In response, Clifford slowly opened the passenger door, got out, and came around to Wayne's side of the car.

Wayne rolled down his window. "Yes?"

"Wayne," Clifford said, like a serial killer who is finally revealing to detectives where all the bodies are, "if you don't get out of that seat and let me in I'm going to sneak into your house some night when you're asleep and shoot you in the knees." Inside the Samoa the remaining crowd felt their perseverance had been justified. Janelle picked up another four dollars for being closest in the pool to Clifford Fed Up Time: 56 minutes into Lesson Number Two.

From almost any other person Wayne would have written off the threat as mere bravado. But he knew Clifford well, knew when he was completely serious, and knew he had a key to the Whitley house. Wayne believed him. He stepped out, handed Clifford the car keys, held the door, and Clifford stepped in.

"This should be good," Frank Forcade said, standing inside the Samoa's glass door.

As Wayne ran around and got in on the passenger's side—a place he had never sat before—Clifford carefully inserted the "key" into the proper orifice. He twisted a quarter turn and the Chevy's engine once more blurped to life. Instantly Wayne said, "Good! I think that's enough for the second day, don't you?" and reached for the ignition. However, he had underestimated his student. Clifford had been watching his friend drive the Chevy for more than a year. He knew what to do next and he did it quickly before Wayne could stop him.

Clifford threw the automatic transmission into 'R' so fast he didn't have time to put his foot on the brake. Not being a car guy, and used to his father's limp Saab, Clifford didn't realize that Frank Forcade had set the idle speed on the Chevy very high so the engine would growl impressively whenever it was running. In this way Wayne hoped to impress girls without actually having to speak to them.

The Chevy, Clifford and Wayne shot backwards out of the Samoa parking lot and across the street that fronted the place. That street ran parallel to a freeway exit ramp, separated by a sidewalk and curb, which the Chevy leapt like a hippo, making an impressive show of sparks underneath. They came to the freeway exit itself, going backwards across the lane rather than forwards down it, as was customary.

"Jesus Holy Christ!" we heard Wayne yell. "Brake! Brake!" Clifford stamped down with both feet, hitting the brake and the gas simultaneously, so the Chevy's engine growled even louder but her speed remained more or less the same, until the two-by-four attached to the rear bumper smacked into the freeway wall and splintered.

At any moment someone was likely to come over the hill of the exit ramp and discover a large Chevy blocking the road, far too late to do anything but plow into it. Realizing this, and realizing that Clifford wouldn't be affecting any helpful change in their situation with suitable speed, Wayne quickly reached over and popped the transmission into 'F1.' At that same moment Clifford took his left foot off the brake but kept his right foot where it was on the gas, exactly the opposite of what he intended to do. The Chevy came barreling back even faster across the exit ramp, the curb, the sidewalk—more sparks—and into the Samoa lot, two-by-four first, slamming into the short concrete wall that surrounded the outside eating area. The building shuddered, and dust from the 1950s fell from the ceiling into everybody's eats.

Clifford's first drive lasted fifteen seconds and covered 175 feet, round trip. But it was definitely over. In the kind of graceful motion that Clifford would have admired under different circumstances, Wayne turned off the ignition, grabbed the keys, and leaped from the car. From the floor where he had fallen because he was laughing so hard, Frank Forcade gasped, "That's gotta do it for Lesson Number Two."

Clutching the ignition key like it was the Koh-i-nor Diamond, Wayne walked around the corner of Art's Food Center next door and disappeared. We found him an hour later, sitting in Art's Home and Garden section, just quietly smelling the flowers. He was very unhappy. By then Clifford had also walked away, with a look of studious concentration. Neither man came into the Samoa, where for the next six hours all somebody had to do was yell "Jesus Holy Christ!" to reduce those present to tears.

Eventually Wayne came back to check out the Chevy. The damage was minimal, thanks to the two-by-fours, but for Wayne there was no such thing as minimal damage to that car. On previous occasions he had reacted to the slightest scratch as if the Chevy was totaled and nothing would ever be right in his world again. This time he backed her out from the wall and then walked around his beloved mechanical friend very slowly. From his calm, curious manner you would have thought he'd found a dead whale on the beach. He inspected the tires, looked at the scrapes and dents in the undercarriage, and finally popped the hood. I thought Frank Forcade would go out, help in this inspection and buck up his friend, but Frank stayed where he was at a booth inside.

"He wants to be alone," Frank said. He could be very sensitive in automotive matters.

Clifford told me he tried all that evening to call Wayne. He sincerely wanted to apologize for what had happened and promise it would never happen again. But—odd for the Whitleys, who were not telephone people—the line was always busy. Clifford finally got through around 10:00. Wayne's mom answered.

For a lot of guys, the Best-Friend's-Mom played a unique and important role in teenage life. Like your own mom, she was an adult who had power over you, but not much power, not often applied. Quite often she became your own friend too, the first real adult female friend you would have. Some teachers tried for that kind of connection with their students, but they had an educational agenda that affected the relationship. They gave you assignments and sent quarterly reports to your parents. Friends don't do such things. But as long as you were decent to her children, the Best-Friend's-Mom came at you as close to an equal. I know a lot of guys who talked to their Best-Friend's-Moms about things they wouldn't have considered discussing with their own parents.

Clifford and Doris Whitley were like that, and not just because Clifford's own parents were so uninvolved in his life. Their relationship started very early. One Saturday in 1958 Doris drove little Wayne and Clifford over to Bellevue for a kid's movie matinee. Doris went shopping, lost track of the time, and was an hour late to pick the boys up. She found them sitting on the curb outside the Kandy Kane Restaurant, down the street from the Bel-Vue Theater. Wayne was reading a *Baby Huey* comic book and sucking on some red licorice. Clifford was reading *David Copperfield* and eating some celery he'd brought from home. From that day on Doris thought Clifford was the best thing that ever happened to her son. For his part, Clifford recognized in her that rare adult he couldn't snow. He respected her for that, and for her obvious intelligence in a milieu where intelligence wasn't necessarily prized.

"What did you ever see in Whit, Doris?" he once asked her.

What do you see in Wayne, Cliff?" she answered immediately. She was the only person I ever knew who called him Cliff.

"Doris, it's Cliff," Clifford said when he finally got through that night. "Is Wayne around?"

"He is. But he told me that if you called he didn't want to talk to you, and wouldn't tell me any more. What's going on?"

"If he didn't tell you then I don't think I should..."

Doris cut him off. "Cliff, maybe you didn't hear me. I said what's going on?" So he told her the whole story. She was frightened by what might have happened but glad they were safe. "Give him time," Doris counseled. "These Whitley men usually do the right thing when you give them enough time."

"I've only got six months to learn."

"And it sounds like you're going to need every second of it." She was sorry the moment she said it, and so was he. To make amends she tried her hardest to coax Wayne to the phone but he was adamant that he didn't want to talk.

"For some reason he's spent most of the evening on the phone, too," Doris told Clifford. "Maybe he's just tired of talking."

"That isn't it, and you know it."

Doris heard a sadness and desperation in Clifford's voice she had never heard before. But there was nothing she could do except volunteer to teach him to drive herself. She valued their friendship far too much to jeopardize it with a doomed alternative like that.

"Don't worry," she insisted. "He says he'll see you tomorrow. Get some rest."

I didn't know if teacher and student were going to show up at the Samoa at 3:30 the next day when Lesson Number Three was supposed to begin. Given what had happened the day before Wayne's appearance was especially in question.

Clifford arrived first, with his don't-talk-to-me face, and took a table alone outside. A few minutes later Wayne drove up. And Curtis drove up. And Frank Forcade, Jesse, Stackhouse and two other guys who had cars drove up too, all pulling into the Samoa lot and parking side by side. Wayne had removed the splintered two by fours from the Chevy's bumpers. Now there were two-by-sixes on the front and back bumpers of Curtis' Dodge.

Clifford began to get an inkling of what Wayne had been doing on the phone all evening. His suspicions were confirmed when the seven guys came in, ordered Cheese Deluxes, and went out to his table. Wayne told Curtis that they had formed an organization to teach him to drive, involving as many guys as possible to minimize the risk to any one guy's life and car. Frank Forcade would oversee the operation and do any necessary repairs to the cars but he wouldn't be directly involved in instruction.

"They'd nail us, Clifford, the cops would stop us before we got two blocks from here."

Clifford had understandable doubts about this plan. After all, one of his proposed teachers was Curtis, and appointing Curtis as a driving instructor was like appointing Governor Wallace to be the Honorary Chairman of Black History Month. In that sense the plan seemed doomed.

At the same time Clifford was genuinely touched by the group offer. He'd helped all of these guys at one time or another on some academic problem. The previous year he wrote a two-page paper for Stackhouse on 'The Sense of Family in Charles Dickens' *Cricket on the Hearth*' in the twenty minutes before it was due. Stackhouse got a B+, his best English grade ever, an achievement made even more remarkable by the fact that Clifford, like Stackhouse, had never read a single word of *Cricket on the Hearth*. As an intellectual challenge he based the entire paper on the dust jacket copy. Almost every Samoan had used the crib sheet Clifford prepared for the Bonehead General Science final exam. Still, his voluntary instructors were much better friends to each other than they were to him. Yet they stood before him, ready to sacrifice their time and possibly their wheels so that he could learn to drive. He agreed to the plan because to do anything else would have been churlish.

Even with seven instructors the daily lessons stopped immediately. Clifford wouldn't be able to take the driving test for another five months and 28 days, and as Frank said, "We don't want you to peak too early." Twice a week, starting with Curtis because Curtis had more time on his hands, one of the sacrificial cars would pull into the Samoa with the two-by-sixes attached. (Eventually they ran out of lumber, and went to railroad ties.) Clifford would go out, get in the driver's seat, and after a brief period of Vehicle Re-Orientation, off they would go.

His first trip with Curtis lasted two minutes. They drove around the Samoa, hitting and destroying three of the garbage cans out behind Art's. That was enough for Curtis. Clifford's instructor on the next trip was Stackhouse. That journey lasted a little more than five minutes, and consisted of driving around in circles in the vacant lot next to the Samoa, where the only thing Clifford could possibly run into was a large rock way off in the corner. He ran into the large rock twice, once going forward, once in reverse. Stackhouse retired from the field.

It became apparent that each driving instructor was replaced not according to any planned schedule but when the instructor couldn't take it any more. After only a month, Clifford had been through the entire rotation two and a half times. Frank called a meeting of all the instructors at the Samoa. He made sure that Clifford was otherwise engaged that night, but asked me to sit in as Clifford's de facto representative.

"So what's the problem?" Frank inquired of the group after all the Cheese Deluxes had been handed out. "This is a very smart guy here, he should be able to do this no sweat."

"Smart's got nothing to do with it," Curtis grumbled. "You don't have to be smart to drive a car. Look at some of the other people on the road."

"For many of us, Curtis, you are the other people on the road," Jesse said.

"And sca-rew you," Curtis responded warmly.

"He's smart enough to drive," Wayne offered, "I mean he knows the rules and about the engine and all, it's just… it's just he can't do it, he can't get it together, you know, his legs and feet and stuff."

The memory of six years in gym loomed up before me, six years of watching Clifford try to get his appendages to do anything together, much less do two different things at the same time. I was there to represent Clifford's interests, but I was coming to a painful realization.

"It may be..." I stopped, then started again. "We've all been in P.E. with him. We've all...seen him." The others nodded. "Well, driving takes coordination. Not a lot, not all the time, but some. Like...parallel parking." A shudder went through the group. "You're looking one way, you're going another way, you're turning the wheel, you're tapping the gas and the brake. You have to have everything engaged. Clifford's never been able to do that anywhere else. He may be—I hate to say this—he may be a guy who's simply too uncoordinated to drive."

Curtis wasn't buying it. "That's nuts," he said. "I'm no goddamned athlete; none of us are, except Wayne. But we drive."

Wayne looked very sad. "Yeah, but there's a difference, there's a difference between being just kind of clumsy, and not being able to do anything. Maybe that's why his father never gets out of second gear. He's just like Clifford and he knows it. He probably got his license before you had to take a test."

We talked for a long time that night. Some of the instructors were for giving up, but it was Frank, Wayne and Curtis who said no.

"Let the state tell him he can't drive," Frank insisted. "That's a job for the cops. Not us. We're his friends. We teach him as well as we can, then let him go take his chances with the state."

"Goddamned right," said Curtis, who had become oddly passionate about the issue. For the first time in his life, he and Clifford had something in common. People were trying to write Clifford off just as they'd written Curtis off for years. He wasn't going to sit there and be a part of it.

"Any of you other guys, you want to drop out," Curtis said, "I'll take your shift." With that, the gathering broke up, except for a final word from Wayne.

"Anybody tells Clifford we had this conversation behind his back, I'll come for you."

Four months passed. Clifford worked hard, and the instructors—all of them stayed with it—worked harder. There were a lot of dented fenders, frayed nerves, and one night, a whole row of roadside mailboxes down on West Mercer Way that was sideswiped down an embankment. Frank Forcade eventually had to do some kind of work on everybody's car, and three or four times at the Samoa we passed the hat around to pay for parts or tires. Clifford did get better, no question about that, but when his sixteenth birthday arrived there wasn't a person in the Samoa who would have voluntarily ridden anywhere with him, especially any member of The Seven.

Saturday morning after his birthday he had an appointment to take the driving test in Bellevue. All of us who were involved in The Clifford Project gathered at the Samoa to see him off, wish him well, and assure him that no matter how good a driver he was he would fail the test the first time, just as we all had. Clifford arrived with his mom—I noticed she was driving—and while she waited in her '61 Olds he dashed in and thanked everyone for everything they'd done. Then they were off.

It would make a great finish to say Clifford passed the first time and stuck it to the rest of us. But in fact his first test lasted no more than a few minutes. It came to a premature end when the DMV examiner told Clifford to turn right and he did instantly, directly up onto the sidewalk and into the flank of a pedestrian. Fortunately he was only going six miles an hour at the time—he had decided he wouldn't exceed ten for the entire test—so the pedestrian wasn't hurt badly.

Clifford took the test nine times, smashing the record set by Curtis (5) the previous year. He didn't even get as far as parallel parking until try number seven. Before that he failed for a variety of reasons, including accidental speeding, shooting across some train tracks with a freight coming, inadvertently hitting the examiner in the eye, and once, when he was told to make an emergency stop, stepping on the gas instead of the brake with such force that the examiner got whiplash and was out sick for two weeks.

My favorite failure was the cat one. Clifford was driving cautiously up a slight hill in a residential area when a cat stepped out into the street in front of the car and sat down. Clifford stopped and stared at the cat, which stared back. Then he turned to the examiner and said, "How much do you people pay that cat?" The examiner answered solemnly, "It's not our cat. Proceed with caution." The cat stayed where it was, and there was no way to get around it. So Clifford got out of the car and shooed the cat away. Then he turned back to his car, only to see it slowly rolling away down the street, tail first. He'd forgotten to put it in park or set the emergency brake. The examiner was busy writing something on his clipboard so he didn't realize the car was moving until Clifford threw himself on the hood in a desperate attempt to stop the vehicle. The examiner jumped in surprise, hitting his head on the ceiling of the car, and then threw himself to the floor to operate the foot brake with his hands. That was one of the times when they just went back to the DMV Examining Station without bothering to see if Clifford could parallel park or not.

After he failed the eighth time it looked like Clifford would never pass the test. His scores were actually getting worse, not better, and his mother was tired of driving him over to Bellevue, sitting in the waiting room while the test was conducted, and then driving him home. Understandably he was not in the best of moods on those homeward journeys, and they had some snappish conversations. So after the eighth test, she said, "Let's just forget it then," and stormed into their house without him.

The next evening The Seven met at the Samoa, with their student present this time, to discuss the situation. Frank Forcade and one of the other guys were gone by then. Janelle and Steve had taken their places. Somehow it didn't seem right if there weren't seven. Clifford was talking about giving up, becoming one of that handful of people in the Western World who don't drive and are intimately familiar with the bus schedules. Some of those present at the table were secretly relieved that he wanted to quit. But Curtis and Wayne wouldn't hear of it, and not only because they didn't relish the idea of driving Clifford around for the rest of their lives. There was a solution and they were going to find it.

Because the Saab had a stick shift, Clifford had always taken the test in his mother's Olds. Wayne thought maybe that was the problem. The car was a jinx. The minute the examiners saw it they knew their lives were in danger again and were looking for ways to cut the test short and minimize their personal risk.

"Next time you should try it in some other car," Wayne said. "Change your luck."

Clifford considered. "I suppose I could take the test in Wayne's Chevy."

"No, no," Wayne answered hastily. "I wasn't suggesting the Chevy. Too big, uh, too powerful, uh..." Wayne looked at the rest of us in desperation.

"And too 'kid', Clifford," I said, trying to help Wayne out. "When an examiner sees that hog, he's going to think of every teenage jerk who ever cut him off or brought his daughter home after midnight."

It was the subsequent discussion of available cars and what they would bring to the examination process that led to The Idea—that discussion, and Janelle's eagerness to help—Janelle, the daughter of a Ford dealer.

For his next test a month later, Clifford didn't go to the DMV office located in upper class Bellevue. He went down and around the lake to the examining station in Renton, a hard-knuckle working-class town on the back side of a Boeing Company plant. And he didn't go with his mom, and he didn't go in the Oldsmobile.

Clifford took the test in a 1965 Lincoln Continental with 26 miles on the odometer and every bell and whistle you could get for that model. It was pale blue outside, with a white top and wire wheels. Inside was red leather upholstery, soft and sensuous. The Lincoln had a polished mahogany dash, a tape/radio player better than most people had in their homes, and even a car telephone, the first one we Samoans had ever seen. It was the kind of car you don't just 'ride in' or 'drive,' it was the kind of car you *experience*. And with Clifford at his side, experiencing it to Renton was Jolly Jack The Ford Fanatic himself. Janelle's Daddykins had come through, and come through in very grand style.

Everybody knew Jolly Jack from his ubiquitous television commercials, so he was only the second celebrity who had ever entered the Renton Department of Motor Vehicles Examining Station. (The first was Jimi Hendrix, before he was famous.) And he knew how to work a room, meeting and greeting the staff and examiners, laughing his big laugh, introducing Clifford as his 'protégé,' "just an outstanding young man who's learning the car business from the ground up." This was an important part of The Idea, presenting Clifford not as a rich kid from Mercer Island driving a car that was worth more than most of the examiners' homes, but a worker who just needs to get this little test out of the way so he can go back to his duties at Jolly Jack the Ford Fanatic's Fantasia of Fords.

"Soon as we're done here," Jolly Jack told the DMV staff confidentially, "Young Clifford will be breaking in the Lincoln for...well, for security reasons I can't tell you who's purchased the car. Let's just say he's in the very highest echelons of state government."

The examiners had a little scuffle about which one would get to conduct Clifford's test. Finally one guy claimed seniority, and he and Clifford went out and got in the car. Jolly Jack stood in the window watching, beaming his 14,000-cars-a-year smile in all directions.

Clifford's biggest problem during Test #9 was getting the examiner to tell him what to do. The old guy was so busy playing with the various features of the Lincoln that Clifford kept having to ask, "Do you want me to turn here?" and getting in response, "Oh yeah, sure, wherever." For a while Clifford just drove along streets that looked interesting to him, waving pleasantly to the people who would stop and stare at that car.

Just before they got to the parallel parking test, Clifford, as planned, told the examiner that Jack said it was okay if he wanted to make a call or two on the car phone. So while Clifford was knocking over all four of the pylons marking the parking test area and bouncing up over the curb twice, his examiner was on the phone saying, "Hey, honey! It's me! You'll never guess where I'm calling from!"

All of his driving life, Clifford has been a Ford man.

Curtis

WE DIDN'T GET a lot of parents in for Cheese Deluxes. Certainly no Samoa regular ever considered bringing the folks in for eats. Some Samoa habitués didn't seem to have parents. Or their parents influenced them about as much as they were influenced by the *Tibetan Book of the Dead.*

While his father was busy writing Letters to the Editor about fluoridation and the Lost Tribes Geoff apparently could do anything he wanted, any time, with any one. He seemed to live in the dark corners of the Samoa. Twice that summer I found him asleep in a booth when I opened up Sunday morning. He'd been locked in all night and never knew it. Most guys disappeared to the Samoa, but because Geoff was always there he could only disappear from it. Which he did, all weekend sometimes. His parents never called to find out where he was. I assumed they were like the rest of us. They didn't care.

Parents existed for most of the regulars, but more spiritually than physically, like the dead ancestors of the Kaliai people of Papua New Guinea. We got messages from our parents and heard their voices in the night. But we believed actual personal contact with them was beneficial only during tribal rituals like Christmas and Thanksgiving.

Close continual contact with parents was simply out of the question. One of our group, Jesse, was afflicted with a "pal"-style dad he'd been trying to shake for years. Together they had experienced Peewee Football, Indian Guides, Boy Scouts, Sunday School and Little League, and it was driving Jesse nuts. His father even chaperoned school dances. That meant Jesse had to go too. His only alternative was getting laughed at because his father had a more active high school social life than he did. If he didn't go he also had to endure the post-dance report down at the Samoa when happy couples told him about all the cute crap his father had done at the dance. He could avoid that humiliation, or at least be prepared for it, by going, but that led to an altogether different kind of anguish.

Jesse was built like the baseball catcher he was. His calves and thighs were huge compared to the rest of his body. As a result he was gorilla-esque, an impression that wasn't helped at all by his proto-Beatle haircut. On some guys the Beatle-look worked but you had to have a good strong brow for the bangs, and Jesse didn't. They gave him a sort of permanent Neanderthalian glower, like a young Kirk Douglas only much more hirsute and without the chin dimple. Perhaps because of his appearance, as well as an awkwardness around girls so overpowering he once complimented Robin Strauss on the shine of her braces, young ladies were not clamoring to be held by Jesse at a dance or any other time. He went through agonies looking for dance dates.

"Why do you do this?" we asked. "Why not just go stag?" But Jesse explained that if he went alone his father would insist on hanging out with him throughout the evening. He could stand that; he was used to it. But Dad's pimping nearly killed him.

"He'll start prowling the hall," Jesse moaned, "asking any girl who's standing more than five feet away from her date if she'd like to dance. The girl says to herself, 'It's that cute old chaperone. Sure I'll dance with you,' she says. 'Oh, not me,' he says laughing, 'I'm way too old for the likes of you, ha ha ha,' and then he drags them over to me. You should see the look on their faces. They think I put him up to it. He doesn't care who they are either, he goes for the most beautiful ones, girls who wouldn't pull me off a fire. Christ, at the Winter Ball he asked Missy Sagerson! As soon as they got near me Missy suddenly said she had a rock in her shoe and sort of hobbled away. And for the rest of the evening whenever my dad or I came anywhere near her she went into her 'Chester' routine from *Gunsmoke.*"

Eventually Jesse reached an understanding with Tess, a Samoan whose father insisted she go to all the dances too because by God when he was in school he couldn't go to dances because he had to work in the coat hanger factory to support his parents by God. Tess' dad was a former professional football player, a huge, barrel-chested, broad-shouldered man. She looked just like him, half a foot taller than Jesse and 20 pounds heavier. They were just friends, but that friendship solved both of their dance date problems. Even with Tess in tow Jesse was still mortified at the affairs because his father danced too, usually with the faculty chaperones. Watching your father jitterbug around the floor to "Bye Bye Love" with ancient giggling Mrs. Cunningham at the same time you're failing her Spanish class and know she hates your guts can cause a lot of stress. He was a real horse's ass of a Dad.

One evening the boys were sitting around the Samoa having a frank and open discussion concerning Yvette Mimieux's acting career. We had been especially impressed by the previous night's *Dr. Kildare* episode in which Guest Star Yvette played a surfer with a brain tumor and a baby blue bikini. Dr. Kildare's concern was the brain tumor but our discussion centered more on Ms. Mimieux's apparel than her diagnosis. Stackhouse had just made what we considered a kind and compassionate remark—"I wouldn't kick her out of bed because she has a brain tumor"—when a booming voice from nowhere said, "Mind if I join you?"

It was Jesse's dad. He pushed in next to his son because "It'd be groovy to hang out at the Samoa with Little Jesse and his friends. If you all don't mind." This was a brutal thing for a father to do. And though we felt very sorry for Little Jesse we have all called him 'Little Jesse' since that moment. In 1978, over the strenuous objections of his wife Kristin, he named his own first-born son Lorenzo.

One of us, however, probably envied Little Jesse his Big Jesse. Curtis was a splotchy underachiever whose negligible fine motor skills had caused him difficulties since kindergarten. He was one of our regulars, vying with Geoff for the title of Guy Who Has Wasted The Most of His Life at the Samoa.

Curtis' father, an immaculate corporate attorney from the German part of Switzerland, had two principal hobbies; tennis, and being deeply disappointed in Curtis. Practically anything could make him deeply disappointed, from dirty socks on the bathroom floor to Grand Theft Auto. Being the considerate lad that he was Curtis provided his father with almost daily opportunities between sets and corporate mergers to wallow in Deep Disappointment.

The Fuehrer (that's what Curtis always called him) tried to help his son. His first idea was to bribe Curtis with a 1958 Plymouth. Bribery didn't work, or at least the car didn't work as a bribe because all it did was give Curtis the opportunity to screw up in more places in a shorter period of time.

The Fuehrer next turned to outside experts. Curtis may have been the only seventh grader in history to have a private tutor for Mechanical Drawing. He got a D+.

"I'm deeply disappointed," said the Fuehrer.

"I passed," said Curtis.

Every summer for five years the poor kid was exiled to a mosquito-infested Idaho bog called Camp Commitment, where the nurse was Rocky Graziano's old cut man and the camp accomplished its mission of "Turning Boys Into Men" principally through brutality and starvation. Decades later, when the neo-Nazi activities near Idaho's Hayden Lake were in the news, Curtis' friends had an uncomfortable sense of familiarity with the area, its people, and their singular preoccupations.

The most lingering method Curtis' father used to turn his son into himself was psychiatry. From about age seven Curtis spent an hour twice a week with a shrink named Willi, an immigrant Swiss like the Fuehrer and just as loving. One night at the Samoa Clifford figured out that for what Dad spent over the years on Willi he could have bought his son a Ferrari. This fact so enraged Curtis that for the next month, instead of his usual routine of calling Willi every vile thing he could think of, he didn't speak a word. He and Willi just sat and stared at each other for fifty expensive minutes. The doctor was so moved by this behavioral change that he called the Fuehrer at his office downtown. "At last we're making wonderful progress," he reported proudly.

Neither of them needed to speak anyway, because Willi had nailed Curtis' problem some years before. "My problem," Curtis explained one evening, "is that I'm trying to compete with my father. But it's impossible, because he's perfect in every way. No matter how hard I try I will always lose. So I don't try. I want to fail, because failure is the only thing I can beat my father at. For me failure is victory. It's what I do better than he does." As a result of this insight Curtis never made the slightest effort in school ("Why should I?") and those of us who knew him never had the slightest respect for Willi, or psychiatry in general.

Although Curtis' success at failure was his raison d'être he did have three other areas of expertise: smoking, drinking, and driving. He still holds the record for running the stop sign at the foot of Gallagher Hill. He was going 118 miles an hour when he shot through it. We wouldn't have believed him, but there were witnesses, some of them terrified occupants of the car.

Although smoking, drinking and driving were the principal sources of Deep Disappointment for Curtis' dad they also led to the only known cathartic moment between Fuehrer and son. Curtis was a guest at a party in Seattle. The host was his cousin, whose parents had made two mistakes. They had gone away for the weekend, and they had assumed their son was mature enough to be left on his own. So the party had been going on since an hour after Mom and Dad drove away Friday afternoon, which was when the first keg was delivered. By Saturday evening Curtis was refreshed to the point of incoherence and ready to come home.

A not-unattractive Seattle female, emphatically just an acquaintance of Curtis, volunteered to drive him back to the Island in his Plymouth. It was a good deal for both of them. Curtis was in no condition to drive. Curtis was barely in condition to breathe. And the young lady had just failed her State Driver's License test for the second time and needed practice at the wheel, especially the wheel of somebody who wouldn't mind a little damage. Off they went together, the girl driving, the guy slumped over in the seat next to her.

At that same moment Curtis' parents were just leaving home for a fête of their own. Theirs was a semi-formal affair in town, so the Fuehrer was wearing a stylish black suit and hat, and Mom, a quiet woman who was dominated by her husband, was outfitted in a sincere dark frock.

These two parties crossed paths in the middle of the floating bridge that connects Mercer Island to the rest of the world. The grimy brown '58 Plymouth was going east, the sleek black '64 Mercedes was headed west. At the moment of confluence Curtis was staring intently at his shoes. He knew from experience that if he moved his head just an inch in any direction he would hurl all over himself, his car, and the young lady. Curtis wouldn't have noticed his parents going the other way if they had been riding camels and leading a circus parade.

But his parents noticed him, or rather his car, being driven by a young woman they had never seen before in their lives. Curtis' mom thought for a moment that the girl was a car thief, but then she spotted the lump in the passenger seat.

"That was Curtis," she said, referring to the lump. This was the same Curtis she thought was back on the Island helping Wayne Whitley build a tree house as a Boy Scout project.

The Fuehrer considered this situation in silence as he went another hundred yards, and then he made a spur of the moment decision. It was probably his first impulsive act in a long life of careful planning and calculated risks. He did a tire-squealing U turn in the middle of the bridge and began to follow his son and the mystery girl. Many years later he told Curtis why he did it. There in the middle of the bridge he suddenly realized he knew almost nothing about his only offspring after sixteen years together.

Like a sick old dog staggering home to die Curtis was heading for the Samoa. But it was dark, the young lady didn't know the Island, and Curtis' mumbled directions were understandably confusing. So instead of staying on the freeway until the Shopping Center/Samoa exit she took the first off-ramp she came to and headed up Hosner Hill into clusters of homes. Behind her in the dark the Mercedes shot off the same exit, and then ducked into driveways and alleys to avoid detection. Even in his slowly recovering state Curtis couldn't have detected a Sherman tank following him, but The Fuehrer didn't know that so he was using defensive maneuvers. Actually he was having a hell of a good time playing Spy. Corporate attorneys have rich fantasy lives, believe it or not. Curtis' dad imagined himself as James Bond behind the wheel of a super-charged Aston Martin, diving in and out of the back streets of Gstaad. With a beautiful blonde at his side he was in pursuit of Ernst Stavro Blofeld. He even made a mental note to trade the Mercedes in on an Aston Martin when the market went up again. The real blonde (well, sort of) at his side was just scared, worried that her son was sick and her husband had gone suddenly, inexplicably mad.

After some aimless neighborhood meandering the lost young lady spotted the Shopping Center down the hill and turned for it. The Mercedes, cruising slowly through the parking lot of the First Congregational Church, followed discreetly. She drove up the main drag while her Swiss shadow ducked in and out of Shopping Center side streets.

By this time the young lady's interest in both the Plymouth and Curtis had bottomed out. When she finally found the Samoa she was inside before the gravel settled, scanning the menu and being intensely scanned herself. Curtis was left alone in the vehicle, staring at his shoes. But he was beginning to think he would live.

Burgered up, the young lady asked the assembled Samoans if anybody could give her a ride back to town. Volunteers were numerous. Geoff offered to hot-wire Wayne Whitley's car to accomplish the mission even though he was sitting across from Wayne at the time and didn't have the slightest idea how to hot wire anything. Stackhouse asked whether she'd ever had a Big Joy Burger, one of America's best. Jesse complimented her on not throwing up as so many might have in her condition.

Eventually Wayne got the assignment because Wayne had the Chevy. It was a wasted opportunity, because girls scared the bejesus out of Wayne. An hour later, back at the Samoa for debriefing, he said he never put his full weight down for the entire drive. Curtis went unnoticed by all of us, because he often spent hours sitting in his car in front of the Samoa, smoking. His only alternative was to go home.

Meanwhile his mom and dad were discovering what a lot of other parents already knew. It was very difficult to observe activities at the Samoa discretely. The restaurant fronted on a freeway exit, so there was no street parking, and even on Mercer Island, a big black Mercedes would have stood out in the Samoa's small parking lot like a Brahma bull. Finally Curtis' folks parked in an alley half a block away, where they could just glimpse the rear fender of the Plymouth. And there they sat, waiting for something to happen.

Half an hour later something happened, but it was not what they expected. The building they were hiding behind was the local branch of the Seattle First National Bank. Back then it was calling itself "The Friendly Bank!", but not so friendly to dark figures in a big black car parked by the back door on a moonless night. Police cruisers suddenly blocked both ends of the alley. Enthusiastic officers took up defensive positions behind their car doors, and an authoritative voice rang out in the night.

"You in the black sedan. Don't move. This is the police."

There was a dramatic pause. Curtis' father said quietly, "I'll handle this," and Curtis' mother said "You bet your ass you will." (This response was one of many surprises Curtis' father experienced that night.) Then the police said, "Throw out your weapons and come out very slowly with your hands on top of your heads."

There was another dramatic pause. The Fuehrer glanced around the car, considering what he might have on hand that police officers would consider a weapon. Finally a Swiss Army knife flew out the driver's side window and clattered to the pavement. The little plastic tweezers popped out. Curtis' mom threw her purse out the other side because she didn't want the officers to think she might try to hit them with it. Then mom and dad did what they were told, slowly emerging from the Mercedes, keeping their hands in view at all times. They turned together and as ordered spread-eagled themselves against the bank wall.

Like her son, Curtis' mom was a big fan of *The Untouchables*, and she knew what came next: frisking. She would have nightmares about this anticipated event for the rest of her life. But frisking never actually occurred. As the police approached cautiously it was clear that the perps spread-eagled before them were not the upscale version of Bonnie and Clyde. Even late at night, even pinned up against the wall like spiders, Curtis' folks still looked like bank executives, not bank robbers. But the officers were curious as to why these seemingly normal types had been driving slowly through back alleys and parking lots for the previous 45 minutes.

It was then that the Fuehrer's legal experience kicked in. Mercer Island had a lot of lawyer dads in the mid-60s and even a few lawyer moms. The best of them always treated their kids as clients whenever third parties were involved, especially if the third parties were governmental or educational authorities. Later on you could discipline your child in your own way for his transgressions, but outsiders automatically got the "innocent babe" defense.

So instead of telling the cops that they were spying on their drunk 16-year-old son, Curtis' father improvised a beauty. Nervously clutching his Homberg he smiled at the officers in a shy, embarrassed, almost groveling way.

"Shucks," he said. This opening was so completely foreign to his nature that Curtis' mom turned and stared at him. She had never seen this person before, but then just like her husband, she was having her own series of surprises that night.

The Fuehrer did all the talking. He told the police that their son was out on a first date with an older girl he met in church camp who made them a wee bit nervous, sophistication-wise. That's why they were shadowing the young couple, who had been attending the Youth for Christ Awards Banquet and were now on their way home with their trophies for Community Service and Dedication to the Lord.

As an attorney the Fuehrer believed implicitly in the corporate lawyer's maxim: If you are in court, you have failed. He never failed, so his only real courtroom experience was 25 years before; a Yale Law School mock trial when he unsuccessfully defended Lindbergh kidnapper Bruno Hauptmann. But he rose to the present occasion. His story played so well and was so well played that the cops never even asked the name of the son in question. Which was just as well. "Curtis?" they would have said. "Curtis, out with a girl? Slap the cuffs on these lying bastards."

When the Mercedes eventually pulled into the Samoa lot, Curtis was in his regular booth, almost alive. "Oh Jesus," he said when his father peered into the Samoa, rather like Dr. Watson peering into an opium den. "I'm dead. I'm jus' very dead. So dead."

What Curtis didn't know was that the man in the doorway was a slightly changed man. For a few minutes in that dark alley behind the bank Curtis' father hadn't been a successful attorney with two secretaries, a beautiful house and a powerful backhand. He'd been a bad guy, a guy somebody assumed was up to no good. It was a completely alien experience for him. Standing there with his hands on his hat, being interrogated by men with guns, he had a flash of what his son's life was like, what life was like for all those kids whose parents are so eager to assume they are villains.

Now he walked up to the booth where Curtis was sitting and looked down at his son with almost a smile.

"Good evening, Curtis."

"Goo' evening, father," Curtis mumbled, ready to hear how deeply disappointing his behavior had been.

"I think maybe we should go home now," the older man said. "If you're finished here."

"Yes, father," Curtis answered, confused by not hearing that edge he was expecting in his father's voice. "I certainly think I'm finished here."

Then instead of just turning and walking away, the Fuehrer waited for Curtis to stand up and join him. They went out side-by-side; a couple of guys. Dad asked if he might drive the Plymouth just this once, Mom cranked up the Mercedes, and they were gone.

Curtis was back at the Samoa a few days later. In the interim there had been a lot of conjecture about what horrible punishment the Fuehrer would inflict. Curtis had barely ordered before somebody asked him what happened.

"Nothing," Curtis said. Then he picked up a Cheese Deluxe and two chicken baskets to go, and went home.

The Bunny

WAYNE WHITLEY'S FATHER worked in a Seattle shipyard. Because almost all of our parents were professional people we assumed Whit Whitley was too—a shipyard executive, a supervisor, at least a foreman. But Wayne said no, his old man spent the day punching holes in massive sheets of steel and then attaching them to the hulls of large ships. Wayne said it like his father performed these tasks alone, except for Babe, his big blue ox. Whit Whitley was an Elk, not an ox, with a GED, one blue suit, two ties, and a dedication to Chevrolets that had been going on for 35 years. He was a worker, and Wayne was proud of that. On the rare occasions when we'd see a big ship Wayne would look at it the way John Muir must have looked at the Sierras.

"That's what my old man does, right there," Wayne would say with a little catch in his adenoids. "Without him that baby would be on the bottom." And when one of those babies did occasionally go to the bottom Wayne was quick to point out that the deeply departed wasn't from his dad's shipyard.

The progeny of Boeing workers were the same way. When a plane went down and hundreds of people were killed in terrifying gruesome bloody burning agony, the first thing these kids looked for in news reports was who made the plane. If it was a McDonnell/Douglas product, a true Boeing family felt a little surge of satisfaction. Nobody actually said, "Well, what can people expect if they're going to fly around in crap like the DC 9?" but a lot of Boeing people felt that way.

The Whitleys were practically pioneers on the Island. They moved over from Renton in 1939, even before the floating bridge to Seattle went in. (According to the local joke, there are three kinds of people on Mercer Island: The BBs, who came before the bridge; the ABs, who came after it; and the SOBs, who run the school system.)

The Island was a different place in those days, mostly truck farms and houses that were really cabins. When the wind came up you filled your bathtub with water in case the power lines fell and the pump in the lake stopped working. The only fancy houses on the Island were the summer 'cottages' of big city rich folks. The Shopping Center where the Samoa would eventually sit consisted of a general store with a post office window, Hamilton's Flying A gas station, and the White House Drive–In, where they made chocolate milk shakes out of chocolate ice cream because they didn't know any better.

Most of the Before Bridge dads hunkered down and did what they did on the Island. Whit Whitley was an actual commuter, one of the first of a daily migration that would become thousands of people by the 1990s. His commute was 55 miles each way, and he called it The Drive. It was the big reason he loved Chevys. They got him where he had to go.

"Never had a Chevy crap out on me on The Drive. Never. Had to use a Ford once. A loaner while the Chevy was getting her annual checkup. Ford crapped out on the first day, in the middle of the bridge, five miles from this very spot where I sit now. Not even five miles, more like four and a half. Made it four and half miles in a Ford. Had to push it off the bridge in traffic. Missed two hours of work and was docked for it. Ripped my pants. Goddamned Fords."

The Whitleys lived in a small house on top of the Island, with a nice vegetable garden bordering where the front lawn should have been. Whit Whitley thought lawns were a waste of time. He used to say a tree was from God and a lawn was from fertilizer. That's the way he said it around us kids, anyway.

Whit Whitley's passion in life, besides Chevrolets and Doris, was hunting. Each season he ventured forth into the tall-and-uncut to kill pheasants, ducks, geese, quail, partridge, doves—pretty much anything that took to wing when he came walking up. As a young man he'd hunted deer as well, but after secretly sobbing through *Bambi* in 1942 he swore off killing ruminants forever.

As a builder of ships Whit spent WW2 at home doing what he always did. He agreed with his draft board that a skilled shipyard worker was more crucial to the war effort than "just another grunt." But it was tough on his son, who was a romantic about such things.

Wayne owned three G.I. Joes when he was a little kid. He re-clothed one of them in a little blue work shirt and Sears work pants that Doris made, with an aluminum foil hard hat. Doris padded the work shirt with some cotton so the figure had a pot gut; her little joke. Wayne used a cigarette lighter to melt off some of Joe's hair, but he didn't get the 'balding' effect he wanted. The result looked more like a hideous scar from an industrial accident. But Wayne was satisfied. He played with the figure often—not war games, because Shipyard Joe wasn't in the fighting. Generally the scenario was that Shipyard Joe would go into his neighborhood bar (a cardboard box with BAR written on the front) after a hard day making Victory Ships. The other two G.I. Joes, home on leave, were already in there. They'd see Shipyard Joe come in, an able-bodied man who wasn't in the military. The G.I. Joes would give him gas about shirking his duty and not being a real man and how they were putting their lives on the line every day just so he could sit on his fat ass and drink beer. Clifford and I played these two loudmouthed G.I.s many times. Clifford even did research on the role, developing a stream of condescending he-man soldier invective that David Mamet would have admired. His line of abuse was all historically accurate, too, from the University of Washington archives and based on police accounts of fights between soldiers and civilians during the war.

Wayne's scenario always ended the same way. Even though Shipyard Joe respected the uniform of his abusers he would feel compelled to beat the hell out of them, just wipe the place up with these two guys. When Wayne got a little older a Barbie he swiped from the girl next door became Rosie, the date of one of the G.I. Joes. After the fight she'd leave on the arm of Shipyard Joe for a tour of the dry-dock, marriage, and one large son.

That large son was ten when he first went hunting with his dad. They'd been in the field for about an hour when he shot his father in the head. It was unintentional. For the rest of his life Whit had a buckshot pellet in his earlobe which he would invite people to feel if he was in the right mood. His other injury from that first hunting trip was a thin red line Doris Whitley alone was allowed to feel if she was in the right mood. Wayne and his dad were heading for the car to go have the bleeding earlobe attended to. Properly shot an earlobe puts out a lot of blood, so Whit looked like Carrie at the end of the prom. Wayne was so horrified at what he had done to his father that he wasn't paying attention to where he was walking. He slipped in a fresh cow pie and fell heavily into Whit, who sat down abruptly on the top wire of a fence so powerfully electrified that a herd of Tyrannosauri would have avoided it. Sparks flew, and four hours later other hunters passing by that spot sniffed the air and thought somebody was branding cattle nearby.

Dad and Son Whitley were duck hunting on that first trip, but the only ducks they saw all day were the ones that lived in the Whitley yard back home. This was an irony most Mercer Island sportsmen endured. They sat all day in freezing blinds far from home in hopes of shooting exactly the same kinds of ducks that were leaving green slimy duck crap all over their beautiful lawns back home. The Mallard's Revenge, we called it.

Despite the bleeding, the burning, and the absence of any dead ducks to show for their labors, father and son had a great time together on that first hunting trip. Wayne went on every murderous outing thereafter, and became quite good at it, although he was to shoot his father twice more. Both times were unintentional.

One soft summer night in August a group of guys were sitting around the Samoa making up obscene verses to "On Top of Old Smoky" when Wayne arrived with Good News For All. "My old man says you guys can come hunting!"

He had never mentioned this possibility before, nor had anyone asked, but he'd obviously given it a lot of thought. "We have four shotguns, besides mine and the old man's. So four of you can come this first time. Whatdya say?"

"Just a minute," Clifford said, alarmed. "Your family has six shotguns? Your family?"

"Yeah, I guess," said Wayne. "So what?"

"Do you have other guns too, a lot of them like that? Revolvers, pistols, bazookas?"

"No, not a lot of them. Just the ones in the cars. And my old man's got one in the bedroom. And there's the one hidden by the front door. What's the big deal?"

Clifford was becoming a little hysterical. "My God, don't they do tests or something, suitability, intelligence, something like that, before people can go out and buy an arsenal? People like you?"

"Hey, look," said Wayne, beginning to steam, "do you guys want to go hunting or not?"

Of course we wanted to go hunting. Screw around in the woods, make a lot of noise, fire off guns at flying objects—it was hard to find a downside in there for a bored teen male. But it wasn't as easy as just picking up a Whitley weapon and going where the wild things are. We would have to take a course in gun safety run by the State Game Department before we could get a hunting license. And Whit Whitley insisted we come over and get checked out thoroughly on the available weapons before taking to the field.

"We don't want any accidents out there," he said, with the concern of a man who's been shot three times by his son, unintentionally.

These prerequisites thinned out the number of troops who were interested in going. Geoff thought this hunting might be a beer-drinking opportunity, but when Wayne said even his father didn't drink with loaded guns around Geoff said "Screw it then." Stackhouse was extremely eager to kill something, which is exactly why his mother wouldn't let him go. That left me, Clifford, Curtis, and for a surprise fourth, Janelle.

"Yeah, I'd like to go," she said. "Why not?"

"Steve," Curtis said.

"Mr. Steven Derdowski is no longer a part of my life," Janelle answered with dignity, as she had so many times before. "Any other reason?"

Clifford, Curtis and I couldn't think of one, but Wayne was worried. Spending a day in the woods with Janelle intrigued him, even if he was terrified around girls and this one would be packing iron. But he wasn't sure what his father would say. His mom had shown outright loathing for the sport. As a present on their nineteenth anniversary Whit gave Doris a little Lefever Side by Side 20-gauge shotgun, perfect for the delicate female hand. Whit insisted nineteen was the Gun Anniversary. What he learned was that nineteen is also the anniversary when your spouse no longer feels she has to be gracious and accommodating about her gifts. Doris wasn't going to fake it any more.

"What am I supposed to do with this?" she inquired after opening the beautiful calf-leather case and staring down both barrels. "Other than what I'd like to do with it?"

"It's yours, Doll,' Whit cooed. "Now we can hunt together. As a family."

"Whit," Doris said, with gun barrel steel in her voice, "the only thing I like less than cooking birds is killing them. Where's my real present?"

"It's out in the car," Whit answered instantly. He jumped up, ran out to the Chevy, drove into the city, bought the first pair of earrings the saleslady at the fanciest jewelry store in town recommended, and was back home in less than an hour.

"Good work, Whitley," Doris said. "And here's your present." She handed him a little Lefever Side by Side 20-gauge shotgun she happened to have. She was happy, and Whit had a spare gun. The family always called it 'Mother's Gun' even though in her entire life the only time Mother ever laid a finger on it was to get rid of it.

"I suppose you could use Mother's Gun," Wayne told Janelle, "but my old man isn't used to girls hunting. He might say you can't go."

"Let me handle your old man," Janelle said confidently.

"Okay, I guess we'll see what happens." Wayne was far from convinced. "Just one thing, Janelle. Whatever you do, don't tell my father that your father sells Fords."

The next day Geoff and Stackhouse came bursting into the Samoa and begged me to help get them into the hunting party.

"I made a hasty decision," Geoff admitted. "I didn't realize how much I want to go into the woods with my buddies, whether there's beer or not." His mouth said 'male bonding,' but his eyes said something else. Stackhouse's leer was nearly identical and just as familiar to me.

"And you," I asked him, "I thought your mother wouldn't let you go."

"For this wonderful experience," Stackhouse said nobly, "I am prepared to, well, I'll admit it, I am prepared to lie to her. I'll tell her I'm driving to Cle Elum."

"I see. This sudden interest in hunting wouldn't have anything to do with Janelle, would it? The fact that she's going?"

"Janelle's going? Is she? Is she really? Fancy that." Stackhouse apparently thought I was an idiot.

"Gentlemen," I said, "Let's be honest with each other. Your interest isn't in sport. It is in what I believe used to be called 'sporting.' And though personally I would never stand in the way of true love, Wayne Whitley would. He has decreed that there are six guns, six hunters, and one station wagon. That's it. So I speak for Wayne, Janelle, Curtis, Clifford and myself when I say, if you really want to go hunting, you will be going by yourselves. I suggest you try up a creek."

Curtis drove us all over to Wayne's house one evening a few weeks later. I thought Janelle would wear something in the Tight n' Sexy line to encourage Whit Whitley to want her to come along. I was looking forward to it, in fact. But Janelle was a lot smarter than I am about such things. When we picked her up she was wearing a white blouse with a Peter Pan collar and a full skirt that looked like it was made out of pool table felt, only baby blue. There was a matching blue satin bow in her hair, a little gold locket in the shape of a heart around her neck, and no evidence of makeup or mail order lingerie anywhere. Janelle looked like the poster child for Waiting Until Your Wedding Night. We hardly recognized her.

"Nobody speaks," she warned us, and got into the car.

Wayne still hadn't told his father that one of the hunting party was female. Whit was under the impression that four of the guys were coming over to learn about the family guns. When we walked in he was standing behind the dining room table laying out the Whitley weaponry before him. He looked up, saw us, saw Janelle, and his jaw dropped onto the top of his gut. Clearly this was a man who all his life had wanted a daughter who looked ... just...like...that.

Janelle didn't wait for Wayne to make introductions. "Mr. Whitley!" she squealed with very un-Janelle-like glee, skipping across the room. "It's so nice of you to let me come along on the expedition. I'm Janelle." She floated her arm out over the table and the guns. For a moment I thought Whit was going to kiss her hand. Instead he took her digits in his like he was cradling a kitten, and smiled the way he smiled when Doris made Bacon/Tater Tot/Velveeta Casserole.

"Young lady...Janelle is it...I had no idea a girl was part of...Wayne didn't tell me that...I don't think he's ever mentioned you before...well, I think we're all going to have a very good time on this...ha ha...expedition."

The rest of the hunting party had dropped onto the couch, watching these performances in awe. Two people we thought we knew pretty well had turned into two very different people before our eyes. The always-commanding Whit Whitley had become a moonfaced, stammering Daddy, blushing to where the roots of his hair used to be. And Janelle had turned into Shirley Temple in *The Little Colonel*, flashing her megawatt dimples and turning the old curmudgeon into a pussycat. She was so proficient at this that I figured she'd had a lot of practice. Later that year when Clifford took his driving test I met her father, late night television's own Jolly Jack The Ford Fanatic. No bigger Daddykins ever lived.

Whit turned back to the table. "I have just the gun for you, Janelle." He snatched up Mother's Gun and was waving it around when Doris walked in from the kitchen with a plate of cookies.

"This baby is a Lefever Side by Side," Whit was saying, "which means the two barrels are...oh, look, cookies!" If he hadn't been holding the gun I swear he would have clapped his hands together in girlish glee.

"Doris," Whit bubbled, "You know these guys"—the rest of us got a perfunctory wave, even though by this time we all had guns in our hands and were pointing them at each other—"but I don't think you've met Janelle. Janelle, this is Mrs. Whitley. My wife. Doris. Wayne's mother. Doris, Janelle is going hunting with us. She's a friend of Wayne's! Can you believe that?"

Janelle turned and faced Doris Whitley straight on. Doris looked at Janelle's blue dress, at the little blue bow and the gold locket, at Whit Whitley standing behind the weapons table grinning like a performing chimp. The two women exchanged a glance that no male in the history of the world has ever fully understood.

"How do you do, Mrs. Whitley." It was an entirely different voice than the one she was using on Whit.

"Hello, Janelle." That was all they said out loud, but they'd already spoken a lot to each other with that look. Wayne told me that hours after we left his father was still going on about Janelle.

"That's just the kind of girl for Wayne, Doris, for Wayne to build a life with. Respectable, intelligent, pretty, a girl I'd be proud to have in the family. Don't you think so?"

Doris laughed. "Whitley," she said, "you're just damned lucky I cut you out of the herd early." And she grabbed up the leftover cookies and took them up to bed and Johnny Carson.

"What does that mean?" Whit asked the place where she'd been standing. And when he got no answer he asked Wayne. "What does that mean?"

"What does that mean?" Wayne asked me the next day at the Samoa.

"It means women can be really, really scary, Wayne."

"I thought so."

We took our class in gun safety, got our hunting permits, and the big weekend arrived. By then it was fall, which meant we wouldn't be hunting ducks, but doves. The doves were making their annual migration from Canada to Mexico, and each hunter in our state was allowed to kill ten a day throughout the month of September. A guy who had a lot of ammunition and spare time on his hands could have 300 doves in the fridge by October first.

"And a divorce," Doris said, as she saw us off that Saturday morning. "You kids, any doves you kill, you take them home with you. Don't assume that just because some of us hunt the damn things that all of us want to eat them for the next six months. You kill it you keep it. That's the rule."

We agreed, but it was four in the morning, cold and dark. We would have agreed to anything.

Clifford vowed some years before that he would never voluntarily take up any activity that required him to rise before nine a.m. He was breaking his own rule, and he was cranky about it.

"Are these birds nocturnal?" he whispered to me as Whit and Wayne were loading the guns into the back of the car. "Or are we going to surprise them as they sleep soundly in their nests and blow their brains out before they know what hit them? Is that the kind of sportsmen we are? What exactly is the Christian purpose of that?"

"Shut up," I counseled.

"Aren't doves some kind of pigeon? I believe I have seen pigeons walking around in the daylight hours. Just a few."

"Don't complain to me, complain to the Whitleys. Am I in charge here?"

"All right, but you should know something right now. I'm not killing anything. I'm here to have a cultural experience. To experience the hunter culture. Besides, my mother says anything you kill yourself can't possibly be kosher, and she won't let it in the house."

"You don't eat kosher anyway."

"Don't turn anti-Semitic on me, Bub," Clifford snarled, "this is my mother we're talking about."

Curtis' arrival stopped Clifford's agonies, since Curtis had given Janelle a ride. In a cloud of cigarette smoke they climbed slowly out of the Plymouth like two people who have never gotten up at four in the morning in their lives. Up 'til four, sure. Up at four, hardly.

Janelle surprised me once again. She had dressed for the occasion, and not just in the jeans, sneakers and parkas the rest of us were wearing. She'd created a hunting ensemble, based on an article in *Gentleman's Quarterly* titled "The Hunt for Fashion." She wore a beautifully tailored tweed jacket with a brown leather pad covering the right shoulder, rugged wool trousers in an earthy brown and black check, and sturdy but stylish boots. Around her neck was a scarf of pure white, and over her shoulder she carried an empty game bag that was as chic as canvas gets. The whole outfit must have cost as much as the rest of the hunting party's clothing combined, including the guns. Janelle looked like Princess Anne off to pot a few grouse before teatime.

With one exception. To Janelle, it looked like the *GQ* models never came any closer to real woods than cutting across the corner of Central Park. She was worried that her outfit, though stylish, lacked practicality. There was only one person she'd ever seen actually hunting: Elmer Fudd. So she added her personal touch to the GQ look; a forest green Elmer Fudd hunting hat. She hoped it worked for doves a lot better than it worked for wabbits.

Whit and Wayne were struck speechless by the vision of her. Clutching a cup of hot coffee and peering out from inside her dark kitchen, Doris Whitley was speechless too. Then she started laughing so hard she woke up Gretl over by the refrigerator. Doris really didn't stop laughing until late that afternoon.

"Janelle," Whit said, swooping up, "I'm so glad you could join us. You look ...enchanting."

"It's my pleasure, Mr. Whitley," Janelle tried to coo. But it was very early in the morning for a dedicated smoker and Janelle was still growling more than cooing. Whit didn't notice. He squired her over to the car, opened the passenger side front door, and in she went. This was a disappointment for the rest of our party, who had imagined squeezing into the back seat with her for the long ride to the killing fields. Wayne was especially surprised because he always sat in the front next to his dad, even when Doris was along on trips to IHOP for international cuisine. But as Clifford correctly deduced, on that particular hunting trip the rest of us could blow each other's brains out and Whit Whitley wouldn't care, unless some of our brains spattered onto Janelle's hunting ensemble. Then we would be in big trouble.

We four guys squeezed into the back seat and off we went, east for Wenatchee, about two hours away. There wasn't much talk on the way over. Curtis fell asleep against the window glass before we were off the Island. Clifford knew it wasn't wise to complain about the early hour around the Whitleys, and that was all he cared to discuss. Wayne and I both came from families where the tradition on long car rides was complete silence. When I was thirteen my family drove to California, four of us in a Volkswagen bug, and didn't exchange a word from Tacoma ("Did you turn off the stove? You said you were going to turn off the stove.") to Eugene ("Look, any motel will do, just pick one for Christ's sake.") It was our collective personal best.

Up front alone with Whit Whitley, Janelle wasn't talking much either, just looking out the window at the world going by in the dark. She started fidgeting after twenty miles, and shooting glances at Whit. She was sizing him up about something, picking her moment. And then it came.

"Mr. Whitley, I'm afraid I have a little confession to make," Janelle said as sweetly as she could. Wayne, Clifford and I were instantly alert. What could Janelle possibly have to confess to a parent she barely knew?

"I...I have a naughty little secret."

"Oh my God," Wayne whispered to himself. "She's going to tell him about the Ford business."

"I can't believe that, Janelle," Whit said graciously.

"No, it's true. I'm afraid I...I smoke cigarettes. Sometimes. On trips."

Whit Whitley turned and looked across at his passenger for as long as the traffic would let him.

Really," he said. A half-minute of silence went by. All of us, including Janelle, wondered how Whit would deal with his dream daughter's slight touch of sin. Then he reached inside his coat pocket, pulled out a pack of Old Golds, and held them out towards her. She grabbed the Zippo in her own coat pocket, expertly lit two cigarettes, and handed one back to him in less time than it takes to blow your nose. It was like a scene from the movies. It *was* a scene from the movies.

"Jesus," Janelle said to herself, taking a drag that started somewhere near her heels and then rolling down the window. Sitting right behind her, a blast of cold morning air hit Wayne Whitley full in the chops. He didn't even notice it. He was too flabbergasted to notice anything. His father had never offered him a cigarette, had in fact lectured him on the evils of smoking and drinking. Often these lectures took place late on weekend evenings, when Mr. Whitley had been smoking and drinking for most of the day. The message to us back seat commandos was clear. We guys were kids, but as far as Whit was concerned, Janelle was an adult.

We didn't stop when we got to Wenatchee but drove straight through to the Airport Road. The rising sun was still low in the sky. The brown hills up behind town looked like giant loaves of pumpernickel bread, freshly baked and lined up neatly side by side. Even Curtis, who had successfully slept through the entire journey and awakened at precisely the right moment, was impressed. With the windows down, the car filled up with the smell of sage and dirt, wiping out the smell of smoke and Curtis.

Shortly before we got to the airport Whit turned up a dirt road. We went a few miles into the hills and pulled over. When the Chevy engine stopped, we heard nothing—the kind of silence only the Whitleys among us had ever experienced before. We sat in the car for a moment, feeling the place, hearing the occasional meadowlark. Way down below I could see the airport just coming to life, lights blinking on, a few people walking around the small planes tethered at the far end of the field. Other than that it seemed like there were six people in the world, all of them armed.

Whit Whitley was not one for extended meaningful moments. "Those birds aren't going to come to us!" he boomed. "Gimme a hand, Wayne." The two of them rolled out and started pulling gear out of the back like the veterans they were.

Sitting next to me, Clifford closed his eyes. "I may just stay here," he said. "I may just become a part of nature, instead of attacking it. Nature, here in the car. 'See a Chevrolet, in the USA...'" He sang to nobody in particular. Outside, Whit was decanting shotguns, putting shells into belts, zipping open large bags. I invited Clifford to observe.

"Does that look like a guy who's going to let you stay here?"

Clifford opened one eye and peered out the window. "I may be the one who shoots him this time," was all he said, and then closed his eyes again.

Pulling Clifford along with us, we tyro hunters got out slowly and stood around blowing on our hands, stamping our feet, waiting for instructions. Whit had already told us we were going to hunt in pairs, going off in separate directions so we couldn't accidentally shoot each other. But he hadn't named any specific duos. It was a subject of considerable interest to us young men. After their bonding I guessed Whit would take Janelle for himself, or maybe put her together with Wayne in hopes that love would bloom, followed by marriage and grandkids. But I was assuming that Whit would create the teams because he was the only adult present. No similar assumption was made by our adult-du-jour. Just as we were lining up in front of Whit with our assigned guns and shells Janelle grabbed me by the arm.

"Why don't we go up that way," she said, pointing to a small hill a few hundred yards off. It wasn't a question. It was a command.

"Me? You want me to go with you?" I was so very suave at that age.

"Uh, sure, okay, that'll be good," Whit Whitley said. He'd been caught by surprise, not being accustomed to take-charge teens. "Sure, and uh, Clifford, why don't you and...it's Curtis, isn't it? You and Curtis go that way." Whit Whitley had lost the chance to hunt with Janelle, but he was not about to spend the day with Curtis. Curtis made him nervous. Curtis with a shotgun in his hands made him very nervous.

"Then Wayne and I will go over to the other side of the valley. Keep your partner in sight all the time, and slowly work your way down toward the airport. We'll all meet up there." Whit started off, and then stopped to drop a hydrogen bomb on the rest of us.

"Oh, one other thing," he said pleasantly. "Watch out for rattlesnakes, especially after the ground heats up. We saw a beauty last year, right around here, must have been four feet long."

"Four and a half easy," Wayne offered.

"If you have a problem, Wayne and I have the Snake Bite Kit. Good hunting!"

Whit Whitley walked away before anyone could say anything. And we had a lot to say. Especially Clifford.

"Did he say rattlesnakes? Why didn't anybody mention rattlesnakes before? All these classes, this long drive, nobody mentioned rattlesnakes. How many rattlesnakes are there? Are they all four feet long or are there little tiny ones you can't see? Did they shoot the big one last year or is it out there this year and it's six feet long now? If I'm over here and the Snake Bite Kit's over there what the hell good is it if I have a 'problem'? I'm supposed to run over there with a snake hanging onto my ass?" These were the questions Clifford asked Wayne, but Wayne didn't stick around to hear them. He took off after his father.

"Come on," Janelle said, pulling me away. As we left, Clifford and Curtis were discussing climbing up on top of the Chevy and staying there until either the hunt was over, or St. Patrick arrived on his long overdue mission to drive the rattlesnakes out of Eastern Washington.

Janelle and I started slowly up the hill, slowly because we were watching the ground so intently. "You know, I don't care for snakes," she said.

"We have that in common," I said. "But they say a snake won't bother you if you don't bother it."

"Nobody who's been bit by a snake says that." Janelle had a point.

We kept moving. I was concentrating on terrain that was suddenly alive with rattlers, and at the same time trying to figure out Janelle's thinking. Why did she choose me? The answer took some analysis, or at least an attempt to think like Janelle. Whit Whitley was an adult and a parent. He wouldn't hustle her, but she probably didn't relish the idea of having to act like Julie Andrews for ten hours. Curtis was the only one of us likely to keep hitting on her all day. He wasn't that way under normal conditions, but he might think it was his duty, something he owed to Geoff and Stackhouse and all the other guys back at the Samoa. And Clifford—I think Janelle was a little afraid of Clifford, afraid that he'd talk all day about things she didn't understand or turn vicious about some mistake she'd made. So of all the available men I was the least problematic; the least likely to hustle her and the least likely to go back to the guys and lie about my steamy day in the hills with Janelle, frolicking amongst the sagebrush and the rattlesnakes. She could trust me.

I was proud of that. I was also kind of sorry for her. Janelle had to deal every day with young men whose interest in her was entirely physical. Whether she was eating a Cheese Deluxe or hunting for doves, around her there were guys who were thinking of nothing but putting their hands on her, of getting her 'in the mood,' of seeing her horizontal. And telling their friends afterwards. I don't know whether she really liked Steve or not, but he served a purpose. He was that ominous presence keeping a lot of creeps at bay. But Janelle had decided that I was not a creep. She and I walked along together as two people who didn't want anything from each other, and that can make for a pleasant time.

We heard the first gunshot just as we got to the top of the hill. It didn't come from the Whitleys but from Curtis and Clifford. By that time they'd moved ten feet from the car. As the smoke cleared I saw the two of them walk over and look intently at something on the ground, Curtis with his gun at the ready in case he had to shoot it again. And then, whatever it was, he shot it again. If it was a dove, there was probably a half-pound of buckshot in it by now. I thought that was likely to affect the flavor.

Clifford had quickly grown to dislike hunting because it was an activity where you got up before dawn. I was growing to dislike hunting because it was an activity where you never had a place to sit down. Dirt and dusty knee-high bushes surrounded Janelle and me up on our hill. The bushes were some kind of gorse, I guess, if gorse comes in kinds, and they smelled like sage. It was a wonderful smell for the first hour or so. Then you felt like you were drowning in sage-scented bath salts. There were no convenient rocks of the right height for sitting, and even if there were Janelle and I wouldn't have sat on them anyway. You don't have to be a herpetologist to know about snakes and rocks. We stood the whole time, something neither of us enjoyed.

When we weren't just standing, we wandered around looking intently at the ground. A million-dove flock could have been circling five feet above our heads and we wouldn't have seen it. The Whitley guns, way to our left, were going off fairly frequently after a half hour, but my partner and I were still firepower virgins. Then Janelle gave a little "Eek!' She brought her gun quickly to her shoulder—the unpadded shoulder, because Janelle was left handed in a right handed world—and fired at the ground ten feet away. She killed a stick. It was a stick that had the bad luck to look like a snake. Janelle was embarrassed about shooting the stick, but I told her we were better safe than sorry. That's when the stick slaughter began.

Without talking about it she and I decided that we would rather waste ammunition blowing away anything that might be a snake rather than have a lot of doves to eat at the end of the day. Eating doves might be nice, but not if you have to do it while you're nursing a snakebite in the Snake Bite Ward at Sagebrush General Hospital. So as we walked around, cries of Eek! and explosions of Blam! filled the air, from both of us.

Janelle got the first actual dove we saw. Its fatal flaw was to take wing right after she shot a nearby stick. ("There's one! Blam!") She was a good natural shot; the dove dropped from the sky like a rock. I trotted over to fetch it, a harmless-looking little bird, not much like a city pigeon at all, with a huge breast, a tiny head, and a crop full of grain. I brought it back and showed Janelle her kill.

She glanced at the little ball of feathers in my hand. "There ya go then," was all she said, and walked on.

The day progressed. We shot a few more birds, missed a few others, and killed a dozen sticks. Except for the guns going off, and a plane taking off low over our heads every ten minutes or so, it was very peaceful. Janelle and I had a nice chat about this and that.

Below on the right I could see that it had taken Curtis and Clifford three hours to move another fifteen feet from the car. They looked like duelists, standing back to back, guns at the ready. But not ready for birds. Just like Janelle and me, they were concentrating on the ground. It's interesting the effect one little offhand remark about rattlesnakes can have on a group of people who haven't had a lot of snake experience. We didn't feel like the hunters at all, but the hunted.

Over on their side of the valley Wayne and his dad had covered a lot of ground, going down the hill towards the airport. I told Janelle we'd better start that way ourselves.

"How many doves do we have?" she asked, as if either of us cared.

"Five total. Two for me, three for you."

"Good enough."

We started moving faster than we had before now that there was some place to go. In all the hours she and I had been tromping around that hill we hadn't seen one real snake. Maybe there weren't any snakes. Maybe the snake they'd seen the year before had escaped from a zoo, or was really a four-foot long stick that had fooled even the Whitleys. Maybe this was the snakes' day off. Or quitting time. We felt like we were done trying to kill birds so maybe the snakes were done trying to kill us. They were slithering back to their homes under the small rocks, ready for a nice dinner and a good night's sleep. Then they'd get up early tomorrow morning and try to bite a whole new crop of hunters. But Janelle and I would be gone, the ones who got away.

We were barely over the crest of the hill when there was a sudden rustling close behind us. I had just caught up with Janelle and we were walking side by side. Before I could even look back to see what it was she whirled and fired from the hip in one graceful motion. It could have been anything back there. A few moments earlier and it would have been me. So I guess we were lucky, because ten feet behind us a rabbit was flopping around in its death throes. There was a hole in its head the size of a quarter. Janelle had hit it right between the eyes; another perfect shot, unless you count the fact that she never saw what she was killing until after she fired.

"Oh my God!" she cried. "I thought it was a snake!" She ran to where the rabbit was lying, with thick red blood oozing out of its head. "It's a bunny!"

Actually it was a big no-frills jackrabbit, about as far from a bunny as a Rottweiler is from a Pekinese. But to Janelle it was a soft, furry creature with big, brown eyes. She squatted down beside the rabbit, dropping Mother's Gun in the dirt, gently touching the creature's side. I could hear her whispering softly to it, telling it how sorry she was. Then she picked the rabbit up and held it in her arms, the blood from the wound running out onto her sleeve, dripping down the front of her hunting jacket. She didn't even notice.

"I wasn't supposed to do this," Janelle whispered, as much to the rabbit as to me. She was crying now, stroking the rabbit's rough, filthy fur.

"You, you were startled," I said. "You reacted automatically. Anybody would have…"

"I didn't want to do this. I never killed anything. I never wanted to kill anything." It's not that she had forgotten the three doves in her bag. It's that they were birds, just far enough away when they died to be objects, not living creatures. In the ways to deliver death Janelle had gone from bomber pilot to foot soldier, and the change horrified her. She stood up and looked at me, tears still running down her cheeks. I felt like holding her in my arms, telling her it would be okay, telling her that as soon as we walked away the rabbit would jump up and take off. At that moment, more than anything else in the world we both prayed for the resurrection of one large bunny.

All I could do was gently take her arm. All I could say was, "Come on, let's go meet the others."

"What about the...the rabbit? Should we take it with us? Or should we bury it?

"Bury it?"

"Yes. You're right. We should bury it."

"But Janelle, we don't have a shovel, we..." She was already digging in the dirt with the heel of her boot, holding the jackrabbit in her arms and kicking the ground hard, almost frantically. Working together, eventually scratching away with our hands and gun butts, we clawed out a hole that was about a foot deep. It was enough for her. It was the last and only thing she could do for her victim.

Janelle took off her white scarf and wrapped it around the rabbit like a shroud. Then she gently laid the body down in the grave. We covered the rabbit with dirt and a few rocks and then stood and looked at what we had done.

"Rest in peace," Janelle said. I was no outdoorsman but I was pretty sure not much resting in peace was going to take place. I figured ten minutes after we left the hill a coyote would come along, dig up the rabbit and eat it. If Janelle thought so too she didn't say anything. We'd done what we could, and life went on.

I picked up her gun, she took my hand, and together we walked down the hill toward the airport. We just walked. We didn't worry about snakes any more. That was over.

And when a few doves jumped into the air in front of us we stopped walking and watched them fly away. It was a strange thing. I felt better about letting those doves get away than anything else I'd done that day.

Curtis and Clifford were waiting a hundred yards off the end of the airport's main runway. We probably looked odd to them, holding hands, Janelle's arm and legs speckled with blood. Clifford gave me a very odd look.

"Having fun, kids?" he asked.

"Doing okay," I said. Janelle squeezed my hand very slightly and then let go.

"So we were watching you up there, and suddenly you both dropped from sight for a while," Curtis said. He took a big drag on his cigarette, looking up at the hill we'd just left. "You just...disappeared."

"I found a rock." Janelle's tone precluded any further discussion. Then the Whitleys arrived, toting bags full of dead birds.

"Well, how'd we do?" Whit boomed. "Janelle, did... Jesus, is that blood? Are you hurt?" Whit gave me a look indicating that if I had anything to do with an injury to Janelle I should start running as fast as I could.

"It's not...I'm fine," Janelle said. "I accidentally shot a rabbit."

I tried to help her out. "A big old jackrabbit. It didn't seem like much to eat. We left him up there."

Whit looked closely at Janelle and me. He could tell something was wrong but he couldn't figure out what it was. "Well, that...that's good," he said slowly. "The Game Department wants us to shoot the jackrabbits around here when we have a chance. Some of 'em have turned up rabid. You didn't mess with it after you shot it, did you?" He was looking at the blood on Janelle's jacket.

I sneaked a glance at her. She was looking at the blood like she had no idea what it was. "No," I said. "We didn't really touch it. We just walked away."

A half-mile away at the airport a large commercial plane had been doing its final pre-flight check. Now, with a great roar, it came down the runway right for us and took off over our heads. Watching it go Wayne suddenly pointed and said, "Look at that!" He brought his gun up and fired at three doves that came shooting out of a clump of bushes between us and the runway. One dove hit the ground and Wayne went to get it. A smaller private plane took off a minute later and two more doves popped out of the bushes. One of them survived, one of them became Whit Whitley's twelfth of the day.

"Wayne and I thought we'd take a few over the ten allowed because I didn't think you people would limit on your first day." He was certainly right about that. Clifford hadn't even fired his gun, and besides shooting a lot of kindling Curtis had been skunked in the dove department.

Wayne picked up Whit's latest kill and then looked at the airport. Another big plane was taxiing out to the runway. We all watched in silence. Just as it started to take off Wayne and Whit brought their guns up. Sure enough, as the plane lifted off the ground a few more doves popped out of the bushes. Wayne, Whit and Curtis fired away and hit two of them. The Whitley men very graciously said one of the two belonged to Curtis. When we got back home he put it in his glove compartment. It was there for three weeks, and by then it didn't smell like sage anymore.

"Well now," Whit said, "I think we'll just stay here at the airport for a little while. That okay with everybody?" It was a rhetorical question. Curtis stood ready to shoot. Clifford was deep into his cultural experience. Janelle handed me Mother's Gun and walked a short way back up the hill. She found a little mound to sit on and there she stayed, watching the horizon with red-rimmed eyes. She looked very sad and very alone, but I was the only one who noticed. The others were watching the airport so intently they actually forgot about her. And I just stood there with the two shotguns, hers and mine, four barrels pointed at the ground.

For the next 45 minutes, every time a plane took off doves would come flying past us and get shot. Some made it, some didn't, and the Whitleys were as happy as larks. After a while I happened to glance at the airport building itself and saw a jeep with four guys inside come screaming out from a hanger. Only they didn't go out to the airport road. They came straight down the runway towards us.

With a sense of approaching doom I said "Mr. Whitley, I think we're about to have some visitors." Whit saw the jeep bouncing off the end of the runway and coming very fast. He looked into the sky and thought for a moment. The he put his gun carefully on the ground and told the rest of us to do the same. He sent Wayne up the hill to get the car.

When the men in the jeep arrived they identified themselves as airport security officers. They were extremely angry. The problem with letting aircraft beat the bushes for you is that the flushed doves are right over your head, but at just a little more altitude so are the planes. Apparently a pilot had radioed back to the tower that much to his surprise Cascade Airlines Flight 189 to Pocatello was under fire. We went down in the tower logbook as "possible terrorist activity."

The Whitley family tradition was to take no gas from anybody. But on that occasion, standing in the dust at the fringe of the airport, Whit Whitley took gas by the carload. The airport men started by telling him we were all under arrest on Federal charges. Whit was astonished and chagrined. They asked him if he was a complete idiot. He said he certainly was and thanked them for setting him right on that score. They demanded to see every piece of identification he had. He pulled out his hunting license, his driver's license, his union card, and a certificate for one free game at the Leilani Lanes Bowling Center. He apologized five or six times. They wanted to know if he was ever going to hunt in that area again. He said, "Certainly not, Sir," and thanked them for their consideration. They finally climbed back in their jeep and drove away. Throughout the entire conversation Janelle never moved from her place on the hill.

Wayne arrived with the car, having missed his father's humiliation, which I suspect is why Whit sent him away in the first place. We got out of there fast. All the way home hardly anyone spoke, even when we stopped for dinner at Leonard's Big Joy in Cle Elum.

Back at the Whitley's house Janelle thanked Whit for the day. She was most gracious about it, but he could tell she wanted to get away from that car and the rest of us as fast as she could.

"I hope you had a good time, Janelle," Whit Whitley said gently, taking her hand a last time. "I've enjoyed meeting you very much." There was a sadness in his voice. I think he realized that he would never see her again.

She shook his hand and thanked him once more. Then she came over and asked me if I could give her a ride home. Curtis and Clifford shot me that odd look again, and we were gone.

"Would you do me a favor?" Janelle asked as we pulled up in front of her house. "Would you take my...things? I don't really want them."

"I'd be happy to." And I watched her walk slowly into her house. She gave me a little wave as the door closed. From that moment on, we have been friends.

The next night my mother cooked the doves using a Whitley family recipe. Doris may have disliked game birds but she knew her way around them in the kitchen. My father, mother and brother ate the five doves eagerly. I had a grilled ham and cheese.

Frank Forcade

A LAWYER FRIEND of mine is one of the most civilized people on earth, and courtly around women in an Old World way that is utterly charming. I've seen the top gals of the Lesbian Feminist Radio Collective blush and giggle like sorority girls around this man, because he exudes such civility and respect for women.

Unless the women are waitresses. With them he flirts shamelessly and generally acts like a teenage boy whose parents are away for the weekend. It doesn't make any difference if the waitress is 16 or 65, gorgeous or over the counter. It is her essential "waitress-ness" that does it. He's been devotedly married for more than 45 years (no, she wasn't) and is the most upstanding, moral of persons. His fascination with waitresses is strictly part of the restaurant experience for him, but he's never outgrown it.

I know a woman who is courteous to everyone she meets except paperboys, whom she automatically despises. For three decades she has been accusing a long succession of deliverers of intentionally hiding her newspaper. She made one of them so angry that on his last day on the job, before he went off to divinity school, he set fire to her paper before he threw it on the porch.

A cousin of mine couldn't walk down the street without being followed by every dog in the neighborhood. He was ambivalent about dogs but no dog was ambivalent about him. They'd abandon their beloved masters without a second's hesitation whenever my cousin passed by.

So there's just something about some people. They give off a scent that is undetectable to the rest of us but turns them into slightly different beings for select groups.

Frank Forcade was such a person. He used to hang around the Samoa considering a career in automobile repair after wasting twelve years of public education. Frank was tall, broad at the shoulders but skinny thereafter, with thick brown hair he rarely cut and a wardrobe that ran exclusively to black high top sneakers, sweat socks, grease-stained jeans and a way-off-white tee shirt. He was quiet and easy going, not a playmaker intellectually but not particularly concerned about that or about anything else, either. Mostly Frank wanted to mess around with cars, his sweetheart Stacy, and his friends, in that order. There was something about him, however, that drove a particular group of people into an irrational frenzy of animosity. Unfortunately for Frank that group of people was the police.

Even our local bulls had enough to do without looking for unwarranted villains, so I have to believe there was some initial incident that led to their Frankophobia. There had to be some reason the name Forcade went down on a list at the cop shop as a guy to watch. Frank didn't know what it was, though. Whenever he discussed his situation over a Cheese Deluxe he couldn't recall any heinous act that so enraged the cops that they never forgot or forgave him. But if there was such an act, Frank must have been a precocious son of a bitch when he committed it, because he insisted the cops had been after him since he was seven years old.

"I'd be walking along the road with my towel, heading for the Beach Club, and they'd pull up and hassle me," Frank said once, perpetually kind of confused by it all. "Every day, all summer long." By the time he reached high school there was no question the cops were after him on general principles. Many times I saw him pull up in front of the Samoa, followed immediately by a police officer intent on giving him grief. When our cops wanted to round up the usual suspects, they went looking for Frank Forcade.

It would take a great man not to resent the police for their incessant hostility. Frank Forcade was not a great man. Resentment and revenge were never far from his few non-automotive, non-Stacy thoughts. So over the years a series of incidents occurred which in their recounting could always perk up an otherwise dull evening at the Samoa. The actions of the police were documented and well known, but Frank's retributive acts were a combination of truth and legend. While the police blamed him for everything that ever happened which they couldn't otherwise explain, from a flaming sack of dog crap on Chief Gilmore's front porch to the big earthquake of 1964, Frank would confirm or deny nothing. He never bragged. Friends, acquaintances and even complete strangers frequently presented him with diabolical schemes to get-the-cops. Frank always feigned disinterest. "That's chicken shit stuff," he'd say. And if what was suggested eventually happened you couldn't attach Frank's name to it. You just knew.

To offer the most famous example, late one night an unidentified youth was driving past the Roanoke Tavern, the Island's only beer joint. A police car was idling out front with an officer inside. But something was wrong, because this particular youth had hardly ever passed a police car without being chased and stopped. This time the officer didn't stir. The intrigued teen circled back and took a closer look. The officer seemed to be asleep. His observer pulled up across the street from the tavern and the cop, and waited.

Five minutes passed. The officer snored while the youth sat in his car watching carefully. He thought it could be a trap, that if he took any action at all every other officer on the force would come bursting out of the bushes, like the "arrest" scene in *Bonnie and Clyde*. But as the minutes went by it became clear that it was what it was. This particular policeman was confining his patrol to the precincts of Morpheus.

An idea took form. Being a youth who liked to work on cars, he always carried a heavy chain in his trunk for towing purposes. That chain was all he needed. Without re-starting his own engine he rolled his car fifty yards down the street. Then he got out the chain and walked back to the tavern. After wrapping one end around a concrete pillar that was part of the Roanoke's foundation, he took the other end and wrapped it around the rear axle of the patrol car. He returned to his own car, fired it up, and laid the most magnificent patch in local teen history. Three years later you could still see those dark streaks burned into the asphalt. It was so extraordinary a patch that two miles away at the Samoa Curtis looked up from his Cheese Deluxe and said, "Who the hell is that?"

The officer jolted awake in time to see the taillights of the offender disappearing rapidly down the road. He threw his black&white into gear, stomped on the gas, and instantly turned his patrol car into a patrol sled. In an explosion of sparks, the new two-wheeler rolled to a complete stop twelve feet away in the middle of the street, effectively blocking traffic for the next hour. Inside the Roanoke the jolt to the foundation was such that nine guys went home with wet laps.

Some years later almost the exact same scene was recreated in George Lukas' *American Graffiti*. For us Samoans it was like seeing history come alive. But unlike *Graffiti's* audience we knew what happened later that night, when Chief Gilmore came down to the station with his pajama top tucked into his Sansabelt slacks, seeking an explanation. Waiting for the city tow truck the officer had plenty of time to conjure up how such a thing could possibly have happened. Naturally his thoughts turned to Frank Forcade. When Chief Gilmore inquired at the top of his lungs just what the hell was going on, the officer claimed Frank had somehow slipped dangerous drugs into his Pepsi during a routine stop at the Roanoke. Frank was apparently in an elaborate disguise when he did this so the usually sharp-as-a-tack officer didn't recognize him. The whole caper—he actually used the word 'caper'—had taken weeks of meticulous planning, and the officer was simply an innocent victim.

Given the cops' irrational feelings about Frank the patrolman might have gotten away with it if the bartender at the Roanoke hadn't come forward. "Yeah," said the bartender, who disliked cops almost as much as Frank did, "I saw what happened. The officer was drugged by the four free beers he asked me to slip into his glass."

A month later, just as the same policeman was coming off suspension, he discovered Frank and Stacy, a pleasant, healthy young lady, parked in a remote area. They weren't breaking the law, at least not quite yet, but the officer still rousted them. He couldn't help noticing that Stacy was buck naked and so was Frank, if you don't count sweat socks. So he stood them up against Frank's car, got on his radio, and over the next two hours police officers from a three county area came by to shine their flashlights on the young couple and make remarks. Finally, when their amusement faded, the cops got back into their cars and drove off without so much as a good-bye. No arrests were made.

Numerous small incidents followed, usually having to do with what was called P&C: possession and consumption. Although Frank was not a thief, a vandal nor a hoodlum, he did enjoy an underage beer now and then, his only persistently illegal act and thus his Achilles Heel for law enforcement personnel. The cops watched him so closely for this activity that eventually even Frank's best friends wouldn't drink with him. They were afraid they'd be tagged when the cops inevitably arrived to get Frank. The police tried very hard to get him, too, in many different ways. Every six months or so Frank was approached by guys in their mid-20s with crew cuts and black leather shoes who said "Groovy" a lot and offered to buy him beer. In this way Frank got to meet every new recruit to the Mercer Island police force.

Frank eventually stopped drinking, partly because his mom told him that drinking alone can lead to problems, and partly because of the "Friskies Tuna" incident. On that occasion, Frank was having a few frosties at the home of his one remaining drinking buddy, whose parents were out for the evening. After an hour there was a rough knock at the door. Frank was in the kitchen at the time, preparing a mayonnaise-and-ketchup sandwich. Through experience he knew instantly who had arrived and why they were there. He looked around for something to cover the smell of beer on his breath. Frank had a lot of expertise obscuring the telltale aroma of Budweiser. He knew a hundred mayonnaise-and-ketchup sandwiches wouldn't do the trick, but there didn't seem to be anything else handy.

Just before all was lost he spotted a plate of Friskies Tuna Cat Food down on the floor, being eaten by Max, his friend's massive cat. Frank kicked Max out of the way, grabbed a handful of the pungent brown chunks and stuffed them into his mouth, swishing them around a little. Max was shocked. By the time the officers made it through the house to the kitchen, their quarry was sitting in the breakfast nook, reading the Betty Crocker Cookbook and delicately dropping the last morsel of Friskies down his throat. Max was beside him on the table, happily licking mayonnaise and ketchup off a slice of white bread.

They grabbed Frank anyway. He was handcuffed, marched through the house and out to their patrol car at the curb. He rewarded them for their tenacity on the ride back to the station. It was a bumpy ride, not easy on a tender stomach full of Friskies. After about a mile, Frank hurled the half-digested remains of four beers, the cat food and a Cheese Deluxe into the wind. Because of the handcuffs, he was leaning forward at the time, so the effluent of his illicit evening splattered through the wire screen that separated the front and back seats.

Half-digested-beer-soaked-Tuna-Deluxe stuck to the dashboard, the radio, the shotgun in the door, and Officer Maxwell.

We ruled that one a draw, but Frank was the ultimate loser. A week later at the Samoa he announced that his beer drinking days were over. "It all tastes like cat food to me now," he said sadly.

Frank Forcade's last skirmish with the police was the most satisfying for his friends. Early one morning on the way home from Stacy's he passed a large orange road grader parked in a vacant lot. Always interested in machinery, Frank stopped to look the grader over. He was inspecting the engine when the contractor who owned the beast arrived. The guy was furious because his regular driver hadn't shown up and the equipment was due immediately at a construction site on the other end of the Island. So after showing Frank how to run the thing, he hired him for 20 bucks to drive the road grader up there.

A few minutes later Frank was in the cab high above the street, moving majestically up the center of the Island at fifteen miles an hour. As luck would have it a police officer passed by going the other way and spotted him. He was hard to miss.

The officer sped up, executed the high-speed U turn he'd recently been taught in Police Car Driving School, and gave chase. He was undoubtedly thinking that this time he really had Frank Forcade where he wanted him. Heisting construction equipment worth many thousands of dollars was no slap-on-the-wrist P&C. It was grand theft, trespassing, reckless endangerment, and if he played it right, resisting arrest as well. Frank Forcade was going to jail—real jail. And he was going to make the collar, for the glory of the Mercer Island Police Department and not coincidentally for his own glory. Visions of a sergeant's badge danced in his head. He would be known from now on as The Man Who Got Frank Forcade.

"Pull over!" the officer shouted as he came up alongside the road grader, towering over his cruiser. Frank didn't even look at him. "Pull over, I said!" the officer barked. Frank looked down and smiled.

"Pull over right now goddamn it Forcade!" the officer requested, flipping on his lights and siren. Frank waved warmly, and tipped his baseball cap like he was Mickey Mantle acknowledging the crowd after a homer. It went like that for about a mile, until the officer got the bright idea of darting out in front of the road grader and blocking the road. He assumed this would force Frank to stop.

In the following months, whenever Frank and The Road Grader was discussed at the Samoa, there were some who argued that the officer was correct in his assumption. No matter how much he resented the police, Frank would have drawn the line at destroying Mercer Island municipal property and personnel. Others argued just as vehemently that Frank would not have hesitated to grade the police car and its occupant into a grease slick, and then grab up Stacy and run like hell for Brazil.

We will never know. Certainly the officer came to believe that Frank wasn't going to stop. As the huge orange machine loomed closer and closer without any sign of slowing down, the officer's fantasy switched from The Man Who Got Frank Forcade to The Man Who Got Turned Into Pâté By Frank Forcade And Died A Horrible Death For A Lousy $525 A Week. So at the last second he gunned his engine to get out of the way and slammed into the drainage ditch that ran alongside the road. Eventually he required a tow back to the police station garage. His radio still worked, however, so that Frank, the road grader, and the combined majesty of the Mercer Island Police Department arrived at the construction site at approximately the same moment.

Waving their shotguns, the officers got ready to shoot Frank off the seat of the grader, much as you'd pick a beer bottle off a fence. But before they could get a bead on him, the contractor came running over and dropped his bomb. This was no theft, no teenage prank. This was a worker performing his assigned duties, and why were the police harassing his employee?

The police regrouped. Nobody in any suburb in America during the housing boom of the 1960s wished to offend construction companies. They brought people, and people brought jobs, even for cops. But a lot of constabulary face had been lost, as well as a front axle and a tranny. The cops had to do something. They argued with the contractor that Frank had failed to respond to an officer's request to pull over. Frank explained that road graders are mighty noisy and he couldn't hear too good up there, what with concentrating on the safe and legal operation of a potentially dangerous vehicle with which he was unfamiliar.

"That makes sense," said the construction boss, and all his workers nodded their heads.

"Ya can't hear a goddamned thing when you're drivin' one of them," said a worker with grader experience.

"But the officer turned on his lights and siren," the sergeant in charge bellowed. "Even a dumbass like you could see and hear that, Forcade."

"I thought he was offering me a police escort," Frank said innocently. "Isn't that what he should have done?"

"Yeah," a huge dozer driver asked. "Isn't it?"

The officer wasn't there to answer that question. At that moment he was sitting on the hood of his police car waiting for a tow truck. But the rest of the force knew the answer. They knew that in ten years of harassing Frank Forcade, Frank had never openly defied them. He'd taken their crap in silence and done what he was told, no matter how unfair, because he was smart enough to know he couldn't win. Their officer assumed that this time was just like those times and Frank would do what he was told. The cops also guessed that their brother officer was so busy licking his chops over arresting Frank Forcade on a major felony charge that he went a little stupid. But they couldn't say any of that, especially with the entire construction crew watching. So after a little more hissing and spitting, they pulled out in file, just like Broderick Crawford and his boys used to do it on *Highway Patrol*. Frank picked up his twenty dollars from the contractor for driving the grader, although given the way things worked out he would have paid hundreds of dollars for the opportunity. He bought a good, heavy chain with the money. Apparently a while before he'd lost the one he usually carried.

After such a total defeat, the police force went into full "Get Frank Forcade" mode. Officers would park across the street from his house for hours and just sit there, watching. Frank finally had to stop driving, because no matter where he was or what he was doing they would cite him for something.

Frank graduated from high school the year before me, and he and Stacy got married. It was a very nice ceremony in the VFW Hall. Stacy looked beautiful in her grandmother's wedding dress, even though it had to be let out in a lot of places.

At the party afterwards the bride and groom were standing in the reception line doing the traditional hand-shaking and hugging. Frank noticed a strange guy in his twenties lingering by the punch bowl, looking around, but not lining up to say hello. Frank assumed it was a friend or relative of Stacy's but she said she'd never seen him before.

"What are you two talking about?" Frank's father whispered from down the line.

"That guy over there," Frank answered. "Do you know who he is?"

"Never saw him before. Who is he?"

Frank pondered the guy in the corner; then he looked back at his father.

"Dad," he said, "you've been telling me for a long time that the cops wouldn't hassle me if I didn't give 'em a reason to. Am I doing anything wrong now?"

"What the hell are you talking about?"

"If I'm not doing anything wrong why is there a cop here?"

Mr. Forcade looked at his son and then looked over at the guy. He turned to Stacy's mother next to him, excused himself for a moment, and walked across the room. He stopped in front of the stranger.

The bridal party watched the two men shake hands and then chat. From where they stood they couldn't hear what was being said but it seemed like a normal conversation, or at least it did until Frank's father took a step back, brought a roundhouse right from somewhere downtown and caught the stranger hard on the point of the chin. The guy rose up a little from the force of the punch and then went directly to the floor, out cold. For a moment everything in the room stopped, but the moment didn't last long. The Forcades and their friends were the kinds of folks who don't interfere in other people's business no matter how interesting that business appears to be. Two of Mr. Forcade's army buddies, plus old friend Whit Whitley, strolled over casually to see if there was anything they could do. After conferring quietly with Frank's dad, each one took a limb of the unconscious crasher. They carried the guy out and dumped him on the front lawn of the VFW. Whit brought along a glass of the cheap Scotch and carefully poured it over the cop's white shirt. Then he went to the VFW's pay phone and called the police station.

"Yeah," Whit said to the answering officer, "this is a concerned citizen over at the Forcade wedding. I'm sure you know where it is. Some gatecrasher got in here, drank up a lot of our booze, and then passed out on the front lawn outside. Come and scrape him up, will you? He's giving the place a bad name." And he hung up.

When Frank's father came back from outside he went straight to his son.

"I'm sorry," Mr. Forcade said, and the two men shook hands.

Six months later Frank, Stacy and Frank Junior left home for good, driven away from their families and friends for no reason. I've never known what happened to them, whether another police department in another town had the same reaction to Frank. Somebody told me once that he'd become a policeman himself in one of those tourist-trap towns on the Oregon coast. Frank certainly knew all the procedures, but that's still a cheap irony I refuse to believe.

For a simple, unpresuming guy, Frank Forcade had a lasting effect on the people at the Samoa. There were the stories of his teen years, of course; of cat food and road graders. But there was something else. Forever after, those of us who knew Frank and knew what he went through would instinctively distrust the official version of events. We would always be jurors with an inclination towards the defense. That's not what the police were trying to do, but that's what they did.

Hadley & Elliot

WHEN WE WERE LITTLE KIDS we used to hang out at each other's houses a lot, playing with the home toys, ignoring or torturing younger brothers and sisters. By the time we got to high school home visits were rare. We'd become too sophisticated for that, so the Samoa became a family room for us without the family.

We sacrificed a few things for the proximity of Cheese Deluxes and our own exhilarating company. Back home there was free food, television, older brothers with interesting things hidden in their dresser drawers, and older sisters who might forget we were visiting and walk around in their underwear. The other thing I missed at the Samoa that I found in my own home and the homes of almost all my friends was animal life. We were all pet people and the descendants of pet people, with beloved beasts playing an important role in our kindred structures. My family had a Springer Spaniel, a Black Lab, and Siamese cats named Sibby and Tootoo. The night Tootoo gave birth to seven kittens she chose the middle of my bed for her labors. For the next month I slept on the floor because my mother didn't want to disturb the new family. And I was proud and happy to make the sacrifice. One of those kittens, Timothy Anne, died 19 years later. My mom took care of her cats.

Some Mercer Island people were identified more than any other way by their animals. The Loebs were the Beagle People. The Taziolis had full size poodles, and were always "those people with the big poodles." The Garners were famous for a randy Samoyed named Eli who nailed practically every bitch on the east side of the island, including a blue-ribbon-winning Dalmatian show dog. Her owners thought she was impregnable behind a chain link fence. Eli somehow chewed through the fence and found her very pregnable indeed.

Most of the male Samoa regulars had their own dogs or a big percentage of the family dog. Wayne Whitley's was a German Shepherd bitch named Gretl that he insisted was a retired Army attack dog.

"All I have to do is give a secret command and she'll rip your throat out," Wayne told me one day when we were twelve. I might have believed him if Gretl wasn't carrying 35 extra pounds and none of it brains. To rip my throat out Wayne would have had to hold her up and show her where my throat was, then keep holding her up while the ripping out took place. Gretl spent her days lying in front of the Whitley refrigerator, hoping the door would pop open and a pot roast would fall out into her mouth. Underneath her the linoleum wasn't just stained. It actually sagged.

"My father says retired army are all like that," Wayne explained.

Stackhouse's mother was devoted to Chihuahuas. They had four of what Stackhouse pére called 'show rats,' brainless little beasts that never got the concept of "on the paper." One night the family was awakened by a strange voice downstairs in their living room. The voice said clearly and distinctly, "For Christ's sake, it's dog shit!" Then there was a thump, a rustle, and a slamming door. When Mr. Stackhouse descended a few minutes later brandishing his son's Red Ryder beebee gun he found a canvas bag on the dining room floor with most of Great Grandma Stackhouse's good silver in it. Chihuahua-crap footprints trailed out the back door. (The police refused to take a plaster cast.) It may have been the only time in criminal history that a perpetrator stopped in mid-perpetration out of sheer disgust.

The next morning Mother Stackhouse was extremely proud of her fecally irresponsible pets for "protecting the priceless family heritage." Father Stackhouse pointed out with asperity that during the entire incident, "not one of the little bastards barked even though they bark at me every night when I come home from work. Every damned night."

Curtis got a Weimaraner as a gift from his father, so of course he ignored it completely. His psychiatrist Willi suggested, "It would be goot for the boy to haff a dog." His mother took responsibility for the pup, named it Tref, and they became very close. So Willi was half right. It was good for the mother to have a dog.

Time passed. We outgrew our homes. We outgrew our pets. We became far too sophisticated for stick throwing and kitten baiting. Except one of us.

Hadley Greene was bright, gentle, pudgy, and one of the first guys I knew who carried his books in a rucksack. He was a very good oboe player in the school orchestra, but he would have been the orchestra oboe player whether he was any good or not because the competition was nil. Every high school has to have one artsy female literary magazine editor, one kid willing to dress up like the mascot for sporting events, and one oboe player. Hadley was Mercer Island High's 'go-to' guy on the oboe.

Whenever Hadley came into the Samoa I knew who it was at the counter without looking around the bun warmer to see because his order was always the same: a Cheese Deluxe and a plain Smo burger, with two strips of crisp bacon on the Smo and the whole thing cut into small pieces. The Smo was for Elliott, and I always served it in person. Whenever Hadley dropped by, in fact, a bunch of us would take that burger out to the parking lot so we could chat with Elliott and find out what he'd been up to.

Elliott was a cat. According to Hadley he was a pure-bred 'American Domestic'—a handsome cat, with brown/black/white/orangey fur worn long and luxuriant, a very expressive face and tail, and a strong personality. There were people he liked and people he would have buried if he could. You knew your status with Elliott pretty quickly and you were damned pleased if he liked you. I saw Dennis grin like a two-year-old because Elliott gave him The Big Purr on their first meeting, and Dennis was not in any way a guy into grinning. But that was another thing about Elliott. He had a savoir-faire that made it all right for us big tough sophisticated high school men to accept him and his owner. Nobody ever gave Hadley any gas because his best friend was eight pounds and fluffy. This was no powder-puff Persian. Elliott had as much grit as a guy with no balls can have.

Hadley and Elliott first met and started sleeping together when Hadley was four. Through elementary school and junior high Hadley took the bus every day. I was on that route too and always looked forward to Hadley's stop because Elliott would be standing there with him, saying goodbye for the day. There's something very encouraging about seeing a bright, friendly cat out and about early in the morning.

Six hours later it would happen all over again when Elliott welcomed Hadley home. If Hadley had after-school oboe lessons or other commitments and wasn't on the bus Elliott would watch all the others get off, wait until the bus pulled away, and then stroll home alone. They trusted each other. By the time his partner was in junior high Elliott would be waiting only on those afternoons when Hadley was on the bus. I never figured out how he knew.

Right before his senior year Hadley bought an ancient Ford sedan with his savings. Over and above the desire of any red-blooded teen male to have his own wheels, I suspect Hadley's principal interest in getting the car was so he could go places with Elliott. Certainly they were always together after that.

After he bought the car Elliott even came to school, although not inside. Vice Principal Murray wasn't about to let a cat disrupt classes. Elliott would have disrupted, too. He just couldn't help drawing attention. Instead he sat in the Ford all day in the parking lot, waiting, snoozing, nibbling from the bowl of kibble that Hadley left on the back seat. Hadley would come out at lunchtime with his lunch sack and he and Elliott would dine together. When he finished eating Hadley would take out his oboe and practice until the bell rang. Elliott loved the oboe. When Hadley played the cat would close his eyes and purr. Then one glistening drop of saliva would form in the center of his lips and just hang there.

After a month Elliott's days in the school parking lot were over. He'd been an indoor/outdoor cat since kittenhood, and he didn't care at all for the litter box behind the passenger's seat. He started missing it, just a little, with his fragrant deposits. He was sending Hadley a message. A way had to be found to make the car accessible to Elliott but inaccessible to rain or intruders of any species.

The Auto Shop boys volunteered to put a cat door somewhere in Hadley's Ford. They saw it as a unique challenge to their vehicular skills. There were days of discussion and argument, many drawings, and at least one experiment. Leaving for work one morning Police Chief Gilmore was surprised to discover the passenger side door of his daughter Glennis' car was missing. The next day the door was back with a one-foot square hole cut into it. Chief Gilmore assumed Frank Forcade was the culprit, but we'll never really know for sure who did it.

Eventually the auto shoppers had to give up the project. Unless Elliott spent his waiting time in the trunk (which he most definitely was not willing to do) there was no way to cut a cat door in a car door without compromising the structural integrity of the vehicle. Hadley's parents vetoed that, and you couldn't blame them. Cat Door Project Director Frank Forcade, who had the original idea, felt so sorry about his failure that he brought Elliott a whole rabbit to eat as a consolation for raising the cat's hopes in vain.

A cat door wouldn't have solved the real problem anyway. The fact was that Elliott was bored waiting. Cats are so proficient at amusing themselves we forget that once they hit the boredom wall no species hits it harder. Not many friendships can survive the mind-numbing tedium of sitting in a parked car seven hours a day, five days a week. So Elliott stayed home after that. As soon as school was out Hadley would rush back and pick him up for an afternoon drive. That was part of their deal. Often that drive was to the Samoa.

When I was cooking and DeeDee was the Counter Personnel I let Hadley bring Elliott inside. DeeDee didn't care. DeeDee didn't care about much of anything at the Samoa, being worldly as she was. And I figured that the chance was slim a health inspector would visit the place while Elliott was there. If a health inspector did show up I was prepared to argue that Elliott was probably the cleanest living creature on the premises, given the Samoa's regular clientele. Nobody I knew was as well groomed as Elliott. Except DeeDee.

The cat obviously enjoyed the opportunity to escape the car. He'd sit on a back booth table, eating his Smo burger off a china plate I stole from my mother. It was the only real plate in the Samoa, and Elliott appreciated the gesture. He even ate the bun, the only cat I've ever known who enjoyed bakery products.

After he finished dining we would gather to pay our respects, scratching him on the top of the head, under the jowls, and between the shoulder blades. You never touched him past the mid-back, however. He didn't care for that, I think because it was an approach to his tail. That tail was absolutely off limits; not even Hadley was allowed to touch it. Like most cats Elliott spoke with his tail, sometimes eloquently. To grab it would have been like sticking your hand in somebody's mouth while they were talking.

The only trouble we ever had in the Samoa because of Elliott wasn't his fault. Hadley had run over to the supermarket on a mother's errand, and Dennis, who had been sitting with Elliott, had to go to the john. A guy named Burton in the next booth over decided that this was the perfect opportunity to find out what the big deal was about the cat. He was not a Samoa person.

He was also not a cat person, something Elliott sensed immediately when Burton jumped booths and they were together. It was a sudden move, and cat people know about cats and sudden moves by strangers. But to look at Elliott, only if you were his friend would you know he was on edge, alert to every possibility. Burton didn't have a clue.

"It's just a cat," he said to DeeDee, who was standing at the counter, looking closely at the skin on her arms. "What, it does tricks or something?"

"Are you talking to me?" DeeDee responded with mild astonishment. She did not chat with us. She took our orders. Period.

"So why's everybody so nuts about this stupid cat?" Burton was sticking his own face into Elliott's, blatantly violating Elliott's personal space. Cats invented the concept of personal space and hold it sacred. Yet Elliott still seemed unconcerned. But it was an illusion. His tail was going slowly but steadily back and forth. His ears had flattened out slightly. A cat person would have known what these signals meant and backed off. But again, Burton was clueless. And stupid too, because the next thing he did was grab Elliott's tail.

Dennis was just coming in from the can and saw it all from that moment on. Elliott rose up a little on his hind legs, and with a fast right cross etched three deep parallel lines on Burton's left cheek. Before his target could get out of range Elliott hit him a second time with his left, a claw down the nose from brow to tip. Both shots took less than a second. If Dennis didn't have the quick eyes of a boxer he would have missed them. Then Elliott assumed his original position. He calmly watched his attacker, waiting for a response.

Burton roared and fell back. He let go of Elliott's tail and grabbed his own lacerated face. He looked at the blood on his hand and lunged for Elliott. At the last instant Dennis grabbed Burton by the back of the shirt and held him out at arm's length.

"Fight's over," Dennis said. "You lose."

"But look at what that cat did to me, that goddamned…"

"That's nothing compared to what I'll do to you if you mess with the cat."

Dennis' voice was an odd mixture of menace and joy. He wanted Burton to understand that if he put hands on Elliott again he would be leaving the Samoa on a gurney. At the same time Dennis was very pleased to get the opportunity to do something for Elliott that nobody else could do, not even Hadley.

"But I'm bleeding, for Christ's sake!" Burton was bleeding a lot.

"We're outta Band-aids. Pick up your food and get out of here."

Burton was obviously outclassed by both man and cat. Holding paper napkins to staunch his wounds, he skulked away, all the time muttering that things weren't over yet. His one pitiful act of defiance was to not take his food as directed. He left a perfectly good Cheese Deluxe right there on the table.

While I cut Burton's burger into chunks the victor carefully washed himself from nose to tail, like Marciano taking a long shower after a ten-round title fight. Then Elliott ate most of the spoils of war, even though he really preferred a Crisp Bacon Smo.

"Kids," DeeDee said.

It was one of Dennis' best moments at the Samoa and he talked of it often, always giving credit to Elliott. "He stood his ground, you know?" Dennis would say, with the admiration of one tough little bastard for another. "Even when that asshole was cut and coming back for him, I mean the guy had, what, 170 pounds on Elliott, the cat stayed where he was ready to nail him again. You gotta admire that." Indeed you gotta, and we did.

I saw Burton a few days later. Elliott's shots had scabbed up by then and from the left side the kid looked like a Maori warrior. Hadley was worried that some kind of trouble would come from the incident, that Burton might report a vicious cat to

Animal Control or even get the police involved. Being a gentle soul, Hadley just didn't understand the Tough-Guy-Teen-Male ego. A sixteen-year-old boy who's been beaten up in public by a house cat is not looking to prolong the moment. Every giggle he hears in the halls is aimed at him, every guy who says, "What the hell happened to you?" already knows what happened and is just rubbing it in.

Besides our own growing sophistication and outside interests, as high school teens we drifted away from our animals for one other reason. We were going to live forever and they were dying. Most of us had gotten our pets "when you're old enough to take care of it," so anywhere from age four to seven depending on the parent and the pet. Ten years later the fish had long since been flushed away, most of the birds had dropped from their perches, and the mice and snakes were in back yard graves under cardboard headstones with crayon epitaphs. Those dogs and cats who shared our beds, ate our vegetables under the table and chased balls around for our amusement weren't moving so fast any more. They were senior citizens, going through a lot of the pains and disappointments of human senior citizens. They were circling the drain.

Wayne Whitley's Gretl didn't make it to graduation. The Stackhouse Chihuahuas were as energetic as ever, but that's because Mrs. Stackhouse was secretly replacing them as they dropped, knowing that only she could tell them apart. She died at home in 1998, and at her bedside were allegedly the same four dogs. I figured they were 56 years old each, or 392 in Chihuahua years.

One winter day Elliott and Hadley were in the Samoa. Elliott was wolfing through a Smo burger with more than his usual enthusiasm.

"Look at him go," Curtis said. "Haven't you been feeding this cat?"

"In fact I've been feeding him more than usual," Hadley answered. "He just seems hungry all the time these days."

When Elliott finished his own meal he walked around the table trying to get at other people's eats. I'd never seen him do anything like that before. At least until then he wasn't a cat who begged for food, and he eschewed all other dog-like behavior as well. But now he was all over us. He looked odd, too. There was something different about his appearance. For the first time Elliott looked like an old cat.

A week later he was back and just as hungry. But something was wrong because even though he was eating a lot more he was noticeably thinner. Hadley said they had an appointment at the vet the next day, and promised to come by afterwards and let us know what was going on.

"It's something to do with his thyroid," Hadley explained the next afternoon, holding up a small brown bottle. "I have to give him these pills four times a day." We were sitting in Elliott's booth watching a Bacon Smo disappear. Elliott was chewing frantically through the bacon as if it might slither away at the slightest opportunity. Hadley was obviously relieved. It wasn't meningitis, cancer, distemper, or any of the other possibilities that had been scaring him so much.

So he's okay, yeah?" Dennis wanted to know. "He's going to be okay?"

"Well, there's always the chance that the pills won't work, and then he might need an operation. And he's got a touch of arthritis which is completely normal for a cat his age. But yes, they think he's fine."

Dennis picked up the plastic bottle on the table and looked at the tiny white pills inside.

"These are very small. They're very small, Hadley. Can they be any good if they're that small? Maybe you should give him eight of these mothers a day instead of four." Pharmacology was not Dennis' forte.

"It's going to be hard enough giving him four," said Hadley. "I have to pry his mouth open and stick a finger way down his throat with the pill on the end. He isn't going to care for it."

I was in the can at school a week later when Hadley came in. Under the bandages there were bites and scratches that went all the way up to his shoulders. He and Elliott were friends, but a friend who sticks his finger down your throat four times a day has to put up with a little grief.

Hadley came in with Elliott a few times during the next month, and on each occasion we could see that our friend was still just as hungry and still losing weight. After a while his ribs stuck out through his fur and his face had a hollow, desperate look that broke your heart. He always allowed a few of us to pick him up, but now it was like holding a piece of fur. There didn't seem to be a cat there anymore. The pills weren't working.

One day after school Hadley dropped Elliott off at the Samoa. He was going to the vet to ask about the thyroid operation, and he didn't want to take the cat along with him. Elliott had developed an overwhelming dislike for the drive to the vet's, the vet's parking lot, the vet's waiting room, the vet's nurse, the vet, the vet's smell, and those damned pills. Hadley took off for his appointment a mile away, and Dennis, Janelle, Geoff and I entertained Elliott. I cooked up some Bacon Smos, and we all had one, the only time in his life Geoff ate anything in the Samoa besides a Cheese Deluxe. Elliott had two. Then he went to work on a plate of spare bacon bits. He climbed down off the table after that and curled up in Janelle's lap, purring loudly. Dennis sat beside them, scratching Elliott between the ears. He was so worried about the cat that it didn't even occur to him to give Janelle a little feel at the same time.

Elliott was sound asleep an hour later when the Ford pulled up in front of the Samoa. Hadley, pale and shaky, came in slowly. He told us the vet finally admitted that even though there was an operation he could do it was never really a possibility as far as Elliott was concerned. Hadley took a sheet of paper out of his jacket; the evaluation the vet had written up for his parents. After a lot of doctor crap describing Elliott's condition, the key sentence was: "Given the patient's age a surgical procedure is contra-indicated."

"What does that mean?" Dennis whispered so Elliott wouldn't wake up. "What the hell does that mean?" He was furious, and he didn't know why.

Hadley took a long time, like a guy who wants to give any other answer but the only one he can give.

"It means Elliott is fourteen years old," he said finally, "and if the anesthetic didn't kill him the operation would."

There was a horrible moment. Then Janelle put her arm around Hadley's shoulders and just left it there.

"I'm so sorry," she said softly.

Hadley gently stroked Elliott's head. The cat's tail twitched a little. He wanted us to know he was still awake and listening.

"Isn't there anything we can do?" DeeDee had come up behind us, and her voice was kinder and softer than I had ever heard it before, or would ever hear it again.

"No. We just...we just wait."

Dennis suddenly stood up and marched out of the Samoa without a word to anybody. That woke Elliott up completely. He peered into the faces looking down at him in Janelle's lap, and then climbed back up on the table. He walked back and forth a few times, rubbing his back on Hadley's chin, slapping Hadley in the ears with his tail, saying hello. Then he went back to the leftover bacon.

I knew about old animals, and somebody had to ask the question. "Is he in pain?"

"He may be. We...we don't know. Maybe. I...I have to go now. I have to tell my parents." Hadley gathered Elliott up, cradling him on his back like a baby. "Thanks for taking care of him today."

"Absolutely any time, Hadley," I said. They went out to the car. Instead of sitting on the back of Hadley's seat as he usually did, Elliott curled up on the passenger seat, down and out of sight.

Elliott's deterioration seemed very fast after that. He lost the ability to retract his claws completely. He kept getting stuck in carpets and upholstery and had to be helped. Hadley told me he'd started crying in the middle of the night. He was restless too.

"He can't seem to get comfortable," Hadley said. "He goes in and out twenty times a day, like he's looking for something and doesn't know what it is or where to find it."

He also started serious hunting, an activity he'd never really shown much interest in before. Every morning there'd be a new dead creature in the Greene family kitchen; a mouse, a bird, a mole. It was the hunger driving him, I guess, but Hadley said the carcasses were whole. It took the Greenes a while to realize that what Elliott wanted to do was trade what he caught for more of his regular food, the canned fish, kibble and burgers that had been his nutritional life. In his hunger and desperation Elliott was trying to make deals with the only gods he knew.

Except for the hunting, the crying, and the restlessness, his personality didn't change that much in those last months. He was still kind to his friends and oblivious of his enemies, still quick to purr and preen, still interested in the world around him. But when his personality began to change for the worse Hadley realized that Elliott was suffering. He could see that his friend's life no longer had any joy. It had only desperation, intense hunger, confusion and pain. It was then that Hadley made the most selfless decision I ever saw a high school kid make.

They hadn't been in the Samoa for some time, but one warm Friday afternoon in early spring I was at the grill and saw the Ford pull up. The regular crowd was standing in the parking lot, and Curtis was sitting in his Plymouth. Hadley got out slowly, but instead of getting Elliott and coming in, he just stood by his car. Janelle, Wayne and eventually Curtis wandered over. I saw them looking through the passenger side window, talking with Hadley. I finished up the orders I was working on and went out.

Hadley looked at me, and I knew.

"I wanted to bring Elliott here. To say goodbye. He...he liked it here a lot. Well, you know that." Then he couldn't say anything else. We went around to the other side of the car. Hadley opened the door and I squatted by the seat while Janelle stood over me looking in. Elliott was there, curled up on a blanket. He tried to stand up but I don't think he could any more. I reached out and gave him a little scratch under the jowls. He put his nose in the air as much as he could and purred, a soft purr, more felt than heard. It was the way he had always responded to a good jowl scratch. He was, to the end, Elliott.

Before Hadley drove off for the vet, Janelle hugged him. Then she went and sat with Curtis and sobbed. I was sorry Dennis wasn't there to say goodbye, but perhaps that was for the best. Watching that Ford go off down the road, taking Elliott away from us forever, was a very hard thing to do. Somebody who even looked funny at Dennis later that day could have gotten badly hurt.

We Samoans weren't the only people who supported Hadley during those last months. At school the music director was a good guy named Jack Hibbard. He realized that something was wrong and finally got Hadley to tell him what it was. Jack was a musician, but like all smart musicians he had a backup career. In his case he was a counselor with a degree in psychology. He made it possible for Hadley to get out of school early when there was Elliott business to take care of. He understood about the priorities of life, and for him fifth period Geology and sixth period Orchestra were inconsequential when the alternative was taking care of a sick friend.

After Elliott was gone Hadley didn't snap out of it. He was absent a lot and his schoolwork suffered. He took to sitting alone in his car in the parking lot at lunchtime.

Twice when the bell rang, he didn't come back in but fired up the Ford and drove off somewhere, and never to the Samoa. No amount of commiseration by any of us seemed to help, and the school just wasn't set up to give counseling to a student who'd lost his cat.

I got a call to go see Jack not long before school was over for the year. "The last orchestra concert of the year is this Friday," he said without any preamble. "You going?" I told him I was sorry, but I had to work that night. It was actually true.

"I see." Jack looked at me hard for a moment and then said, "I want you to do me a favor. I want you to come to the concert. Call in sick at work if you have to, ask for the night off, do what you have to do, but come. This will be more important than one more night of flipping burgers. More important to you."

Jack Hibbard was usually not an enigmatic man, but he was being positively inscrutable about this concert.

"That's not all," he said. "I want you to bring those people, those people you hang out with at the Samoa. Janeen and Dennis, Whitley, all of them."

"It's Janelle. And I don't hang out with them, I work there," I started to explain. "So it's just natural that you think..."

"Yeah, right. Just bring them. Bring Cathy too. You'll all be glad you came. Now take off."

We went as a convoy—Wayne Whitley, Janelle, Dennis, Clifford, Cathy and me in Wayne's car, with Curtis, Geoff, Roger, Jesse and Tess following. Frank Forcade and Stacy drove alone, in case they got stopped by the police and were delayed.

I don't know how I talked the others into going. After three years of high school none of them besides Clifford and Cathy had ever heard the orchestra play except at mandatory assemblies. They hadn't missed a thing as far as they were concerned. But there was something so compelling and mysterious about Jack Hibbard's invitation I guess they couldn't resist any more than

I could. We certainly didn't have anything better to do that Friday night.

We filed into the auditorium and took seats in the back row. Some of the students who were already there stared when they saw us. Vice-Principal Murray, skulking around the edges of the hall as he always did, assumed we were there for some nefarious purpose. I saw him go around the room and speak quietly to the few teachers on hand, pointing in our direction. Then he stationed himself in the aisle directly behind us, standing with his legs apart and his hands clasped behind his back like a military MP. When Dennis went by on the way to the john Murray snapped, "What are you doing here?"

"I don't know," Dennis said truthfully, and kept walking.

On the way back he grabbed programs for us and handed them down the row. The mimeographed sheet had all the standard year-end stuff about "Saluting our graduating senior musicians," "Last chance to contribute to the Instrument Fund" and "Have a great summer!" On the back side of the sheet was the program for the evening, with a list of the selections to be played. We all looked at it about the same time, and we all realized at once why we were there. The final number of the concert didn't mean much to the rest of the people in the auditorium but it was everything to us.

SELECTIONS FROM
Death and Transfiguration
BY RICHARD STRAUSS
SOLOIST: HADLEY GREENE

And then below that, with no further explanation, it said:

In Memory of a Friend

I saw what Jack Hibbard had done, for Hadley, and for all of us who knew and cared about Elliott. He had turned a standard high school concert into a memorial service, into a celebration of a unique friendship and a spirited life now over. Jack was a wise man, and knew that what we all needed was a way to say goodbye together. Attention, attention must be paid to such a cat.

I don't remember what else was played that night or have any sense of time passing after the program began. Hadley wasn't anywhere to be seen for the first part of the evening. Jack Hibbard had selected a repertoire that only needed one oboe, one time.

When that time came Hadley walked out of the wings and sat down in his usual chair up front, with the clarinets on one side and the flutes on the other. He glanced out towards the audience and there we were in the front row. During intermission, Dennis had gotten up and moved as close as possible, clearing out everybody who was already there simply by asking them to move as only he could. We all followed him. I doubt Jack Hibbard had told Hadley we were coming because he couldn't be sure we would. Whether Hadley knew or not, for the first time since Elliott died I saw him smile. Jack saw it too. He waited until Hadley looked back at the podium. Then Jack raised his baton, and they began.

I don't think Hadley ever played better than he did that night. Nobody who heard him could ever again think of a duck when somebody played the oboe. To me it sounded like a small boy, lost and crying. Dennis had to get up and march out of the room again.

When the piece was over Jack waved his hand in Hadley's direction. Then, instead of waiting and sharing the bow like conductors usually do with soloists, Jack walked off the stage. Hadley rose alone, bowed slightly, and then just stood there staring out at us.

We cheered for what seemed like two minutes, long after the rest of the audience stopped, long after Hadley sat back down and the curtain closed in front of him.

We cheered for Hadley. We cheered for Elliott. And we cheered for all those companions of our childhood, who gave us their friendship, devotion and loyalty without question or reservation; the cats and dogs we had lost or left behind.

Lotus Blossom

ONE DAY IN THE SECOND GRADE Miss Parthemann distributed some government forms we had to fill out and took us through them line by line. When she got to the place where you listed your race, she turned to the blackboard behind her, where CAUCASIAN had already been written out in large, neat letters. She was always well prepared, was Miss Parthemann.

"We are Caucasians," she announced, pointing at the word on the board and not having to think about it for a moment. Say it loud, say it proud, she implied. "'Caw KAY zhun.'"

"Caw KAY zhun," we recited in unison. She beamed out over our little white faces as we copied the word onto the form. Then abruptly the beaming stopped.

"Wait a moment!"

Miss Parthemann was staring at Jill Lee, the next row over from me. "Jill isn't a Caucasian!" she said with some surprise. "Jill is uh, let's see…" She turned back to the board and began writing more big letters. "Jill is a MONGOLIAN. Jill, on your form, under Race, put 'Mongolian.'" Jill looked confused, and began erasing the 'Caucasian' she'd just written so carefully. It was intense erasing, so she didn't have to look up at the rest of us gaping at her.

"Everybody, say 'Mon GO lee un' with Jill," Miss Parthemann commanded. This was to be the only multicultural education we would get until the eighth grade, when *And Now Miguel* told us what it was like to be a little New Mexican kid.

"Mon GO lee un," we said.

Jill Lee was regarded as a person who could be a real asset on a kickball team, who wasn't interested in marbles, and who was smarter than most of us. But other than that there was nothing special about her. She wasn't like Willy Arnett, who had six toes and a little webbing on his left foot. Now it turned out Jill was special after all. Not necessarily bad special, we didn't get that sense from Miss Parthemann at all. This 'Mongolian,' whatever it was, was not a disease. But it was definitely something different from everybody else in the world as we knew it. I had a vague notion that Mongolian had something to do with restaurants. Which made sense. A meal in a restaurant was almost always more interesting than a meal at home; Jill was almost always more interesting than your average kid in the next row.

Eight-year-old Wayne Whitley sat right behind her. It was a propitious spot for him. He was passing the second grade in large part due to his height. Wayne was a lot taller than she was, and was easily able to see over her shoulder during tests. "Hey," he whispered to her now, "What's a Mognolian?"

"I don't know," Jill snapped back. She was not having a positive learning experience. In the second grade or any other time it's hard to be declared officially 'different' and not even know why. She didn't burst into tears as some kids might have. Jill was far too centered for that. But when she got home that day she marched directly into the kitchen and demanded that her mother explain this 'Mongolian' business right now.

"I already did," Jill's mother replied. "I just didn't happen to use that word."

"You mean the Chinese stuff."

Her mother nodded. "I mean the Chinese stuff." Then they had a wonderful afternoon's conversation, covering more than four thousand years of family and cultural history. Jill looked at photographs of her ancestors. She listened to the stories that her mother heard from her own great grandmother back in the old country, stories of family that she'd been waiting to pass along to her first-born when the time was right. For that and many conversations that followed they owed Miss Parthemann a lot, although neither of them saw it that way. And the next day Jill came back to class as one proud Mongolian.

The Lees emigrated from Hong Kong when Jill was three. As far as I know they were Mercer Island's first non-caw-KAY-zhun residents, at least the first since the White-Eyes drove the Indians away in the 1870s. When the Lees moved in their neighbors on either side moved out. That may seem impossible to believe fifty years later, but it's true. Less stupid people snatched up the houses. They were rewarded for their 1950 sanity with under-priced homes and Jill's mom as a next door neighbor. She was a wonderful woman, who kept a beautiful house and garden and was a tireless volunteer for worthy causes.

In the spring of 1965 Jill paid the school system back for her second grade embarrassment. As graduating seniors we had to fill out forms stating how our names should appear on diplomas and other official escape documents. Sitting in her Honors Philosophy seminar with the form in front of her, Jill had a flashback to that other questionnaire of a decade before. Inspiration followed, and on this new form Jill Frances Lee put her middle name down as 'Lotus Blossom.'

At the graduation ceremony a month later Vice-Principal Murray's job was to announce the name of each senior during the processional across the stage. He did this every year, based on the school board's false assumption that he knew who we all were. Murray had been a speech teacher before he rose to management. He was very proud of his pipes, and given to using them at their most resonant. The r's rolled like rain off Murray.

The ritual was going along smoothly except for the orchestra. None of Music teacher Jack Hibbard's seasoned seniors were playing because they were all waiting to march across the stage to get their diplomas. Under Jack's viciously slashing baton the underclassmen were stumbling through a bruised and bloodied *Pomp and Circumstance*, not once but over and over again as the procession continued. It's hard to work up a decent *P&C* when your best trumpet player has new braces on his teeth and has only been playing for two years. The kid just didn't have the chops for Elgar.

Chuck Deeter was the regular first chair trumpet and a splendid musician. He couldn't bear hearing the orchestra—his orchestra—playing so badly for their biggest audience all season. He'd given three years of his life to that operation and it was imploding before his ears. So when Murray called his name he dashed across the stage, snatched his diploma out of the Superintendent's hand, and ran to the side of the auditorium where the orchestra was set up. Chuck grabbed the horn in mid-note right off his successor's bleeding lips, yanked him out of the First Chair, and began to blow. This intervention improved round three of *Pomp and Circumstance* by a good 30%, which the audience acknowledged with applause. After Chuck did it the rest of the senior musicians followed him. For a while, with their maroon Sateeno® gowns flapping behind them, they looked like migrating birds.

For some of the seniors and the underclass players who had their places taken it was a moving experience. The little sophomore girl who had become the only oboist stopped playing and stood up when Hadley Greene got his diploma. He crossed the stage, she met him in the middle, kissed his cheek and hugged him. Then she handed him her oboe and went down the stairs to find a seat in the back, sobbing all the way.

It didn't go that well at all positions. Sitting in lead chairs for the first time since Middle School, some of the underclass players were enjoying themselves so much they were willing to overlook their lackluster performance. They didn't want to give up their instruments or their seats and didn't see why they should have to. From the procession line we watched with interest as two sweet little things named Cyndy and Patty squared off, with fire in their eyes and one flute between them. There was some hair pulling, a few music stands got knocked over, and sophomore Fred Nibbelink got hit in the back of the head with the bell of a French horn. (He only had to get one stitch. Fred had a very small head.) For a while *Pomp and Circumstance* sounded more like *The 1812 Overture*, which didn't seem to bother Jack Hibbard at all. He kept conducting as if the group before him was the London Philharmonic Orchestra and not a roiling mass of metal, wood, and kid.

In the end the good players were not to be denied. By the time Murray reached the 'L's the orchestra was composed mostly of seniors playing and underclass musicians standing around in the corner not quite sure of where to go or what to do. *Pomp and Circumstance* was rescued, and Jack Hibbard got a unique tribute from the kids he had nurtured both musically and in a lot of other ways, kids who were now moving on. They were supposed to get their diplomas and go sit in the auditorium like the rest of us. But they defied the school to play for Jack one last time.

On the other side of the stage diplomas continued to spread among the multitudes. Murray had noticed the orchestra situation, and even tried to remember the names of those not following directions so he could get them the next day. But once a kid got a diploma that youth was out of the Murray Sphere of Influence forever, and Murray knew it. There was no 'next day' for these miscreant musicians. So the only post-graduation action Murray planned was against Curtis, who possibly deserved it.

As Curtis was crossing the stage to get his diploma Murray whispered, "I never thought you'd make it." Curtis stopped, looked at Murray for a beat, and then said with feeling, "Up yours, you huge turd," and he didn't whisper at all. Sitting in the third row with his wife and their invited guest, Willi the Shrink, The Fuehrer was deeply disappointed. Willi leaned over and whispered in his ear, "Don't worry. It's the last moment of youthful rebellion only." He took The Fuehrer's hand and patted it gently.

"Rrrrandolf...Frrrederick...Lebkin!" Murray pealed. Randy Lebkin marched across to the Superintendent, got his diploma, and disappeared forever from my life. I could see Jill standing at the edge of the stage ready to make her big cross. She had always been feisty, but open insurrection was not in her nature. The administration would have been happy—and lucky—to have a school-full of Jill Lees. So in Willi terms this was not only her last moment of youthful rebellion, it was her only moment. But only if Murray took the bait.

"Jill..." The Vice-Principal took a long pause, and even from the "P"s I could see he was thinking. He stared as long as he could at the printed list before him. Then he did it, and he did it large. Elocutionally Jill had given him a chance to break free from all the boring middle names on his list, the Williams, Frrredericks, Elizabeths and Margarets that had ceased to be a challenge. This was a unique opportunity and he was going for it. He even repeated the first name, just to get a running start.

"Jill...Lotus Blossom...Leeeeee!" rang through the auditorium. There was a burst of laughter in mid-announcement so some people never heard the 'Leeeee!' A stranger would have thought we had a girl in our class with the intriguing last name of Lotusblossom.

Because she was in the academic Top Ten and a National Merit finalist who had never caused him any trouble (indeed, before that night Murray had always referred to her as "that smart Oriental kid") the VP beamed at Jill as she walked past him across the stage. She gave him her sweetest smile back. I'll bet the dumb bastard still doesn't know he was had.

Jill's parents were not amused, especially later that night when she dropped off the diploma before heading to the graduation party. JILL LOTUS BLOSSOM LEE, it informed them, had just graduated from Mercer Island High School with high honors. Jill promised to give them an accurate diploma in four years, a diploma that actually meant something to her.

And she did, with many more honors, from Bowdoin: Marine Biology.

The Couple

IN THE 1950S, when Ray Kroc took over McDonalds from a guy named McDonald, he told his managers that they were not allowed to hire women. Kroc thought that girls behind the counter would attract boys in front of the counter whose interest in meeting girls far surpassed their interest in buying burgers. These young men would hang around the Golden Arches, drooling but not buying, and drive away paying customers. Ray thought that wasn't a desirable situation when you have billions and billions of burgers you're planning to unload. So his first great grinning work force was female-free, and it stayed that way until the government, I presume, ruled that the all-male McDonalds would not be allowed to continue in these Equal Employment Opportunity times. Drooling guys or not, Ray had to get some women in there. I'd be willing to bet the initial secret memo to store managers "From The Desk of Ray Kroc" said "Hire some women and make sure they're ugly." And the store managers said to themselves, "Screw you on that one, Ray."

A decade later Betty had no such qualms about women employees at the Samoa. When there was an opening on the roster she hired the first reasonably clean person who wanted the job and looked like he or she could do it. Gender was not a factor in hiring, although it did seem to be a factor in staff deployment. Except for Betty herself, all the cooks were men—me, Don, Josh—and all the counter personnel were women—Arlene, Thelma, DeeDee.

So it wasn't the employees who attracted hormone-addled teens to the Samoa. They certainly didn't come in for Don and me. It was the teens themselves, mixing and matching with each other. These youth made more personnel trades than a bad baseball team with greedy owners. And as the cook/confessor I became a clearing-house for romantic news. It was interesting, but tricky. I learned never to ask Mr. A about Miss B, because by the time I did he had already been dumped by Miss B and was getting rude remarks from Miss B's best friend, Miss C, even though she was really madly in love with him and would be forever and a day. Mr. A assumed that by asking I was just trying to rub it in about Miss B, and threaten to punch me in my N.

In their couplings and re-couplings, perhaps true love bloomed. Mostly I think it was true lust, a kind of infatuation that struck like a bad cold, and like a bad cold only lasted for a week or two. Love was an extremely rare commodity at the Samoa, and all too often one-sided. Steve loved Janelle, but her feelings about him were always in question. She was waiting to be swept off her feet by one great romance. Steve wasn't it, and there weren't any sweepers among the rest of us, either. I know Tess loved Jesse because she told me so late one night. He thought they were just friends, and when he finally became aware of his error (you bet I told him) it was almost too late for him to do anything about it. Almost. Curtis loved somebody too, but it was a subject he and I never discussed. We both just realized it. He loved Cathy.

And she loved me. But ours was not really a Samoa relationship. Until we started going together she'd never been in the place except on winter weekend evenings coming home from skiing. In the colder months we regulars saw a lot of the aprés-ski crowd, what Clifford called The Wet Wool Set. When you were tired, damp, cold and achy, there was nothing like diving into a tasty Cheese Deluxe, the gastronomic equivalent of a hot bath. Cathy and her sister Maralyn were regular Wet Woolies back then, only visiting the place for the eats.

Our relationship changed her Samoa status, but not much. She started coming in during the day, but usually only to tell me something, not to hang around. The regulars accepted that. They accepted the fact that I had a life outside the Samoa and she was it. Only Clifford knew her very well, but she made a point of getting to know all the others too. Even before I realized it myself, she understood how important those people had become to me. She needed a sense of them, to get a sense of who I really was. Cathy worked at being their friend as well, and I loved her all the more for it.

In my time at the Samoa, besides Cathy and me, and Frank and Stacy, I only saw one couple whose first infatuation turned into what I thought was true love. Their devotion to each other was all the more inspiring, because given the mostly intellectual caste system that pervaded our teen life, they should hardly have known each other's names.

Mike Visser was a regular, a lanky young man with thick brown hair that usually stood straight up, and an Adam's apple you could hang a picture from. He hadn't quite found himself, and he certainly hadn't found anybody else, either. He was quiet most of the time, a listener, and when he spoke at all he sounded just like Goofy, the Disney dog. Even his laugh was Goofy's, a "guh hilk guh hilk guh hilk" that made his Adam's apple bounce so much the picture fell off.

There was actually an historic reason for his guh hilking. Pacific Northwesterners insist they have no regional accent. But Pinto Colvig, the Disney Jack-of-all-trades who created Goofy's distinctive sound, was from Jacksonville, Oregon, near Medford. When asked how he developed Goofy's voice Pinto claimed that it was natural. He said everybody in Jacksonville talked just like Goofy, with that same back-of-the-throat, bonehead bubble. According to Pinto, Goofy's sound was the regional accent of the Northwest, even if Northwesterners didn't recognize it. Gorsh!, as Goofy might say. Pinto eventually left Disney and created

Bozo the Clown, which is why Bozo and Goofy had the same voice at the beginning. Bozo and Goofy; the Northwest in a nutshell.

So Mike Visser guh hilked because in 1898 his great grandfather Omar came to the Northwest with ten thousand other guys seeking their fortune in the Alaska gold fields. Except Omar got mugged in a Seattle back alley the night he arrived and lost both his poke and his Alaska boat ticket. Instead of heading north, where given his luck and experience he would certainly have frozen to death, he went to work for a local outfitting company. The Seattle outfitters were the ones who really got rich during that Gold Rush. Omar's employer was no exception, making thousands of dollars selling supplies at outrageous prices to miners, and thousands of dollars more selling women of ill repute to loggers. Omar couldn't afford to purchase any of these women, less outrageously priced, so instead he fell in love with one of them. She was a red-haired Irish lass named Belle, with big hips, big brains and big ambition. By the time she met Omar, Belle had endured an average of six stinking, hairy men every night for a year. She thought life would be a lot more pleasant with just one stinking hairy man a night. She married Omar twenty minutes after he asked for her hand. In fact, as the years went by he couldn't remember whether he actually asked for her hand or not. The hand just seemed to be there.

Belle looked around to see what the thousands of new Northwesterners were doing for leisure when they weren't throwing their money away on her former colleagues. She saw that the Americans were playing baseball and football, the European immigrants were playing soccer, and up on the hills where the wealthy had their mansions, the rich were filling the air with shuttlecocks and tennis balls shipped from back east.

"Got it," Belle said to Omar one night over Mulligan stew. She took the money she had saved, rented a storefront, and bought an assortment of balls, bats, and birdies.

Visser's Sporting Goods opened in 1900, three years before the first World Series was played. Through very hard work, careful management, and selling homemade gin in hollowed-out bowling pins during Prohibition, the company thrived. Belle brought over hordes of her relatives from Ireland, who worked for slave wages in the stores until they'd paid for their passage. It was perhaps the only sporting goods chain in America where staff meetings were held in Gaelic.

What really put the company over the top was getting into ridiculously overpriced athletic shoes early. By 1965 Visser's Athletic Supply had fourteen outlets spread from San Diego to Bellingham, selling among other things the first sports bra in America. It was a homemade concoction called the Visser Jambalaya™, designed by Belle herself and sewn up in the big back room of Vissers/Seattle by dozens of immigrant ladies from China. Omar getting mugged, in other words, was the best thing that ever happened to the Visser family. And Belle Shanigan Visser was the second best.

The old bawd spent her platinum years living with her grandson, Mike's father. She moved onto the Island after being ejected from three different nursing homes for, among other things, solicitation. On that occasion she defended herself by arguing that propositioning Old Mr. Hatch gave him such a thrill it increased his life by two years. "I did it strictly as a public service," she claimed.

On sunny days she would stump around the shopping center on her walker, greeting one and all happily. She even came in for a Cheese Deluxe now and then, carefully taking her store teeth out of her burlap purse and slapping them in her gums. We loved her. And she said "guh hilk" all the time, but with a brogue. Eighty-two years in this country and that woman sounded like she got off the boat from Sligo twenty minutes ago. When she died at 103 more than a thousand people came to the funeral, including five generations of Irish-Americans and four generations of Chinese-Americans.

Because of the quiet and the laugh, Mike's friends and teachers assumed he was dense. Even his family said he took after Great Grandpa Omar, and they said it shaking their heads sadly. His academic record supported the assumption that Mike was not banging on all eight cylinders intellectually. He should have graduated that June, but when the sheepskins were handed out he found his diploma holder was empty. Afterwards in the theater lobby Vice–Principal Murray handed Mike and a dozen other people sealed envelopes. Inside Mike's was a Summer School schedule and a registration sheet, plus a note announcing officially that Michael Collins Visser had failed the Washington State General Science Exam. He would be allowed to join the Class of '65 if and when he passed Sunshine Science. They did let him go to the graduation party, which our year was a train ride to Tacoma and back.

Elizabeth was on that train too, and that must be where they met, really met, because like most Island kids they had known of each other for years and had gone to the same schools, but rarely to the same classes. In the ninth grade, when Mike and his educational equals were reading *Swiss Family Robinson* and writing two page essays on topics like: "If you were stranded on a desert island, what three things would you like to have with you?", Elizabeth and her friends were writing papers with topics like: "Support or attack the premise that Mr. Bennet is an admirable character in Jane Austen's *Pride and Prejudice*."

She was brilliant and always had been. She could recite *Goodnight Moon* with feeling and in its entirety at the age of 2 ½. But it wasn't until they got a call one evening from Miss Magnuson, Elizabeth's nursery school teacher, that her folks realized what a very special child she was.

"We are having a problem with Elizabeth that I feel must be brought to your attention," Miss Magnuson announced, with that serious yet triumphant tone so many educational authorities use when discussing a child's transgressions.

Elizabeth's mother was very surprised. Elizabeth had never been a problem to anyone before.

"Today in school I was reading a Curious George book to the children," Miss Magnuson continued. "Most of the children love George's clever antics, and the important message the stories contain about personal responsibility is certainly one children should hear. Even Elizabeth. But I'm sorry to report she was paying very little attention."

"Oh, well, uh..." Elizabeth's mom said, "...you see, she read most of the Curious George books herself two years ago. She's sort of, uh, moved on..."

"As she told me. But it is not her lack of attention that is really the difficulty and the reason I'm calling. It is her lack of respect for my authority. In this particular Curious George story there is a camel. We have a toy stuffed camel in the classroom, so while reading the story I was bouncing the camel on my lap. I like to use visual aids as much as possible. Research has shown that they can have a positive effect, vis-à-vis cognition, in the pre-school child. Elizabeth interrupted the class to inform me that I wasn't holding a camel, I was holding a dromedary." There was a pause.

"It has something to do with the humps," Miss Magnuson concluded. Listening on the bedroom extension Elizabeth's father had to cover the mouthpiece quickly so he wouldn't guffaw in Miss Magnuson's ear.

Elizabeth's mother wasn't laughing. She was not about to be bullied by the likes of Miss Magnuson, vis-à-vis her daughter's cognition.

"And were you?" she asked sweetly.

"Was I what?"

"Holding a dromedary?"

"Well, I...I don't know. I guess so. But that's not the point."

It was precisely the point for Elizabeth's parents. They spoke to Miss Magnuson for fifteen more minutes, but what they said could be boiled down to "Get over it." Later, when they asked Elizabeth about what had happened, she seemed upset and said Miss Magnuson got it wrong.

"I told her all dromedaries are camels but not all camels are dromedaries. And that what she was holding was a dromedary. I'm sorry if I was wrong."

"You weren't wrong. You get over it too," her parents said.

Elizabeth never worried about being too smart again. From the first grade on she embraced education completely and got everything out of it she could. At her level that was a lot. Mercer Island was a very good school system because it had some exemplary teachers. All the good people wanted to teach and not push around paper (or kids), so there were some lackluster administrators—the name Murray springs to mind. And a few teachers like Dimwiddie were just phoning it in, waiting to retire on a pension and dabble in real estate. But there were so many others, like Virginia Nygren and Alan Greiner and Clara Hayward and Jim Wichterman, who thought being a teacher was the greatest thing you could do with your life, and taught like it. And when they asked themselves whether it was worth the low pay, hard work, and shamefully little recognition for their efforts, Elizabeth was one of the reasons their answer was yes. Epictetus wrote: "A teacher affects eternity. He can never tell where his influence ends." Elizabeth was the kind of student who would put their influence to work in extraordinary, eternal ways, and they could see that from her first day in class. Now, with perfect SAT scores and scholarship offers from every college in America that didn't have an Animal Husbandry major, she was getting ready to head east, to a future of grand possibilities.

I remember seeing both of them on the train that graduation night. Elizabeth was writing a letter to someone. Sitting there alone in an almost empty car, dressed in her cotton blouse and sensible shoes, she looked like the faculty chaperone, counting the minutes until she could go home to a good warm cup of cocoa. Occasionally she'd stop and look out the window at the dark valley rolling by. A few cars away her friends were bragging to each other about the colleges they would attend and their plans for the future. Elizabeth had participated for a while, but eventually she wandered off. In the Very Smart crowd she must have been the rebel. She wanted the full high school experience, and intellectually she'd gotten it. Socially, she knew that by her own choices an important part of what high school is supposed to be, and is for most teens, had passed her by. This bleak trip to Tacoma was her last chance to be a kid, with all the other kids. I suspect she realized one last class gathering might be too little, too late.

A train ride is not a great place for a graduation party. The main thing you want to do at such an event is sit around with people you won't see again for the rest of your life, at least not as they are that night; young, bright eyed, and full of hope. You want to say goodbye and good luck without having to shout over all that goddamned clackety clacking, without constantly lurching from side to side. You need a big room with a lot of chairs, not a narrow hallway moving at 40 miles an hour through some dull countryside you can't see anyway because it's dark. So with a hundred others Cathy and I spent most of the night going up and down the train, looking for people, trying to shout something at them that wasn't completely inane. By the time it was over we felt like we'd walked to Tacoma and back. Because we had.

The crowd had split into the walkers like us and those who settled in one spot and let the walkers come to them. There was a small third group who wanted to be alone, mostly couples, but a few singles. That's what Elizabeth seemed to be when we came to her car. We stopped anyway, because Cathy took one look at her and said we were going to stop. They had been good friends and classmates for a long time but were going off to colleges 3,000 miles apart. This was probably it for them, but neither wanted to say so and there seemed to be nothing else to say. So we chatted amiably for a few minutes. Then Cathy and Elizabeth hugged and we moved on, leaving her as we found her. Cathy kept looking back at Elizabeth, deep in her letter. I asked her what was wrong.

"She's been crying," was all she said.

Mike was alone that night too. His friends were all on board and they were going mad. For most of us—Elizabeth, Cathy, and me too—high school was essentially a step in the direction of college. Graduation was nice, but it wasn't that much more meaningful than graduation from the sixth grade. The most important moment in our high school academic lives was the day that letter arrived from a college you cared about accepting you for the four years to come. After that very little about high school mattered much. We were already somewhere else, or halfway so, already Stanford Indians, Yale Bulldogs, Washington Huskies, Pomona Sagehens.

For some graduating seniors, however, including a lot of Samoans, this was the end of a lot of things. There was no college ahead for them, just 9-to-5 drudgery in a world where they would have to pay rent, car insurance, and whatever the hell "utilities" are. This Tacoma train ride was the only time in their lives when they were still under the societal protection of being kids but free at last from the academic responsibilities of being students. They had escaped one world and had not yet been sucked into the next. And they were acting like it.

Mike hadn't escaped, though. Anybody who thought he didn't care about his academic life only had to see him that night on the train, guh hilking when necessary but not really listening to anything the others said. His friends didn't care at all that his high school diploma was one summer school class away, that he hadn't really graduated yet. But he did. He felt apart from them for the first time ever. And there was nobody else he could turn to.

Sometime, somewhere out in the valley, Mike and Elizabeth must have turned to each other. Maybe it was coincidence. They showed up side by side at Ardith Stixrud's Soft Drink and Potato Chips bar and started talking. Whatever was said, they realized they were unhappy in the same way for some of the same reasons. Until that night neither of them had really engaged in the boy/girl game so many of their friends had been playing intensely for years. Mike didn't think he had a chance, Elizabeth thought there were more important things to do. For her a high school romance would have been inconvenient. In that instant of proximity over the Pringles maybe they realized what they had been missing and decided to make up for it with each other.

Two weeks later at the Samoa Curtis mentioned an odd thing he had seen the night before while attending the 7:20 showing of the movie *Darling*. That in itself was intriguing, because *Darling* was a well-known chick flick, the kind of date movie you went to if your date was calling the shots. One of the ways you could tell if a guy had a girlfriend was if he'd seen *Darling*.

"And what were you doing at *Darling*?" Geoff asked. "Did you actually have a date?"

"Up yours," Curtis said with feeling. And to the rest of us, in explanation, "Miss Julie Christie stars, and I am following her career with interest."

That we knew. A year before Curtis had seen a picture of Julie Christie on the cover of a magazine. She was wearing a sheer blouse and an abbreviated black skirt, and he fell deeply in love at that instant—so deeply in love, in fact, that he was to see *Dr. Zhivago* nine times.

"Have you read the book nine times too?" Clifford asked.

"Jesus, you mean there's a book?" Curtis was flabbergasted. He went home and asked his mother for money to buy books. She was so thrilled at the request she gave him every cent in the house—$136—and he blew it all on a paperback *Zhivago* and nineteen Agatha Christie mysteries. Somehow (Clifford) he was under the impression that Dame Agatha was Julie's mother. How many famous women named Christie can there be from any one country? After that Curtis could often be found sitting at the Samoa reading Christie. He became quite a fan of the English drawing room mystery, moving on to Dorothy Sayers, Ngaio Marsh, and eventually discovering Edmund Crispin. At last count he's read *Glimpses of the Moon* eight times.

Julie Christie was why he was at *Darling*, however, and made the interesting observation he did. "I saw Mike Visser there. Mike Visser." This was indeed odd, because Mike had never expressed the slightest interest in Julie Christie. In fact, one of the few things he was known for was his dislike of the British.

"Screw him," Mike had said earlier that year when Winston Churchill died. "Granny Belle says that's one less Brit we have to worry about."

"Ah, the Irish," Clifford said wistfully. "Nobody holds a grudge like the Irish. And the Jews."

"That's because the Irish are the Seven Lost Tribes." Geoff was channeling his father again, which was easy because his father was still alive and talked a lot during dinner.

"Wait a minute," Wayne said. "I thought you said the American Indians were the Seven Lost Tribes."

"They're the same people, the Irish and the Indians," Clifford answered immediately. "Think about it, Wayne. Have you ever seen them together?"

"I'm not biting, Clifford," Wayne Whitley answered. "No sir, not this time, not this boy."

"Good for you, Wayne," Clifford said, and came as close as he ever would to hugging his friend. It was a big breakthrough for both of them.

I tried to get the conversation back to the subject. "Was Mike alone at *Darling* or did he have a date?"

"I'm not sure," said Curtis. "He was sitting next to Elizabeth, you know, The Brain, but it was crowded, it must have been a coincidence. They couldn't have been together. I mean, that doesn't make any sense."

It didn't seem to make any sense, though I'd like to think I had a twinge. Something about it jarred train memories. The Samoa guys had a hard time accepting the idea that Mike had any girl, much less that girl. Although we had to admit he hadn't been around the Samoa much since graduation. Sudden disappearances by regulars usually meant incarceration, parental conflict or romantic entanglement. It took iron bars, the iron fist or the velvet glove to keep a lot of these guys away from the Cheese Deluxe.

During the discussion of this improbable match I tried introducing Marilyn Monroe and Arthur Miller as a possible romantic equivalent of Mike and Elizabeth. The Playwright and the Showgirl didn't work for most of my colleagues, though. They all knew who Marilyn Monroe was but too many of them thought Arthur Miller played professional golf. He sounded like a golfer.

One warm Saturday night a week later Mike's beat-up red Volkswagen pulled into the Samoa lot. Only it wasn't quite as beat up any more. He'd actually spent the day waxing it. The rust gleamed.

He was out and around to the other side before the engine stopped rattling, which was easy in a car that popped for a good minute after you shut her down. He opened the passenger side door and then just stood there, grinning like a guy who was having the best night of his life.

Out she came, taking his hand and smiling up at him like Elizabeth Barrett Browning alighting from a carriage-and-four on Bob's arm. At the same time she looked a little frightened, like she was taking her first step into a dark forest. He said something to her and then he guh hilked softly. She smiled back, whispered to him, and in they came. He ordered for both of them (two Cheese Deluxes, no onions, strawberry shake and a small Tab) and nodded to his stunned friends. Then they went off to a booth as far away as possible from those of us who would have given a week's pay to hear their conversation. She didn't have any friends to say hello to at the Samoa. Neither she nor her crowd had ever been in the place before as far as I knew. I don't know what the hell they did for burgers.

I cooked their order and delivered it personally, which was fine with Counter Personnel DeeDee. She was busy in the back exfoliating her elbows, an intimate procedure for which she wished to be alone. Elizabeth and I chatted about school and our college plans. She asked if Cathy might be coming in. I said it was unlikely. She seemed disappointed about that, for understandable reasons. There were a lot of people in the place trying hard not to stare at her, and she'd never spoken to any of them for more than ten seconds. One more friendly face, on a person not wearing an apron and busy behind a grill, would have made a big difference. And through it all Mike just watched us. You would have thought he was personally sending her to Smith, now that he knew it was a college as well as a cough drop.

He was very clean that night, very showered. His hair had gone from straight up to more or less horizontal. He had the look of a guy who's wearing all-new underwear, fresh and fluffy. There's nothing like new socks and your first girlfriend to put a spring in your step.

The biggest surprise for the Samoans was the way she looked. They had never seen beyond her intelligence before. Now, in their milieu, they realized she was simply beautiful, for reasons that had nothing to do with exfoliation, cosmetics or big rollers. She and Mike needed a prom to go to, but the prom was two months before. She had spent that night at the library working on a paper about Immanuel Kant for Wichterman's Philosophy seminar. The paper wasn't due for a week and a half and she'd already done three complete drafts, but it was the excuse she gave herself to get out of the house. She was not going to spend Prom night alone in her room, wondering about the activities in the gym a few miles away and why she wasn't a part of them. All her life she had found comfort by surrounding herself with books, and that long, sad evening was no exception.

Mike usually found comfort surrounding himself with the Samoa, and Prom Night was no exception. He worked through a Cheese Deluxe and listened as the equally Prom-free Wayne Whitley and Clifford debated how many angels could dance on the head of a pin. Clifford eventually convinced Wayne that the answer was six, or eight if they were really very small and there was no live band off in one corner of the pinhead.

Later that night, after the Prom was over, a few couples found their way to the Samoa for end-of-a-perfect-evening Cheese Deluxes, including Cathy and me. We gentlemen were dressed in itchy, ill-fitting tuxedos, our dates in ball gowns with graceful lines that had been obliterated by the addition of huge, ugly, wilting corsages. It didn't matter. We were giddy with happiness and our own sophistication. Mike couldn't stand to be around us. He left quietly, went home, and was as miserable and lonely as he had ever been in his life.

Now he was joyfully showing Elizabeth his world. I noticed that she had brought a little bit of her world along with her. Sticking out of her purse was the corner a book: *Jude the Obscure*, in the Penguin edition—the only copy of *Jude the Obscure* in any edition to ever enter the Samoa. We didn't have a lot of books lying around, except for the AutoChlor specs, a *Dr. Zhivago* paperback with the pictures of Julie Christie ripped out, and eventually all the Agatha Christie mysteries Curtis and his mother had finished.

An hour after they arrived Elizabeth was out in the parking lot, leaning against Wayne's Chevy, laughing and scratching with the Samoans like she'd been one of them all her life. She and Janelle had a heart-to-heart about East Coast fashions. It turned out they were both *Vogue* readers, but kept it secret for the same reason. Their friends wouldn't understand.

Mike showed her the Chevy's famed engine, lingering over the hemi-heads. It was refreshing to see somebody display a genuine interest in lifters, pistons and valves, somebody who until then was completely ignorant of Detroit's finest efforts.

Elizabeth agreed with Curtis that Mr. Cobb left a lot to be desired as a geometry teacher, although she couldn't bring herself to calling him That Old Bastard Cobb. She said that he'd always been very nice to her. Until that moment it hadn't occurred to Elizabeth that Mr. Cobb and most of the other teachers would treat someone like Curtis entirely differently than they treated her. She was shocked to realize that the high school she attended was almost completely different from Mike's high school, and not just because they worked from different reading lists. The two schools occupied the same physical space, but had different boundaries, cultures and conventions.

Elizabeth contributed to the parking lot conversation too. She told them how the school literary magazine she edited had come close to printing Clifford's poetry submission until the advisor, Miss Carmody, finally admitted to the student staff that she recognized the poem. It was the first paragraph of *Peyton Place*. ("Indian Summer is like a woman. Ripe. Hot. Passionately fickle.") Later they all agreed to go to the drags that weekend—Wayne, Janelle, Geoff, Frank & Stacy, Jesse & Tess, and Mike & Elizabeth—the two sides of an ampersand for the first time in their lives. But only after he did his summer school science homework.

I'll never know what brought them together during that long night on the train. You could tell just by watching them in the Samoa parking lot that it was more than hormones. They found in each other something that was missing in themselves, something they wanted very much, and that was enough to overcome their differences. Those differences weren't that much to overcome, either. Like all good students, at Elizabeth's core was curiosity; a desire to learn, to understand, to walk around in somebody else's moccasins. Knock out the intellectual superiority, the belief that walking around in Jane Austen's moccasins is inherently good while walking around in Big Daddy Don Garlatz's moccasins is useless, and you have a person who can enjoy herself with almost anybody. Elizabeth's intellectual pretensions were thin and brittle. They cracked easily through simple proximity to Mike and his friends. It was one of the best discoveries she made about herself.

She made a discovery about Mike too, that he was far smarter and more sensitive than any of us gave him credit for. It's true he was a lousy scientist, and paid the price all summer long in a hot classroom where thoughts of Elizabeth frequently overpowered his interest in the three classifications of rocks, the names of constellations, and the Periodic Chart of the Elements. But in other ways he was her intellectual and spiritual equal. He was just as curious about everything as she was. Where Mike was silent with the rest of us he talked for hours with Elizabeth about the ways of the world, about things he had seen and considered. He was still Omar's great grandson, but there was a lot of Belle in him too.

The actress Glenn Close once talked about making an entrance on stage, what was in her mind when she walked out there. She said that each new person in a room affects the molecules in that space, makes them quiver, changes them forever, and that's what she tried to do with every entrance. Elizabeth made the Samoans' molecules quiver and change. They treated her with a respect and gentility that was new for them but surprisingly effortless. She reflected the class they had always had, and they realized it and loved her for it.

Especially Clifford. He'd been sitting in the same classrooms with Elizabeth for more than a decade but had never considered her as anything other than a fellow student. Now she was this beguiling newcomer in the world he had chosen for himself. Clifford was not a romantic person—no Outward Displays of Emotion for him—but the more she was around the Samoa the more I could see he was falling in love with her. But he was too late. Someone else, someone he had never considered as a rival in anything, had discovered the real Elizabeth before he could. I think it broke Clifford's heart. He began to drift away from us even before the summer was over.

Elizabeth's regular crowd saw Mike as a temporary eccentricity in her otherwise exemplary intellectual life. They called him her "toy," but they only did it once around her. She responded that she knew some people who would drop by and beat the crap out of them if there was any more of that. No one was more surprised than Elizabeth when she said it. After that they avoided outright insults, but when he was around they still treated him like her pet, as if Mike was a stray dog who'd attached himself to Elizabeth and wouldn't go away. They thought they were making the best of the situation by allowing themselves to be amused. When that wore off they tolerated him and waited for her to come to her senses. He was used to being treated like a piece of furniture, so in their gatherings he would sit in the corner and simply not speak. After a while Elizabeth stopped trying to work him into the conversation, realizing that his reticence to get involved was probably for the best, not because he couldn't keep up but because he didn't want to be in the race. The result was that Mike and Elizabeth drifted towards his friends more than hers for the summer, and at her urging. The intellectual elites just didn't understand what the Samoa regulars knew instinctively. It's not true that opposites attract. What is true is that there aren't that many opposites when you get right down to it.

One afternoon she showed up at the Samoa alone. Mike was to meet her there after summer school, but his car had died again so he was delayed. It was a slow afternoon, so while she waited I came out and we talked.

"You're probably the only person who doesn't find this all that strange," she said. "Me and Mike. It seems strange to a lot of people."

"I've been here six months now," I said. "Nothing seems strange to me."

"No, I mean you and Cathy are kind of like...well... certainly people have often wondered what she, you know..." I knew where she was heading, and didn't particularly want to go there. Elizabeth and Cathy were alike in many ways, but I certainly saw myself as having a lot more on the ball than Mike Visser in practically every way I could think of.

"I think it's very nice you two are together," I said, interrupting. "And you shouldn't worry about anybody else. One of the meanest bastards in Hollywood once said, 'Don't even ignore 'em,' and he was right."

"Mike's a lot smarter than his friends think he is, than anybody thinks he is," Elizabeth said after a while. "Sometimes he just, he just amazes me. He sits here and watches all of you, you know. He's told me things about the people here that they don't even realize about themselves. Do you know what Geoff does when he isn't here?"

"When isn't he here?"

"You don't notice, but he's gone for three or four days sometimes. Mike's the only one of you who knows where he goes. Because he's the only one who asked him."

"So where does Geoff go?"

"I'm not going to tell you. But you're surrounded by people who have secret lives and they don't even know it about each other. And he has that wonderful voice."

"Geoff?" Geoff's voice had been changing for three years, and it wasn't there yet.

"No. Michael."

She was right about that. It may have been Goofy's voice, but it was also deep, resonant, and warm. Drop the gorsh! and the guh hilk and vocally Goofy wasn't that far from Orson Welles.

Elizabeth wasn't finished. "He can be funny too, and incredibly sensitive, even poetic."

"Really?" I said. I wasn't trying to jazz her but I think that's the way she took it. She picked up her purse off the next seat over.

"I want to show you something. If you promise not to tell anyone else about it." She pulled a sheet of paper out of her purse and gave it to me. There was a poem on it, hand-written very carefully.

> *I will*
> *Always love you*
> *Whether you love me or not.*
> *That's all I can give you to keep*
> *My love.*

"That's very nice," I said. "Did you write it?" It seemed simpler, more straightforward than I would have thought was her style.

Elizabeth didn't answer my question. "It's a cinquain," she said instead. "A five line poem, composed of two, four, six, eight, and then two syllables."

"I see that."

"The cinquain was invented by a poet named Adelaide Crapsey."

"Tough name," I said. I'd been around the Samoa too long.

"Mike knew that, and I didn't. About Adelaide Crapsey. And the cinquain."

"Ah."

She looked at the poem again, reading it to herself. "He wrote it. For me."

"That's what I guessed."

When she looked up from the poem there were tears in her eyes. The summer was almost over. The time we'd all be moving on was at hand.

As a couple Mike and Elizabeth were doomed, and it was especially sad to see because I think he realized it from the beginning and she didn't until the end. She was a romantic at heart, a poet, but he'd taken three years of Shop. He knew his place, because it had always been his place and always would be. She thought there might be exceptions. She was right, but exceptions are very rare, and almost impossible to sustain over distance and time.

Mike and Elizabeth still had a wonderful summer together, discovering each other and some of life's possibilities neither of them had ever considered before. A lot of her friends joined the Peace Corps in the next few years, going off to remote places to help the indigenous population, but also to learn more about themselves and who they really were. Elizabeth accomplished that same self-discovery by going all of two miles, eating a few burgers, watching a few drag races, and falling in love.

One night in late July she told her shocked parents that she had decided not to go to Smith after all. She was going to stay home, work for a year, and then go to the hometown university. And because they had always been honest with each other she told them why. She was in love with Mike and couldn't bear to leave him. Her parents vowed to support whatever she wanted to do, even though they were horrified at the possibility that all Elizabeth had worked for might be lost because of a summer romance. They liked Mike, but they didn't think he or any other high school sweetheart was worth trading for the life that Elizabeth had before her.

Her parents never knew why she finally decided to go to Smith after all, they were just immensely relieved when she did. We Samoans knew, though. We knew Mike simply would not allow her to stay home. We were there that night he told her he would go away himself, go work in the Visser's in San Jose if she didn't leave for college as planned. She got very mad at him. She accused him of not really caring about her. And he took it even though it was killing him. They left together, Elizabeth sobbing and apologetic, beginning to realize what he had just done for her, his last gift, far more valuable than another poem or a ring. A month later she left for Smith a much better person than she had been when the summer began. And with his high school diploma finally in hand, Mike went behind the counter at Visser's Sporting Goods the same way, for the rest of his life.

One Saturday morning a few years ago I ran into Elizabeth with her husband. They were in town from Connecticut, visiting her folks. She has a good career now, writing and teaching, with a "gifted" ten-year-old son who goes to some hotshot East Coast private school. Her successful spouse has a firm handshake, clear blue eyes and no regional accent. She seems happy. When the husband wandered off I was dying to ask her about Mike, whether she ever thought about him and that summer of '65. But given the circumstances and the life she had created for herself it seemed like a pointless thing to bring up.

We talked for a while more, and then she said she had to run. She and her son were going on a special outing that afternoon and she had to get home.

"We're going to the drags," Elizabeth said. Then she smiled. It was a particular smile I hadn't seen for a long time.

Gypsies

WHEN LABOR DAY WEEKEND came around at the end of that summer of 1965 I was almost done at the Samoa. Betty knew I could work through Monday night and then she was going to need someone else. She asked if I had any recommendations for a replacement. At first I couldn't think of anybody who wasn't already going off to college, or the military, or at least slightly more fulfilling work than burger cookery. There was one exception, a possibility that seemed so weird it took me a few days to accept it even though it was my idea. So before I talked to the boss I brought it up with Arlene.

She was sitting by the walk-in at the time, reading *The Murder of Roger Ackroyd*. I was leaning against the back wall, trying to get as far away from the smoking grill as possible, watching the counter for her.

"Arlene," I called back, trying to sound as nonchalant as I could, "I'm leaving this Monday. I'm done here."

"Have a wonderful life," she said, not looking up.

"Betty wants me to recommend somebody. You know, to take my place. Do you have any suggestions?"

"Paul Newman."

"Seriously."

Arlene put her book down and pondered. A lousy cook, somebody slow, dumb or touchy, can make a counter personnel's life hell. And vice versa. It was in Arlene's self-interest to find a good candidate, but she really didn't know the available players. And she proved it.

"How about what's-his-name," she finally answered, "the smart ass? Even if he's a lousy cook he'd still be fun to have in the place. You know who I mean. Clifford."

I couldn't believe she'd been around us for so long and still knew so little about us. "Arlene," I said, "Clifford left last Monday. He's going to Stanford. He's going to major in Comparative Religion. And even if he wasn't leaving you'd kill him inside of two weeks if he worked here. If he hadn't already killed himself."

"It was just a thought. How about Jesse?"

"Navy. It's the only way he can escape his father. He's going to ask to be assigned as far out to sea as possible."

"Uhhh, Geoff."

"You won't believe this. He's got a full ride to a maritime college in Maine. It turns out he's a champion sailor. All those times he just seemed to disappear for a few days? He was off at sailboat races, crewing for people."

"He always seemed a little damp to me," Arlene said.

"He wants to be a naval architect, designing yachts. He'd probably rather do that than cook at the Samoa. Go figure."

"Sheer shortsightedness on his part. People have to eat but they don't have to yacht. I'm stuck." She started reading again.

"What about Curtis?" At that moment Curtis was parked in front of the building, curled up asleep in the back seat of his car.

Arlene closed her book and looked at me.

"Until this moment I never realized how much you hate me," she said.

I gave her the pitch I'd worked up for Betty, about how Curtis knew the Samoa better than anybody alive, how he could be pleasant and witty and considerate if you just got to know him. How if somebody just gave him a chance, just trusted him not to screw up, he'd be a good worker. I didn't necessarily believe much of this, but I thought there was a chance it could be true. At the same time I had to acknowledge to myself that there was a possibility that Curtis would accidentally burn the Samoa down ten minutes into his first shift.

I was worried about him. We were all going away, going on to good lives, most of us, and leaving him behind. Given his tendencies he was an alcohol problem waiting to happen. Or a traffic fatality.

I thought I owed him something too, that we all owed him something. At that football game nine months before he said we ignored him, that we didn't really notice whether he was there or not unless we needed him. It was true. I'd tried to make up for it since, but a guy doesn't have a lot of chances to show another guy he doesn't think he's a creep. Getting Curtis the cook's job at the Samoa was my last opportunity to be his friend.

Arlene listened to my pitch. Then she said, "He's a little creepy."

"Arlene, all cooks are a little creepy. You know that."

"True."

"He's always treated you decently, hasn't he? He's never given you any trouble?"

"Also true. He has very nice manners. It's one of the creepiest things about him."

"If you met his father you'd understand."

She finally told me that if I recommended Curtis to Betty she'd support me. I went out to Curtis' car and woke him up.

"Wha's going on?" he asked, immediately lighting up a cigarette.

"Curtis, I've got a problem. This is my last weekend at the Samoa, and Betty says I have to find a replacement or work next week too, even though I need the time to get ready for college."

"You need time? You're going here, aren't you?" Curtis asked. "What do you need to get ready? You gotta get a new pencil box? Put name tags in your underwear?"

"Work with me here, Curtis. I need the week and I need a replacement. Would you like to take over for me?"

"Oh." Curtis looked very calm, like I'd just offered him a fudgsickle. "You mean cook at the Samoa? Be the cook?"

"That's what I mean."

"Just for like a little while, or take your job permanent?"

"That's up to Betty. But as far as I'm concerned you're the guy. And I'll tell her that."

I expected him to leap up and thank me and say I was the greatest human being who ever lived. But all he said was "Yeah, okay, I'll do it." Very matter-of-fact, like he was doing me a favor. What the hell.

With Arlene's support Betty agreed to the new hire. She and Curtis set up a meeting Tuesday morning for training. I had one long weekend left as the Samoa's cook.

Back then the Island held a street fair every Labor Day weekend. People set up booths in the shopping center and sold the kind of artsy stuff, candles and watercolors, that no store would have the nerve to carry regularly. There was a kiddie's parade down Main Street and a general gathering of the families at the end of the summer. There was always one of those traveling carnivals, too. Usually they set up in the city-owned vacant lot outside the Samoa's back door.

That year's carnival arrived Thursday afternoon, a procession of ancient big Pontiacs and Caddies pulling disassembled Ferris wheels, merry-go-rounds, the Octopus and Tilt-A-Whirl, followed by eight or nine motor homes. One of the town cops came into the Samoa that night and warned me to make sure I locked up tight at closing time.

"We've got a different carnival here this year," he said, eating a free Smo in three bites and heading for the door. "Not the Greeks we had last year. Gypsies this time." He rolled his eyes meaningfully. "Gypsies."

Clearly I was supposed to know what he was talking about, but I didn't have a clue. Gypsies were Gilbert Roland to me, tambourine players, Esmeralda in *Hunchback of Notre Dame*. If these Gypsies had Esmeralda over in the vacant lot running the Tilt-A-Whirl, she could come by and see me any time. And bring her goat.

All evening long between burgers I stood in the Samoa's back door and watched the assemblage going on fifty yards away. They put that carnival together with the speed and efficiency that comes from doing something the same way, with the same people, a thousand times over. I don't think the whole Gypsy crowd exchanged more than thirty words in three hours. They just did it. By 10 o'clock, Samoa weekday closing time, they were back in their motor homes and the carnival looked deserted. I was alone mopping the floor, which took me exactly four jukebox plays of The Byrds' "Mr. Tambourine Man."

I felt a little guilty about playing that particular number. The previous fall, after I'd been mopping the Samoa to "Tambourine Man" for a while, a veterinarian who lived not far up the hill from the shopping center arrived in his Mercedes half an hour after closing. He was wearing a plush floor-length mauve bathrobe with just a hint of white jammies underneath, and there was steam coming out from under his toupee. He pounded on the glass door until I opened up and asked him what the problem was.

"The problem?" he hissed. "I'll tell you what the problem is, kid. It's that goddamned song about the tangerine man. Don't you ever listen to anything else?" He offered me twenty-five dollars in quarters if I'd never play "Mr. Tambourine Man" again.

"If I hear it one more time, just once more, I'm telling you right now, I'm buying this place out from under you no matter what it costs and turning it into a spay-and-neuter clinic. I'm not kidding, kid."

I wasn't without compassion. From then on I gave him a Tom Jones medley and occasionally a shot of "Something Stupid," the only Sinatra we had on the juke. But this was my last weekend and I was feeling nostalgic. So I played what I wanted to play, and the hell with him.

In mid-mop there was a knock on the back door. I opened up, expecting to find one furious veterinarian. Instead, standing there was the biggest human being I'd ever seen, except for Shag Thomas on Channel 13's *Northwest Championship Wrestling*. This guy was maybe 25, with jet-black hair and dark skin, wearing a tee shirt full of muscles. He and his tee shirt filled the Samoa doorframe with what seemed like another half foot of guy hanging out on either side. He looked like he could kick Gilbert Roland's ass any time he wanted to and not even break a sweat. I didn't see any bandana or earring, and he wasn't holding a crystal ball or leading a goat. If this was a Gypsy then he hadn't been watching the same movies I had. What he was holding was a baby bottle in one hand, and a baby in part of his other hand.

We nodded to each other and I told him I was sorry but we were closed. He responded by holding up the bottle and the baby and saying something I didn't understand. A 1960s Island youth didn't get many chances to hear a foreign language outside of Mrs. Cunningham's Spanish class. Or in it, for that matter. It took me a while to realize this giant didn't speak English. But he kept waving the bottle and the baby in the air and saying something. Did he want me to feed his baby? Change his baby? Buy his baby?

I finally got it. He wanted me to heat the bottle for him. I invited them in, and the three of us stood there in front of the Samoa grill, silently watching that bottle warm up in a pot of water. I don't know what he and the baby were thinking. I was thinking about what the cop had said, and wondering why all these savvy Gypsy folk had purchased Winnebagos without water heaters, ranges or even hot plates.

When the bottle was ready, he tested it, stuck it in Junior's chops, and said what may have been "thank you." He reached into his pocket and offered me a dollar.

"No charge," I said.

"Thank you again," he may have said. Then he disappeared out the door. I watched him lumbering across the dark field toward the encircled motor homes on the back side of the carnival.

It was my turn to open up the Samoa the next day, which meant firing up the grill and doing a quick sweep before we unlocked at 10:00. When I got there at 9:30 a crowd was already waiting outside the front door. I knew the regulars were still asleep. Regular Samoans were night people, so these had to be strangers. It was the Gypsies, a dozen of them, who waited patiently and silently for me to prep the place and then came in and ordered more food in fifteen minutes than I expected to make in the next six hours.

That was just the beginning. They kept coming all day long, wiry, hardworking, handsome folks with the gastronomic capacity of humpbacked whales. The men would order three Cheese Deluxes at a time, eat them on the spot, and then get ten more to carry back to the ride operators and game barkers. The Gypsy women ate their share of burgers too, but they were partial to the Taco Excellante, even though it was nothing to savor thanks to me.

That first morning I faced the real possibility of having to close before noon because I didn't have any food left to cook. Arlene got on the phone, and just about the time the last hamburger patty hit the grill Betty pulled up in her Lincoln. You can get a lot of meat in a Lincoln, and she had, plus buns, cheese, chicken and fish. We were saved.

When we took the cash register total that first Gypsy night it was four times what it usually was for a Friday. Some of that extra business was from locals going to the carnival, but most of it was Gypsy eating, even though I figured there were only thirty Gypsies in the whole crowd. If I'd owned the Samoa I'd have stayed open all night for those people. But I didn't, so I didn't.

About halfway through the fourth round of "Mr. Tambourine Man," four old men I hadn't seen before appeared out of nowhere and settled around one of the tables outside under the Tiki Hut® canopy where the gas pumps used to be. I mopped over and told them the Samoa was closed for the night. The oldest of the old men looked to be around 110 and in better shape than I was. He answered in thickly accented English that they just wanted to sit for a while, if I didn't mind. It was all right with me, so I left the Gypsy Elders, which they so obviously were, and finished cleaning.

Right before locking up I saw a cop drive by slowly and shine his spotlight on the old men, who ignored him. A minute later he pulled up to the Samoa back door with his lights off, got out quietly and came in.

"We have a situation here," he announced. He looked like he was dying to call for backup and collar the perps.

"What situation are you talking about?" I thought he needed to use the can but was shy about asking.

"You know you got carnival people out there? On the premises?"

"Yeah," I said, "I figured they were from the carnival, because we get so few Rumanians in here, especially Rumanian senior citizens."

Sarcasm was lost on this mook. "They're Gypsies, not Rumanians," he informed me solemnly. "Gypsies." And I was treated to that look again. "And you're closed so they have no business being here." He was already practicing his testimony for court.

"It's okay. I told them they could stay. It'll be all right."

"They could steal that table and those chairs," said the Officer, with a "you dumb kid" tone that pissed me off. The table and chairs he was so concerned about had been sitting outside and unprotected in front of the Samoa for more than two years. Nobody had ever shown the slightest interest in them, possibly because they weren't worth ten bucks total. Betty was not a fool. She wasn't about to put anything of any value out front. I told the officer I'd chance a Grand Theft Furniture. He told me again to make sure I locked up tight.

"I'll keep an eye on the place," he promised me, "just in case."

"You do that," I said. He actually backed out the door, as if turning around would give the old men a chance to whip out their crossbows and shoot him in the neck. The officer never actually drew his weapon but I could tell he really wanted to.

Betty didn't have many rules. One of them was that you never gave food away, except to cops, because the next time people would expect it, like cops. But I'd seen so many Gypsies that day giving their cash to Betty that it seemed only right to do something for them. Just before leaving I got some of the real ceramic cups we had on a back shelf and made a fresh pot of coffee for the old men. When I took the cups and the Java out to them the eldest Elder nodded gravely and thanked me. I didn't ask him for any money and he didn't offer to pay. We both knew what was going on without anybody having to say anything.

For the next three days the carny people ate burgers, tacos, fish, chicken and ice cream like the Samoa was the only restaurant in this part of the galaxy. Betty had to make two more meat runs, and Sunday afternoon she and Chuck showed up to help. He concentrated on the fish and she put on an apron and worked burgers right beside me until closing. The Samoa's kitchen was barely big enough for two people, so the three of us, plus Arlene and eventually DeeDee, were bouncing off each other like billiard balls. I wish Don the Fish Man could have been with us too, and not just because Chuck didn't have the slightest idea what he was doing in the deep fat. Don would have liked the Gypsy folk, because they were just like him; quiet, hard working, proud. He hadn't worked the previous Friday night either. Betty told me he was sick, and the way she said it I knew I would never see him again.

We were punchy by the time it was over. Chuck actually threw a spare halibut nugget across the counter at DeeDee, who caught it in her mouth and then barked like a seal. It was the only time I ever saw her show a spark of joy. Betty took a cash register total. It was the best single day in Samoa history. She handed DeeDee, Arlene and me twenty-dollar bonuses on the spot and then invited us to come have a real dinner with them and forget about the mopping up for one night. But I passed. I wanted to stay for the old men.

They had appeared every night shortly before closing, and sat outside in the court drinking my coffee and talking. I listened on the other side of the wall for a while that Sunday night. In a strange language I didn't recognize they murmured to each other in deep, rich voices. Once they all laughed at something. It was a wonderful laugh, not loud, but rumbling and rolling like thunder, from way down in their bellies—an old-man laugh with a hell of a lot of history in it. It sounded like somebody had just whispered a pretty good joke in the bass section of the All-Welsh Championship Men's Chorus.

The cop told me the Elders usually walked back to the carnival encampment just before dawn. Apparently he sat in Fuehrer Alley behind the Seattle First National Bank for most of the night and watched them, waiting in vain for the moment when they would try to snatch up those ratty plastic chairs and shag it across the field. He was obviously disappointed they never did and kept asking me if anything else was missing from the Samoa. He was a pompous ass for a 25-year-old so I wouldn't have told him if the grill was missing. I could have made his day, too, because every morning when I opened up I'd find the coffeepot and cups, washed clean, on the little table inside the Samoa's back door, the door I had carefully locked the night before.

I wish I could say that the all-white Samoans and the Gypsies had an enlightening cross-cultural experience over that weekend, that we became pals and still exchange cards at Christmas. But the fact is they didn't talk much, either to us or to each other. Not that anybody was unfriendly, but they were intense eaters with no time to chat, and you didn't have to be Margaret Mead to see that they wanted to be treated with courtesy and respect and otherwise left alone.

One of them, a guy about the same age as the Samoa regulars, did tell me why they ate so much. "We travel all the time, so we can't spend our money on fancy houses. We have to pull the trailers and rides so we can't spend it on nice cars either. The Elders won't let us drink, and there's no room in the trailers for anything but work clothes. What's left but food?" And then he endeared himself to all of us by declaring that the Cheese Deluxe was the best burger in America. We already knew that, but it was nice to have confirmation from a man of the world.

I was so busy feeding people over that weekend that I didn't have any time to check their place out the way they'd checked out mine. Monday was the last night of the carnival and my last night as a working Samoan. Betty showed up to say goodbye and then stayed to cook after 8:00 so Cathy and I could walk over to the carnival. For the entire time we were there it was like we were the King and Queen of the Gypsies. They shouted to each other that "the kook" had arrived. They wouldn't take my money for the rides, for the games, for anything. At the Dart Toss the balloons popped before we let go of the darts. Cathy won a hideous stuffed green cat that had to be four feet tall, presented to her with great ceremony and much laughter. They threw in an engraved aluminum bracelet plus a ball point pen with a tiny plastic Fender Bass floating around inside the tube.

I was exhausted from Extreme Cooking for four days, and Cathy really wasn't a carnival-going type. We were done after an hour and started back for the Samoa. But before we could leave the talkative young guy grabbed us and insisted we come see his ride. Besides the fortuneteller it was obviously the oldest attraction on the grounds; a homemade looking wooden contraption with bench seats that spun slowly around in a circle and lifted up a little. He cleared everybody else off it, strapped us in and then whispered, "Lemme show you what this old beauty can really do!"

We began spinning, and in a few seconds the carnival was a blur. Shortly thereafter Cathy was a blur too, even though she was going the same speed sitting next to me. I could hear wood cracking somewhere, and people—us— screaming. We were terrified. When the spinning finally stopped the young guy was grinning all over.

Cathy and I staggered back towards the Samoa lugging the giant cat. The carnival was set up to face the street that fronted the vacant lot, so to get to the Samoa we had to walk through the backside where the Gypsies' motor homes were parked. Outside one of them the big guy from four nights before was sitting in a lawn chair tinkering with a piece of machinery. A tiny dark woman who must have been his wife was in the chair next to him nursing their baby. The kid looked nine months older in her arms, and like the Gypsies I had come to know, he was eating hard and fast. The big guy saw me and said something to his wife, who looked over and smiled sweetly. He stood, wiped his greasy hand on his shirt, bowed to Cathy, and shook my hand.

"Goodbye," he said, without any trace of an accent. "I hope you had a nice time with us tonight."

We moved on, but just before we left their encampment I heard a voice come rumbling out of the darkness.

"Hey, you." It was the very old man, carrying a flashlight, dressed as I had always seen him, in a cloth cap, thick working man's trousers and a heavy long coat, even though the night was warm. He was leaning up against a large rock in the corner of the field. I couldn't tell if he was guarding the perimeter or waiting for us.

"My dear," he said to Cathy, taking her hand and gently kissing it. "How are you tonight?" We said we were fine and thanked him for his hospitality. There was a long pause that was awkward for us and didn't seem to bother him at all. He just stared at the three of us; me, Cathy, and the big cat. Then he seemed to be laughing.

"Let me make you little trade," he said. "You give me this," and he relieved us of the cat. "And let me give you... this."

He reached deep into his coat pocket and brought out a round medallion, twice as big as a silver dollar. It wasn't any cheap aluminum trinket either. It was heavy, solid brass, the color of good root beer. He showed me with the glow of his flashlight that on one side of it were what must have been letters, but not in any alphabet I'd ever seen before. On the other side was a bird of prey. It looked like some kind of hawk.

"It is a falcon," the old man explained. "I am a falconer."

"I...Thank you," I mumbled, "but this can't be a fair trade."

"For the cat? No." He leaned in to us and lowered his voice. "We get the big cats for nine and a half cents each from a place in Taiwan that serves all the families. Little cats four cents." Then he laughed that wonderful bass laugh.

"This is not for the cat. You are very young. You will understand some day. And if not, no matter. Good fortune to you both." And he disappeared back into the shadows.

Many years later I did a television news story about a falconer who went around the country doing demonstrations at sports shows. I'd been curious about the medallion for a long time, so I brought it along and showed it to him when we were all through shooting. He was standing out behind the convention hall by then, smoking a cigarette, with his falcon on his arm, hooded but still malevolent-looking. The falconer glanced at me and then at what I was holding. His eyes went wide. In that instant I stopped being just another local feature reporter who wouldn't know a goshawk from a merlin.

"Where did you get this?" he asked. I didn't want to tell him the whole story so I just said "a friend gave it to me," and let it go at that.

"It has something to do with falconry, yes?" I asked.

"Oh, yes," he said. He told me the medallion was from Georgia, not the one in the South but the one on the Black Sea, where the Caucasus Mountains are. That's what the writing was, the lovely, looping Georgian alphabet.

He kept turning the medallion over in his hand, getting the feel of it. "Some people believe falconry began in Georgia," he said. "And this is the medallion of their organization, the Georgian falconers' union. This word, it's pronounced 'me-me-no', it means 'hawk.' It's a thousand years old—the organization, not the medallion. I'm sure it's one of the oldest associations on earth. And certainly one of the best." He looked one last time at the medallion and handed it back to me.

"I'd offer to buy this from you, God knows I'd love to have it. But that wouldn't be right. Whoever gave this to you wanted it to be yours and no one else's. Was he a Georgian?"

"I don't know. I guess he could have been. He was a Gypsy."

"A Gypsy?" The traveling falconer stared at me. "Was he a very old man? With four sons?"

"I don't know about the sons. He was certainly old. He ran a carnival."

"A carnival." He laughed. "Believe me pal, you've been honored." And with his falcon on his arm he walked back into the hall to do another show.

The carnival packed up late that Monday night. When I drove by the next morning on the way to my rented room near the University you wouldn't have known the

Gypsies had ever been there. I was out of town the next summer, and the summer after that they started building a convenience store in the vacant lot behind the Samoa. The Labor Day carnival that year used space at the other end of the shopping center near the Safeway store. I went over one night, but it wasn't my people. It was Italians. I'm sure the police were relieved, but I was disappointed. I wanted to see that old man again. I wanted to stand in the dim glow of a Winnebago and listen to whatever he had to say.

I never saw the Gypsies again. But I did learn something about them from an Island man who knew the family that ran this particular carnival. Whenever they arrived in a new place they'd send people out to the local restaurants, not to check out the food but to see how they'd be treated. The scouts would have some special request, something that required a little extra effort, something that required a little trust. The old men would listen to their reports when they got back, make a determination, and after that the whole group only went to the place where they were treated the best. It was partially a reward for respect and certainly a way to avoid trouble.

I don't know what happened that first night at the Island Plaza Coffee Shop, the Dairy Queen, or the Whitehouse Drive-In up the road. But I do know that Betty paid her rent for the next six months on what she took in on Labor Day weekend alone. Because of a baby bottle, a big guy, a few free pots of coffee, and a kid who declined the opportunity to be a jerk around strangers.

I avoided the Samoa for a while during that first quarter in college. I told myself it was because I didn't want Curtis to think I was checking up on him. Curtis, of course, wouldn't have cared in the least. My real reason was loneliness. Cathy was gone, a freshman at Pomona College, and I was living in a one room basement "apartment" in a Bed & Board. Every night I had dinner with strangers and then went back down to my room to pretend I was studying. I longed for the old days at the Samoa but I knew they were gone and would never return, at least for me. I began to see why DeeDee was so miserable among us. Moving on is hard, but not quite moving on is worse.

I finally went into the Samoa a few months later on a Saturday night. I was happy to see Curtis there, happy to see he'd kept the job. The weather was typical for the Northwest in January, cold and dank, so business was slow. Curtis came out and we had a Cheese Deluxe together, like old times. He asked me if I'd heard from anybody, and I told him about how Clifford sent me a letter entirely in Greek, how Wayne Whitley was doing at Central playing football, how Roger was somewhere in Greenwich Village. Most of the regulars had just disappeared. It would be years before I heard what happened to many of them, and when I did I was almost always surprised and pleased as well. Yes, there were a couple of guys who spent time as guests of the state, and there was one suicide that to this day breaks my heart. But in that crowd of regulars were a future airline pilot, a nature photographer, a yacht designer, two restaurateurs, three decorated Marines (one posthumous), a children's book illustrator, some excellent parents, and an unlimited hydroplane driver. They were not dumb people. They were just motivation-delayed.

Curtis looked good that night I visited the Samoa, like he was doing okay. It was odd. A guy working a six day nine-to-nine job for the first time in his life looked more rested and at ease than when he slept fourteen hours a day and spent the rest of his time smoking, drinking and driving.

"I am doing okay," Curtis said. "Willi finally got something right." That surprised me, because Curtis had never before said anything even slightly positive about his shrink.

"You know all that crap about my competing with my father, how I kept failing at everything because no matter how hard I tried, the old man would always win? Well, Willi said this job was perfect for me, because it's something my father wouldn't want to win. No competition with dad in the burger cookin' line."

"Makes sense, I guess. Good old Willi."

"That was the last time I saw him. Let him bleed somebody else's parents from now on."

"Your folks ever come in?"

Curtis smiled. "All the time," he said. "Chicken baskets. Go figure." And then for the first time he told me the whole story about that night his parents were nearly arrested. And when he told it he called his father "dad."

Some customers arrived and ordered so Curtis went back to the grill. He seemed happier than I'd ever seen him before, and I couldn't help taking a little credit for that. The only downside I could see was that he'd put on twenty-five pounds of pure Cheese Deluxe.

Curtis gave me a little wave as I went out the door, but he was working fish and you've got to pay attention to fish. I sat in my car outside and watched him through the glass door for a while. He didn't speak to anyone, just concentrated on doing his job, doing a piece of work. I'd seen that style before.

When her lease expired two years later Betty shut down the Samoa for good. Chuck had retired from the envelope game by then. They wanted to move to California to be closer to their kids and grandkids. They donated the grill, bun warmer and walk-in refrigerator to a Seattle shelter for runaway teens. After a developer bought the land he brought in a bulldozer and knocked the Samoa down in about three minutes. And that was that. No more Cheese Deluxes, ever.

I've lost track of Curtis, but I'm not worried. He learned his trade, and a fast, experienced cook can always find work. Where the Samoa used to be there's now a lovely bank parking lot. Island kids hang out at the McDonalds that was put up twenty five years ago on the other side of the shopping center. They're allowed to be on the premises for thirty minutes. Then they have to leave.

They don't know what they're missing, in all kinds of ways.

Printed in the United States
132317LV00002B/93/P